To my wonderful
you have been a
since the day you were born. I am
so happy to share this exciting
new aspect of my life with you.
Love Always,
Dad

The Osprey's Nest

SHELTON "BUDDY" WILKES

PublishAmerica
Baltimore

First printing

ISBN: 1-4137-9008-9
PUBLISHED BY PUBLISHAMERICA, LLLP
www.publishamerica.com
Baltimore

Printed in the United States of America

The Osprey's Nest

SHELTON "BUDDY" WILKES

CHAPTER 1

December 19, 2001

It was too quiet as I stood alone in the foyer. There was a stench in the air. My mother's house had never reeked before, particularly at Christmas. I looked toward the living room and was startled to see our Christmas tree lying on its side with ornaments and gifts spread across the floor.

"Mom, Dad, I'm home!" I shouted loud enough to be heard in every room in the house. My backpack slipped off my shoulder, landing on top of my luggage; they banged onto the hardwood floor. The crashing sound broke the spell that had me unable to move. I stepped tentatively into the living room, my eyes fixed on the overturned tree. Accidentally stepping on a stray package, I stumbled, landing against the tree, but catching myself before my face slammed into an ornament. Only two or three inches away from my eyes, my vision was filled with a blur of something shiny and white. It took a moment to bring the image into focus. I'd nearly smashed the ceramic angel that had adorned the top of our Christmas tree since I was five years old. Her wings were broken, but her perfectly hand-painted face appeared to be staring at me. It was spooky. Goose bumps and a cold chill ran through my body, and I shivered before jumping up and righting the tree in the center of the bay window, carefully placing the angel back over the top branch. Shoving the gifts underneath the tree, I remembered that Dad always had trouble making that red and green metal tree stand work properly.

Where were they? Why weren't they home? I reached towards the blinds behind the tree and lifted a slat up with an index finger. There was no sign of them. A nanosecond before I dropped the blind I did a double take, noticing some movement out of my peripheral vision. Mrs. Mulliner's Siamese cat had jumped off the back of mom's Lincoln and crawled under my car in the driveway. Surely they'd left me a note on the chalkboard in the kitchen.

That rancid smell raced through my sinuses and became stronger with every step I took toward the kitchen. I stopped where the hardwood floor met the kitchen's terra cotta tile. Something was wrong. A chalkboard hung on the wall directly across from me next to the phone had nothing written on it. I could never remember a day that my mother didn't have some kind of note or reminder on that chalkboard. It had been completely erased. I turned to my right and was horrified by what I saw. My knees locked and I froze, staring in utter disbelief.

Dried blood covered the kitchen floor from the entrance where I was standing across to where my father and mother lay. My father was sprawled on his back on the cold tile. She lay face down across his ankles. Blood encircled their bodies and was spattered to the tops of the French doors behind them. The white cabinets over the sink had a large bloodstain surrounding a small hole. It looked like hair was stuck on the cabinets in the blood.

I wanted to scream for help, but I couldn't make a sound. My upper body rocked in their direction, but my legs refused to cooperate. I trembled uncontrollably. The coagulated blood that covered the kitchen was closer to black than red. My mother and father were dead. I couldn't help them.

There was blood everywhere. I looked at the hole in the cabinet again. The hair dried in the blood around it must have come from my father's scalp. Vomit churned in my stomach. Oh God, I had to get out. My feet finally released from the floor. The French doors were closest, but they were covered with blood. I turned and ran back through the living room, grasping my mouth with my hand, trying to keep the vomit from erupting inside the house. Kicking open the front door I fell to my knees on the top porch step. Vomit spewed from my mouth and nostrils. It covered the plants and dripped down all three steps and onto the sidewalk. When there was nothing left inside me, I crawled in the doorway and reached for my carryon bag, tearing at every zipper until I found my cell phone. I dialed 9-1-1, my fingers tingling and my body shaking wildly. I couldn't stand to even be in the doorway, so I retreated on all fours across the small concrete porch to the top step.

"9-1-1 operator, what is your emergency?" the female voice answered. I opened my mouth but nothing came out.

"911, please state your emergency?"

Clearing my throat and taking deep breaths I was finally able to utter the words, "My parents have been killed. Please send help."

"Sir, what's your location?"

"Jesus Christ, my parents are dead. Are you going to send someone over here or not?"

"Sir, where are your parents?"

"They're in my house!" I yelled back.

"Sir, what is your address?"

I gave her my address, threw the cell phone down, slumping over, holding my head in my hands. *Oh dear God, please make this all go away. God, please let me wake up and this all be a dream.* I turned and looked at the door. Maybe this was a horrendous dream. I tried to stand but my strength had been sapped from my body, so I put my hands on the step by my sides and pushed myself up. Before I reached the crouching position I collapsed onto the step. *Did they need me? Could I do anything for them? Why couldn't I move?* My mind was not allowing my body to go back in that house.

Nausea struck again. I hung my head over the other edge of the steps and heaved and heaved, but nothing came out, so I lay my face down on the cold concrete porch, listening to the sounds of sirens growing louder and louder and then abruptly ending.

CHAPTER 2

The patrol car skidded to a stop in front of the house. Bay County, Florida, had a sheriff's department and numerous city police departments. This was a black and white. It belonged to the Panama City Police Department. An officer emerged from his car drawing his pistol, clenching it with both hands and aiming it into the air.

"Put your hands in the air," he shouted. His fierce malicious stare was fixed on me as he lowered his gun and pointed it directly at me. I slowly raised my arms over my head. With every step he took in my direction it became clear this cop thought I was the murderer. I was frightened out of my wits, but I kept the presence of mind to do as I was told and nothing more. A second cop, then a third arrived. Patrol cars were scattered in every direction across the road. The cop with his gun drawn on me had closed to less than fifteen feet away.

Mrs. Burroughs, the neighbor across the street, was working in her yard and had walked close to the road to see what was going on. She held her hand over her mouth, a terrified look on her face. She started to cross the road when the second cop threw one hand in the air and reached for his pistol with his other.

"Lady, stay where you are!" Jesus, I wondered if he thought she was the killer. Surely he wouldn't shoot that sweet little old lady right out here on our street. Thank God, she halted in her tracks at his command. She stood at the curb wringing her hands, her usual warm smiled replaced by a look of helplessness.

I lowered my arms and spoke, "I'm the person who called you."

"I said put your damn hands in the air!" he shouted even louder than before.

"But, Officer—" He cut me off before I could finish.

"Now!" he screamed. *My God, he's going to shoot me.* He wasn't going to allow me to explain. I again extended my arms over my head.

"Good boy. I want you to stand up, slowly come down the steps, turn around, and face away from me." I complied again. "Place your hands on your head and walk backwards toward me."

I took a couple of steps backwards and tried again to explain. "Sir—"

"Shut the hell up," he said.

"Oh my God," Mrs. Burroughs cried out from across the road.

"Down on your knees, keeping your hands on your head." The other two cops jogged past me to the front door. Both were carrying shotguns with short barrels. They stood on either side of the door. The one on the left nodded to the other cop, who pointed his gun inside the house. They entered swinging their guns from side to side as they left my line of sight.

"I'm Officer Martin," the first cop said as he patted me down. "Do you have any weapons on you?"

"No, sir." I started to lower my hands assuming the lack of a weapon meant I could do that.

"Keep your hands on top of your head and lie down," were his next instructions. I lay down on the sidewalk with my hands placed on top of my head. He grabbed my right wrist and I felt cold steel on it. He snatched my left wrist and slammed it into my right one. A clicking sound followed. I'd been handcuffed. *Why were they doing this to me?*

"Dear God, please listen to me—"

"Keep your mouth shut. You'll have a chance to talk at the jail." His large black shoe landed beside my right ear. I looked up as he went by, and I saw him bound up the steps and into the foyer where I'd dropped my luggage. I craned my neck, struggling to lift my head to see what was going on inside the house. With my arms restricted behind my back, my shoulders were forced into the coarse sidewalk as I wiggled around to follow the moves of the officers.

Martin, the cop who had cuffed me, came back onto the porch and knelt down, examining the area where I had thrown up. The front door remained open, and I could see my overturned luggage in the foyer. I realized how I could prove my innocence.

"I'm a law student at Georgetown University and I just got home for Christmas, and I found them in there. The airline ticket is in that bag. My flight landed in Panama City about thirty minutes ago. You can see for yourself. Please, Officer Martin, please don't leave me here. I didn't do anything. I just came home and found them. Oh dear God, someone help me please." Martin bent down with his back towards me, but I could tell from the sounds he was searching through my bag.

He stood, turned, and walked toward me, holding my airline ticket. The other two cops came back out of the house, their shotguns now dangling by their sides. One of them went to his car, returning with a roll of yellow crime scene tape. He began wrapping the tape around trees in our yard, encircling the entire house. The other cop tilted his head towards his left shoulder, talking into a police radio microphone. Officer Martin stepped over me, straddling my body. He clutched the handcuffs, lifted me off the sidewalk, ushering me to the steps where he sat me down.

Mrs. Burroughs couldn't stand it any longer. She scurried across the street. This time no one stopped her. She sat next to me and placed her arm around my shoulders. One of the cops approached her, but she spoke before he could open his mouth.

"I'm Tina Burroughs, his neighbor. I was here the day he came home from the hospital." Her short red hair was brushed back away from her face, and without the cover of any makeup, the wrinkles on her brow and around her eyes revealed sixty plus years of being a mom. She'd spent untold hours in the Florida sun watching her children and grandchildren playing soccer, little league, and cheerleading. Despite a little sun damage, she was in great shape for an eighty-year-old woman. I dated her daughter Amy in high school, and often stayed at the Burroughs' house when my parents were out of town.

"Yes, ma'am," the cop said before going back inside the house as if he had been put in his place. I laid my head on her shoulder and whispered the words, "I can't believe it. They're gone. Someone killed them." Her arm tightened around my shoulders, and we both tried not to cry, but that was impossible. Tears began to trickle out of the corners of my eyes and down my cheeks. Her grip got even tighter, and we started to rock forward and backward together.

Moments later detectives arrived along with a mobile crime lab from the Florida Department of Law Enforcement. One of the detectives went from one cop to another shaking hands with the uniformed officers. He stopped making his rounds when he reached Martin. They spoke for about five minutes, then Martin handed him my airline ticket. The detective stretched a pair of latex gloves on his hands before going inside. A few minutes later he came back to the porch and shouted to one of the uniformed cops.

"How about uncuffing him." An officer responded by reached into a leather pouch on his belt, taking out a key and leaning behind my back. Seconds later my hands dropped to my sides.

"Mr. Downing, I'm Stephen Pittman. I'm in charge of this investigation. I'm terribly sorry for your loss." I wiped a few lingering tears my face. "I'm going to ask you to sit in my car while we finish some things up inside your house. Then I'd like to take a statement from you."

"Yes, sir," I said, standing and helping Mrs. Burroughs to her feet. She and I made our way towards his car. I opened the passenger's side door, sat with my legs stretched towards the curb, allowing Mrs. Burroughs to hold my hands together in hers.

"Scott, I'll be right back. I'm going to make you a cup of hot tea. It'll help settle your nerves."

"Thanks, Mrs. B. You don't have to do that. I'll be okay."

"Scott, I know I don't have to, but I'm going to, so you just wait right here. I'll be right back." I almost asked her not to go, but I was too embarrassed to say it. She crossed the road and disappeared behind the tall, green holly hedge leading to the side door of her kitchen. Ten minutes later she was on her way back with a steaming cup of tea. Another twenty minutes passed before Detective Pittman strolled down the sidewalk.

"Ma'am, I don't believe we met earlier." They shook hands. "I'm Detective Pittman with the Panama City Police Department."

"Tina Burroughs. I was here when Scott's family moved in."

"Which house do you live in, Mrs. Burroughs?" She pointed to her home.

"Didn't happen to see or hear anything unusual last night or early this morning did you?"

"Not 'til you all came screaming up here," she said.

"Mind if I speak with Mr. Downing here in private, Mrs. Burroughs?"

"Oh, no. I'm sorry," she said. "Call me if you need anything, Scott. You're gonna stay with us tonight."

Detective Pittman waited until Mrs. Burroughs reached the end of the sidewalk before he spoke. "Too early to tell anything for sure, but it looks and feels like an intruder was expecting the house to be vacant, and when he broke in to burglarize the house, he was startled to find it occupied. Looks like a scuffle ensued, and the thief ended up shooting your parents at point blank-range. I've just talked by radio to the five officers who are canvassing the neighborhood, but so far not a single neighbor said they heard or saw anything. Right at the moment we have very few clues."

He asked me to ride with him to the Panama City Police Department so he could take my statement.

"Can I take my luggage?" I asked.

"Everything here is part of the crime scene, Mr. Downing. When we're finished processing the scene, one of my officers will bring it to you at my office. I hate to have to do this, but it's procedure. I'll need to cuff you again, and put you in the back." He put the cuffs on in front of me instead of behind my back, and then he opened the back door. I sat and rested my hands in my lap.

He must have driven close to seventy in a thirty-five all the way up Cove Boulevard to Highway 98. We turned east for two blocks and wheeled in behind the police station. Detective Pittman ushered me past a dozen cubicles, each with a small gray metal desk and a matching file cabinet. He opened the door to a long narrow room with a conference table and eight chairs down each side. He spread some papers out on the table in front of him and asked me questions about my university schedule, my flight, and my family. About thirty minutes into the questioning, Detective Pittman's phone rang. He turned away from me and said very little other than "right," and, "yes, sir," before hanging up.

The phone hadn't settled on the cradle when I could hear my grandmother's voice. She entered the room followed by a tall, slender man with graying hair. He was wearing a dark suit with a red tie. I stood accepting a hug from my grandmother. Detective Pittman was also quick to rise from his chair.

"You must be Scott," the man said, shaking my hand.

"Yes, sir."

"I'm David Sasser, chief of police. I'm terribly sorry for your loss."

"Thank you."

"I've known your grandmother and I knew your grandfather for a good many years. They're fine people." My grandmother and grandfather had homesteaded a large tract of gulf front land on Panama City Beach. "I want you both to know that Detective Pittman is one of our best detectives. I promise you we'll work very hard to solve this case."

"Thank you, David," my grandmother said, directing me out of the room.

"Can I go?" I asked, looking at Detective Pittman. His eyes were fixed on the chief. He was unable to disguise the frustration he must have felt due to the interruption of my grandmother and the chief.

"Yeah, okay," he said scooping his papers into a neat pile.

My grandmother and I briskly made our way down the hall ahead of Chief Sasser. Officer Martin was in the lobby with my luggage. I thanked him for bringing it to me, and he apologized for having to cuff me and treat me like a criminal. I assured him I no hard feelings.

My grandmother was a strong woman, but tonight she needed me to stay with her. She declared over and over I was staying at her house because I was upset, but I was confident there was a mutual need for us to be together tonight. I called Mrs. Burroughs to thank her for her earlier offer and tell her I was going to spend the night with my grandmother. She seemed pleased with that decision.

My grandmother's phone rang off the hook the next morning. She told me that one of the calls was from a group of our neighbors who had received permission from the police to clean the house. By the time I showered and went over to see if I could help, they had finished the cleanup. Fumes from some type of pine cleaner permeated every room, especially the kitchen, but the fumes couldn't mask the smell of death. My eyes scanned the cabinets. There was no bullet hole, but there was a spot that didn't match perfectly with the rest of the cabinets. They must have used some wood filler and then painted over it. The touchup paint was a shade brighter than the rest of the cabinets, but the fact that they had gone to those lengths to repair everything was astonishing. I looked away for a second. When I turned back, my mind refused to accept my neighbors' handiwork. I could see the bullet hole as clearly as if it were still there.

A carrot cake, a lemon meringue pie, and a spiral cut baked ham were on the kitchen counter along with a sympathy card from the neighbors. A little before nine p.m. my grandmother called. I hated to tell her she was right. There was no way I could stay in the house. My father's keys were on his dresser, so I drove the Range Rover around the block to her house.

She was standing at the front door waiting for me.

"Gram, do you mind if I spend the night in the guesthouse?"

"Scottie, I don't mind, but why in the world would you want to stay way out there?"

"I'm afraid I might wake up in the middle of the night, and I don't want to keep you awake."

"Scottie, you're not going to keep me awake. I'm up and down all night."

"Gram, I'm scared to death I might have a bad dream."

"That would be understandable, Scottie."

"Understandable or not, we'll both be better off with me in the guesthouse."

"Whatever you want. You just try to get a little sleep."

I was awake all night staring at the ceiling. It wasn't insomnia. It was fear, fear of falling asleep and finding their bodies again during a dream. CNN was the technique I used to stay awake.

Sometime in the wee hours of the morning I was amazed to see a news story about David Collins, a *Washington Post* reporter and a good friend of my Dad's. The news story showed footage of the Collins' Arlington, Virginia, home that had caught fire last night when a gas fireplace exploded. The home burned to the ground with Mr. Collins inside. I thought how ironic it was that these two friends would die in less than twenty-four hours of each other. There was no reason to make a connection because my parents were murdered and Mr. Collins was killed in an accident. They were also seven hundred miles apart, which left nothing more than a coincidence of timing, friendship, and now the final twist of fate—they were both dead.

CHAPTER 3

December 23, 2001

Four days after I'd found their bodies, I was sitting alone in a metal chair under a dark green awning contemplating the events that had changed my life.

I thought about the unexpected and impressive motorcade of five black Expeditions and four black Excursions with blue lights flashing in their grills that had arrived at the cemetery. I reread the letter from the President of the United States that had been presented to me at the cemetery by the Deputy Secretary of State. Following the graveside services, Deputy Secretary Armstrong offered his condolences and those of the President. Then he climbed inside his long, black Ford Excursion and his motorcade was escorted by three local law enforcement motorcycles away from the cemetery.

My parents' graveside services had ended nearly half an hour ago, but I couldn't make myself leave. Two men were sitting on a yellow tractor patiently waiting for me to go. I looked towards the sky and noticed a flock of pelicans in single file soaring in my direction, as though they were offering a flyover tribute. The aroma from the freshly cut winter rye grass nearly tricked my senses into believing this was spring instead of late December.

The caskets of my mother and father rested before me. My mind rambled, and I was thinking how I would forever be indebted to my parents for the wonderful life they had given me. I owed them so much, and I never even got to say goodbye. I was thankful I had called them earlier in the week, which I always tried to do. Right before I hung up from our talk, I told them I would see them in a few days. Then I said, "You two are the best." A strange feeling raced through my body right after I'd said that, but I couldn't figure out why.

I thought about how much easier this would be if I had grown up to be a little tougher emotionally. I got my sensitivity from my mother, and I often felt that was a flaw. I shook my head from side to side, thinking about the injustice of losing them in such a brutal manner, which was magnified by the fact that the police were still at a total loss on the case.

Brushing my hands over the glossy bronze caskets, I knew it was time to leave them, but I needed some kind of sign convincing me that it was okay for me to go. Just then, the late December sun dipped down below the edge of the awning, shining directly into my eyes. I had to smile. Those two hated the cold, and the warmth of the Florida sun shining on them was the sign I was looking for. I stepped out from under the awning and stopped to face them once more. I promised myself and them that I would do something with my life to help other families who had to endure this kind of living hell. I wasn't sure how I would keep that promise, but I was sure that I would.

Grandmother Downing was patiently waiting by the limousine under a gigantic oak tree that stood alone near the gravesite. The big oak had clusters of Spanish moss that hung down like tear drops. The other oaks along the drive seemed to reach out and embrace each other from opposite sides of the roadway, forming a canopy.

"Sorry I took so long, Gram."

"We all say goodbye in different ways, Scottie." I held the door open for her as she climbed into the limo, then I sat next to her. Sitting across from us, wiping tears from her face with a little white handkerchief, was another wonderful woman in my life. Maggie Stewart was wearing a black dress with a matching jacket, and a little round black hat. She had cleaned our house and cooked meals for us since I was a little boy.

Over the years, she adopted our family and we adopted hers. As I gazed out the window, my grandmother's long, skinny, wrinkled hand patted the back of mine, and I looked over at her. I had been apprehensive about looking at my grandmother and getting teary eyed, embarrassing myself.

"I talked to Michael Burke at the church, and he's expecting us at his office tomorrow."

"Is that your lawyer?"

"Yes, and your father's."

"Sure, that'll be fine."

"What day do you have to go back to school?"

"Gram, I'm not sure I'm ready to go back."

"Scottie, ten years ago I promised you I'd pay for your law degree from Georgetown. You're due to get that degree in six months. I don't know how many more years I have on this earth, and I'd sure love to be sitting in that audience in June when you get that jurist doctorate." That was all she had to say. Now I had one oath to keep with my parents and a second one with my grandmother.

CHAPTER 4

Monday, April 5, 2004
Three Years Later

FBI Agent Sydney Sloan had recently worked a case involving a captain of a crime family who'd been trafficking drugs through the Port of Panama City, Florida.

I got involved when the wise guy committed a murder, but the FBI was reluctant to give me information. When the Senate Committee on the Judiciary learned that the chief investigator of the Bay County Sheriff's Department had some tenuous times working with the Bureau, they subpoenaed me to testified before them in a hearing.

The director of the FBI sat with his legal counsel at a long table to my left. I stood at the witness table observing three committee members who had leaned their heads together, each of them giving the director a contemptuous stare. A senator from Massachusetts had an evil sneer on his face when he openly revealed his disdain for the director by pointing directly at him and whispering something to his huddled colleagues. The tension in the air between the democratic members of the committee and the FBI director was so thick you could cut it with a knife. They clearly didn't like this guy. Ronald Reagan had appointed the current director, and I'd been told his bias towards working with republicans was always evident.

Several of the democratic senators on the committee had spoken with me by phone over the past week. They were aggressively seeking testimony of someone from local law enforcement who would blast the way the FBI failed to cooperate with other agencies. The senators hoped to level enough charges against the director to force his resignation.

The chairman of the committee announced, "Lieutenant Scott Downing, raise your right hand." I complied. "Do you solemnly swear to tell the truth, the whole truth, and nothing but the truth so help you God?"

"I do."

"Lieutenant Downing, please be seated." I glanced at my watch. It was two minutes past nine in the morning, plenty of time to give my testimony and head home before lunch.

The committee chairman clasped his hands together, pulled his microphone closer to him, and spoke without making eye contact. "Good morning, Lieutenant."

"Good morning, ladies and gentleman," I replied perusing the panel.

"Lieutenant Downing, for the record, please give the committee your title and the law enforcement agency you're affiliated with."

"I am the chief homicide investigator of the Bay County Sheriff's Department located at Panama City, Florida."

"Lieutenant, can you tell us about the relationship between the Bay County Sheriff's Department and the FBI?"

"Senator, I respectfully submit to you that we don't have an ongoing relationship. I recently had the opportunity to work a case with Agent Sydney Sloan in my hometown, but I don't classify that as a relationship."

The chairman's face turned crimson red, and his glare grew more intense.

"Lieutenant Downing, is Agent Sloan in this room?" I pivoted in my chair and looked over my shoulder. Sloan was attractive, and hard to miss.

"Yes, sir, she is."

"Can you identify her for us?" Sydney was sitting two rows back. She raised her hand when I pointed to her.

"Can you describe for the committee what it was like to work with the Bureau?"

"The FBI didn't share information as openly as I would have liked, but they were consummate professionals, and they were doing their job to the best of their abilities. The fact that they're cautious with the amount of information they disseminate is really just good police work. It keeps the bad guys from having easy access to information that might be detrimental to the citizens of the United States of America."

The look on the face of every democratic senator was pure disappointment. I hoped my answers hadn't set me up for long day of grilling. A young committee member from North Carolina smirked when it was his turn to question me. He looked like he was about to rip me to shreds and enjoy every minute of it when he asked, "Is it not true, Lieutenant, that Robert Ramer, your partner at the sheriff's department, almost got into a fight on more than one occasion with one of the male agents who was working this particular case we're discussing today?"

"Senator, I love my partner, but if there was no one around for him to fight with, he'd probably spend most of his day shadow boxing." I didn't mean to be flippant, because my response was close to accurate. Everyone in the hearing room got a chuckle out of it, except the senator who'd asked the question. He looked furious.

"Lieutenant Downing, perhaps you don't realize the seriousness of this hearing," the young senator fired back.

"Senator, perhaps you don't know my partner." A huge roar of laughter echoed in the hearing room.

The democrats fired their best shots at me all morning while the republicans served up home-run pitches for me to knock out of the park. The committee members took a ten-minute break after about an hour and a half. I stood and stretched, but wasn't interested in making cell phone calls or dashing to the bathroom like most everyone in the room. I wanted this to be over with. It was uncomfortable answering the leading questions from both parties, and the process seemed entirely futile to me.

The ten-minute break lasted closer to twenty minutes before all of the senators returned to their seats and finished chatting. Questions similar to the ones I had already answered continued. I squirmed in my seat, occasionally putting my elbow on the table and resting my forehead in my hand as a senior senator ranted about his years as a district attorney and how much cooperation there was between all law enforcement agencies. I caught myself stretching my legs under the table and pushing one hand against the other like an isometric exercise. Before the senator finished his story, I leaned back in my chair and folded my arms with a genuinely disinterested look.

I was elated when the chairman called for a one-hour lunch break. My law school background was certainly an asset for the kind of day I was having; however, sorting out the bickering between political parties would forever be confusing for me. A senate aide escorted me down to the basement and into the cafeteria. I wanted something light and quick, so I chose soup and salad. I didn't want to give anyone another frivolous reason to tear into me like being late from the break. The young aide sat across me in the cafeteria and flipped over endless pages of a notepad. The pressure on Capitol Hill was ridiculous. I was thrilled to be working in a small town far removed from relentless bureaucratic hustle and bustle of Washington. From the exercise I'd just witnessed in the hearing room, support of party affiliation seemed to be more important than serving the common good of the people.

The one-hour lunch break actually took an hour and twenty minutes before all the senators were seated back in the room. The questioning continued, and it was obvious that no side was going to win, and likewise that no side was going to lose. I was taken aback when the republican committee members unexpectedly called Agent Sloan to corroborate my testimony regarding the case we had worked together. She backed up everything I had told the committee, and following her testimony, the senior ranking republican from Utah asked for adjournment. I was thanked for appearing, excused as a witness, and the senators voted on the motion to adjourn. The hearing ended. The young aide retrieved my luggage from a cloak room and rushed over to deliver it to me. Before I could thank him, he'd scurried to catch up with his senator and the rest of the staff.

I walked into the vestibule where FBI Director Fisher was waiting. He held out his hand and said, "Lieutenant Downing, I wanted to personally thank you for your testimony and how you handled yourself before the committee today."

"Like I said, sir, they were easier to get along with than my partner."

The director thanked me again and moved on with his entourage following him.

Agent Sloan remained, dangling her car keys in her hand and asked, "Scott, are you staying overnight?"

"No. My airline reservation was an open return. I'm going to try to standby for a flight this afternoon."

"Which airport, Reagan National?"

"Yeah. I have to catch myself. I still call it Washington National."

"Can I give you a lift to the airport?"

"Thanks, Sydney, but I can get a cab."

"Don't be silly. My car's in the parking lot." She closed her hand, grasping the keys, and hooked her arm through mine. "Besides, that committee doesn't allow enough per diem for a cab ride and slice of a pizza. Got any luggage?"

"Just this trusty carryon piece."

"I don't want to sound pessimistic, but Friday afternoons are usually a zoo round here with everybody trying to get out of town. I hope that open return works."

"Delta has flights to Atlanta leaving every hour from National. The tricky part will be getting on one of our commuters from Atlanta to Panama City."

"Are they that booked?"

"Always. Sydney, are you sure this is not an imposition?"

"That hearing you just went through was an imposition," she said, pointing back towards the room where we'd testified. My head hurt from being brow beaten and bored all day, and my body was stiff and tired from sitting in the same chair for nearly seven hours. There was certainly some relief in knowing I wasn't going to have to bounce across the District in a cab whose shocks were as badly broken as the driver's English.

"I'd be delighted to take you up on your offer," I said as I pushed against the brass handle of the Dirksen Building door.

We stepped out onto the top step of what looked like a hundred steps leading down to the sidewalk. I marveled at the clear early April evening as dusk settled over the city. There were very few panoramas in our country as beautiful as the one I was witnessing. The Lincoln, Jefferson, and Washington monuments were washed by the remnants of the day's sunlight, and the cherry trees in full bloom looked like an explosion of fireworks.

I followed Sydney towards her car in the parking lot, trying to avoid a conversation about the hearing or politics. Pointing to a cherry tree as we walked past, I said, "That's a Yoshino."

She had a surprised look on her face and asked, "How do you know that?"

I pointed across the street and said, "The one over there with the pink blossoms is a Kwanzan."

"Really!" She sounded more shocked than impressed.

"Sorry, Sydney, I don't know why I decided to bore you with trivial stuff like that."

"Hey, it never hurts to know as much as you can about those trees when you live or work in *this* city. Where'd you learn something like that?"

"Georgetown."

"Not in the law school I hope."

"Almost. I had a political science professor who used the types of cherry trees as trick question material. We were actually studying the consequences of our country having to burn and destroy thousands of diseased cherry trees given to us by the Japanese in 1912."

"I've read the story, but I honestly don't recall much of it. My father was in the Pacific during the World War II, so I know a little more about what they gave us in forty-one." She stopped in front of an older model Toyota Camry. "Here we are," she said, unlocking the passenger's door and opening it. I tossed my bag into the back seat. Sydney went around and sat behind the wheel as I reached down for the lever to slide my seat back. I noticed that her seat was back almost as far as mine. I'd forgotten that she was tall for a woman, probably around five-ten. Her brown skirt rose up on her long muscle-toned legs. I had the urge to stare at her a couple of times during the hearing, but fortunately the senators kept me on my toes, avoiding that embarrassment. Since we worked together in Florida, this was the first real chance I'd had to really look at her. She was a beautiful woman with shoulder length blonde hair pulled back into a ponytail highlighting her gorgeous face and smile.

As she backed out of the parking space and pulled onto the road, she turned her head and caught me staring at her. "Nice job in the hearing today," she said, starting the conversation I'd hoped to avoid.

"Thanks," I mumbled, embarrassed that I'd been caught and pretending to be looking at the windows on her side of the car at the passing scenery.

"I had the feeling you weren't expecting the kind of grilling you got today."

"Actually, I wasn't. A couple of them called me at home and chatted like we were long last relatives. This morning they met with me before the hearing and all but tried to give me testimony instructions. They seemed so friendly. I guess I forgot this was Washington."

"Testimony instructions. Jesus, I thought those guys were smarter than that," Sydney said as she weaved in and out of the heavy rush-hour traffic and over the Fourteenth Street Bridge into Virginia.

"They are," I answered. "They came within an inch of the line but never crossed it."

"A lot of people have that talent around here," she said.

"Talent?"

"Bad word choice," she replied. "Anyway, great job. You're a good cop."

"I'm an American citizen who told the truth, that's all."

She nodded in agreement as she pulled up next to the curb at Washington-Reagan National.

"I didn't think anyone could park in front of the terminal anymore," I said pointing to two airport police officers who were scrambling down the sidewalk in our direction. Sydney bounced out of her car holding her credentials and extending them towards the oncoming security personnel.

"Officers, I'm with the FBI," she said. "This gentleman is in the witness protection program." The older of the two officers was probably in his fifties. He stopped in front of Sydney, bent over close to the credentials and squinted, carefully examining her ID. The second officer who looked to be barely twenty-five was twice as heavy as his partner and was still waddling towards us.

"Let's be quick about getting him on his plane, Agent Stone."

"That's Sloan," she said moving past him in my direction. "Sooner I get him on a plane and away from the District, the better we'll all feel." She grabbed me by the arm and fired a serious look of explanation at the pair. Having acquiesced to her request, the older officer ordered his younger counterpart to stay with the vehicle until she returned.

"Witness protection?" I laughingly asked as she hustled us through the electronic doors.

"Sorry, Scott. If I didn't do all of this, we'd still be schlepping your luggage from the other side of that parking lot. I feel like pulling a string or two is the least I can do after you graciously gave up your time to come here to testify." She stood beside me as I waited in the enormous line at the Transportation Security Administration screening checkpoint. Sydney was right about Friday afternoons being a zoo in this airport. It was filled with people I would have guessed to be high-priced lobbyists and members of Congress in expensive suits trekking their way back home for the weekend.

"Sydney, I really do appreciate the ride, but I'm a big boy. I can find my way from here."

"Don't like my company?"

"That's not it at all. I know you have more important things to do than wait in line with me."

The line moved slowly, but I finally made my way to the screener where I held up my ID and ticket. "Thanks again for the lift," I said, making my way past him and looking back at Sydney, who remained on the non-passenger side of the checkpoint.

"My pleasure. Scott, I need to—" I stopped and waited for her to finish, but she nervously halted in mid-sentence and seemed to lose her train of thought. A woman in a TSA uniform who was operating the conveyor belt was urging me to move ahead.

"Take good care of yourself, Syd," I said looking back her.

"You do the same, Scott, and I—" She stopped again just I reached the conveyor belt. I had to raise my voice to talk over the crowd of people pushing in all around me.

"Sydney, is there something you want to say to me?" Her smile evaporated and a look of distress shrouded her face, but she apparently had nothing else to say. Confused, I turned and placed my luggage on the conveyor belt, emptied my pockets into a blue plastic container, took off my shoes, and stepped through the metal detector. On the other side of the detector, I retrieved my bag and shoes and picked up the contents of my pockets.

Just as I bent over to reach for my things and put my shoes back on, Sydney Sloan shouted to me, "I have information about the deaths of your parents." That was the strangest way to say goodbye I'd ever heard. Before I could turn around, she shouted again, "A burglar didn't kill your parents, Scott." I froze. Lightheaded, my knees buckled and my body began to sway. I grabbed the metal sides of the conveyor belt to support myself. Turning around to face Agent Sloan, all I could see was a mass of dark suits with loosened neckties streaming through the checkpoint.

"You okay, sir?" asked a short TSA security officer built like a fireplug and rapidly approaching me. His voice sounded muffled as though I had cupped my hands and placed them over both of my ears.

I shook my head hard to knock the cobwebs out before I answered, "Fine, yeah I'm fine."

"Keep moving please," he said, backing away from me, but continuing to observe my every move. I slung my small bag over my shoulder and faced the oncoming crowds, still searching over my shoulder for Sloan—she was gone. The flow of the crowd forced me to keep pace moving toward my gate. I sporadically checked over my shoulder wishfully imagining Sydney Sloan was following behind me. She wasn't.

The double murder of my mother and father remained a lingering psychological cross for me to bear. I had never discussed any aspect of their murder with Sloan, so how could she have possibly known a burglar was suspected of killing them? The police said they worked the case hard. Because my parents had worked for the State Department, the Vice President of the United States had asked the FBI to give the local law enforcement any assistance they needed to solve the case. It was never solved. If Sydney Sloan knew something about that case, why'd she leave? How could she do this to me?

I thought about calling Sydney from the plane. A quick check of the people sitting around me made me uneasy. This was not the right time. I was exhausted, but I had some issues with trying to sleep. From time to time, I still had nightmares. I was entering that doorway all over again with the overturned Christmas tree, their bloody bodies on the kitchen floor, and that horrible stench. It was all so realistic. My body was telling me to lean back in my seat and get some rest, but my mind was telling me not to do it. In my law enforcement career, I had chased bad guys, been shot at, cornered and attacked. None of that frightened me as much as what I was about to attempt—closing my eyes.

The flight to Atlanta was uneventful. I rode the airport train from the A gate to the C gate, hoping to have less than a thirty minute wait before getting on my eight-fifty commuter flight to Panama City. The counter clerk at my gate was making an announcement when I walked up. She said the Panama City flight was delayed by thirty minutes. That thirty minutes turned into a little over an hour. I checked my watch when we finally circled over St. Andrew Bay. It was ten o'clock central time. I looked out my window and let out a sigh of relief. It felt good to be home.

With no luggage to retrieve at baggage claim, I was pushing the button to raise my garage door less than twenty minutes after we deplaned. I headed straight down the hall to my bedroom where I laid my bag on my bed before grabbing my day timer from the side compartment, turning, and heading back into the living room. I couldn't wait any longer, so I grabbed a cordless phone off the kitchen counter, flipped through the day timer until I found my entry for Sydney. I punched in the numbers—all but the last digit. I held the handset out in front of me and anguished over hitting the last number. I waited until I heard that annoying sound that signified I had failed to dial the number correctly, so I hung up.

Nothing in my life had given me this much angst. From the time I found my parent's lifeless bodies, I wanted so desperately to know who killed them and why. Now a colleague appeared to have some information about their murders, but for some insane reason I couldn't make the call. Maybe I really didn't want to know, or perhaps I was afraid of what I was about to discover.

This was crazy. I had to know what Sydney knew, and I had to know it now. I'd been through three years of personal angst. That was coming to an end tonight.

CHAPTER 5

It was Tuesday, April sixth, the day after Sydney dropped the bomb on me at Washington's Reagan-National Airport before disappearing into the throngs of travelers. There was no point in staring at the ceiling in bedroom for another hour or two, so I crawled out of bed and went to work.

I assumed the place would be empty at ten minutes before six in the morning. Unless an investigator had been called out during the night, it was unusual to find any of them at work this early. Strolling down the investigations wing, I looked over the top of each gray metal cubicle. No one must have been called out, because the place was deserted. My office was across the hall from the lineup of cubicles. It was a real office with four walls and a door.

I wasn't sure why, but I was a little paranoid about anyone overhearing the conversation I was about to have with Sydney, so I closed the door. I sat in my chair, picked up the phone, and dialed Sydney's number. Pushing away from my desk, I made sure I was out of arm's reach of the phone in case I had another nervous attack. Nervously drumming my fingers on the edge of my desk, I waited for her to answer. A recording with a male voice answered, thanking me for calling, and promised to get back with me very soon. I hung up and checked the number I'd dialed. It was the right number. Why a male voice answered was puzzling. Two minutes later line five lit up. That was the private line I'd just used. The number was automatically blocked to any caller ID system. But the FBI could have easily had the technology to unblock my call. There was only one to find out.

"Homicide, Downing." I answered.

"Morning," my partner Robert Ramer said. "I was going to leave you a message, but it sounds like you're already in the office."

"Good morning, Robert."

"I was going to let you know I'd be in early to cover things in case you were late getting in last night."

"Thanks. I appreciate that, but I got in early enough last night."

"Yeah, I see your car now. I'm in the parking lot. See you inside."

"Sure." We hung up. I stood to meet Robert in the hallway and went with him to start the coffee. Robert was whistling coming towards me. Before I reached the doorway of my office, line five was buzzing and blinking again. I stepped back towards my desk and picked up.

"Homicide, Downing." Robert reached my door, noticed I was on the phone, waved, and drifted over to his office.

"May I help you?" the voice on the other end asked politely. It was the same voice I'd heard on the recording when I'd dialed Sydney's number.

"I believe you called me," I responded curtly.

"I'm sorry; I was returning a call from my cell phone."

"The number you just dialed is a blocked number. There's no way it could have appeared on your phone."

"Then I'm sorry. I must have dialed the wrong number," the caller said before hanging up. My first thought was that her cell phone was being answered or intercepted by another agent, but why? Her cell phone number hadn't been changed overnight. A battle between fear and anxiety was going on in my mind. Until I got some answers from Sydney that mental conflict wasn't going to go away.

I needed to think through this, but I couldn't sit there idly and do nothing, so I decided to use this quiet time to straighten the papers and files on my desk. Three of four files down into the stack, a folder bearing the name Wade poked out. Jesus Christ, I'd forgotten about the Wade case. My preoccupation with yesterday's staggering information from Sydney had caused me to lose focus with my work. I'd never been this sloppy before. The Wade case was a crack cocaine murder case that was due to be turned over to the state attorney's office day after tomorrow. Wade allegedly shot and killed his best friend over a rock of crack cocaine. His estranged wife or girlfriend was the only witness. I made up my mind to clean up the Wade case, and then nothing was going to stop me from reaching Sydney even if I had to fly back to Washington.

I went through all the papers in the Wade case file. Fingerprints, ballistics reports, and crime scene reports making sure they were complete and accurate. The only thing I felt was missing was an interview with Wade's girlfriend. The initial report listed her as Wade's estranged wife, which could have prevented her from testifying. An interview with her could sort out whether or not she met the requirements that would prevent her from being forced to testify in the case.

There was a good chance Mark Graham, the state's attorney who was handling this case, would want to sit in on that interview. I gave him a call.

"Mark, Scott Downing. I thought you might like to sit in on an interview with the defendant's girlfriend in the David Wade case?

"Scott, I'm sorry. I should have notified you. David Wade's attorney called me yesterday afternoon. He wants to plea-bargain the case."

"I hope you told him to go to hell."

"Actually, I have a meeting with him in less than an hour. If I can get a guilty plea on manslaughter, I'll probably take it."

I picked up the file and slammed it back on my desk and it popped like a firecracker. "Was that a gunshot?" Mark asked.

"Dammit, Mark, he would have gotten more time if you'd charged him with possession with intent to distribute. This guy killed somebody."

"Scott, I appreciate your hard work, all the time you put in on this case."

"Mark, it's not about my time. My job is to lock up killers and see that they don't have a prayer in the world of getting back on the streets."

"You do a terrific job of putting your cases together, but the septic tank is flooded, Scott. I'm trying to keep the big smelly stuff contained, which means that some of the smaller, slimy shit is bound to get out."

"Mark, I didn't just fall off the turnip truck. You're blowing smoke up my ass, and you know it."

"Scott, what I'm saying is that we work the hardest on the bigger cases that need more effort, and we get what we can on guys like Wade and his rock cocaine smoking friend. It's all about prioritizing the level of the crimes. You know, picking your battles."

"We had a good case, Mark. I know we could've at least gotten a conviction for second-degree murder on this creep. Tell me we wouldn't be prosecuting the hell out of Wade if the kid he killed had been from a prominent family and not a crack head?"

"That's not the way it is, Scott, but we have to allocate our time and the court's time according to what's before us. I'll talk to you later, Scott." The phone went dead. He'd hung up. I was so pissed off, I threw my phone at the receiver. It bounced across my desk and landed on the floor. I grabbed the cord, pulled it back up, and placed it on the receiver. My mother used to say you can find good in almost any situation. I pondered the Wade case. Maybe my mother was right. At least I didn't waste my time interviewing Wade's girlfriend.

Days like today made me believe that the term *criminal justice system* was an oxymoron. Prosecutors, judges and even cops were all so busy that they had to pick and choose who to take to court. Defense attorneys' requests to plea-bargain their client's charges had become a fact of life for both the prosecution and the defense sides of the judicial system. I tossed the Wade file on the floor by my desk. A few pages leaked out and I shoved them back inside with the edge of my foot. I needed to file it properly, but I knew if I kept it in my hands much longer, I'd be tempted to throw the whole thing in the trash. There was way too much work in the file to do that.

Now that my most pressing case was no longer pressing, I was free to completely focus my energies on Sydney Sloan and my parents' murder. It was time to bring this nightmare to an end.

CHAPTER 6

Wednesday, April 7, 2004

If the Bureau was tracking my phone calls, I was about to give them another opportunity to do just that this morning. I came close to calling Sydney's cell phone a dozen times last night, but that male voice that answered yesterday had me too apprehensive about calling that number again. A call to the FBI from the sheriff's office was the most prudent decision to make. I could always justify my reason for calling since Sydney and I had recently worked a case together.

I dialed the number, listening to the phone ringing in one ear and to a couple of officers talking as they approached up the hallway out of my other ear. Their voices grew louder, and I recognized one of them as Cale Golden, a uniformed deputy who'd been aggressively seeking a promotion into investigations. On the second ring Golden and Ray Stanford had stopped in front of my office door. They were in the midst of a discussion about the Florida State University football team. Golden waved good morning and I motioned to him close my door. I saw him mouth the word *sorry* before he reached for my door and swung it shut.

The FBI switchboard operator answered on the third ring. I explained to her that I was calling about a case that Agent Sloan and

34

I had worked together at Panama City Beach, Florida. I told her that I needed to speak with Sloan about the case. She put me on hold, I assumed she was looking up Sloan in their directory, but it was taking way too long. She came back on the line, "I'll need to take your information. Someone will get back with you as soon as possible." I gave her my contact information. She said she'd have someone, but not necessarily Agent Sloan, get back in touch with me. I'd called Sydney at the Bureau when we worked together, and they forwarded my call to her. I thanked the operator and hung up. I had an uncomfortable feeling about the way my call had been handled. With Congress wanting to fire the Bureau director over the way he worked with other law enforcement agencies, why was I just given the run around?

Cathy Cornwell, my secretary, knocked on the door and delivered my mail and phone messages. I flipped through and stacked them by importance. There wasn't one from Sydney. Nothing was exceedingly pressing, and I didn't want to be on my phone if Sydney returned my call. My beeper buzzed on my belt. It was the code for the SWAT team. Robert Ramer and I nearly collided in the hallway.

"You know what the call is?" he asked.

"No idea, Robert." We hustled to the garage area of the building that was used exclusively by the SWAT unit. Each member had a locker that stored his SWAT uniform and gear. We all changed and climbed into the back of our armored car. Donated by a local bank, the vehicle was perfect for a SWAT unit. Major Holloman was the SWAT leader, and when everyone had changed and climbed into the back of the truck, he secured the door and radioed to Rick Funchess to drive. The major told us that uniformed deputies had responded to a call from a woman who said her boyfriend had set a methamphetamine lab up in her house. She was afraid of an explosion, and with good reason. Meth labs blew up all the time.

"Here's the kicker," the major said. "Now the dope maker is holding his girlfriend and her baby hostage and threatening to kill them." I was the hostage negotiator, so I asked the major if we had any background information yet.

"The woman gave us the boyfriend's name when she called. We're also running their plates through NCIC. Com. center is going to fax us a background sheet. I should have it for you by the time we get there."

"Thanks," I said to the major. It was important to me to have as much background information as possible to effectively communicate with a hostage taker. We drove about a mile farther when the major was radioed telling us to stand down. I inhaled deeply and released a long sigh. Mine wasn't the only one. The back of the armored car was filled with steady professionals, but it was always a great relief to hear the words *stand down* in a hostage situation. We continued to the scene in case the situation had deteriorated. Fortunately the deputies were able to talk the meth dealer out of the house, releasing his hostages. We returned to the sheriff's office.

I changed and went back to my office.

Cathy Cornwell asked, "Everything come out okay?"

"We got a stand-down on the way there."

"Great."

"Cathy, I missed breakfast this morning, so I was going to head to an early lunch."

"Have a good one, Lieutenant." I punched the code into my desk phone to forward incoming calls to my cell.

Across the bay from Panama City Beach was a little fishing village known as St. Andrews. It was the first official location for the delivery of the US mail in Bay County. The mail boat arrived once a week up until the early 1900s, stopping at a dock directly across from the present day location of the best oyster bar in the world. Randy Hunt, the proprietor, was about five feet five inches tall with a broad chest and smile.

He greeted me at the door. "Where've you been?"

"Fighting crime," I said.

"Been missin' some good oysters lately."

"I plan to make up for that today, Randy."

"Gotcha a stool on the end of the bar."

"Randy, I'm expecting a call about a case; mind if I get you to seat me at a booth in a quiet corner?"

"You got it, Scott." He escorted me through the restaurant past the walls that were covered with metal license plates that had been donated by patrons over the years. Most of the plates were from states in the southeast, but all fifty states were represented. The low ceiling was covered with dollar bills bearing the names of the patrons who'd taped them up there.

There were a dozen tables in the center of the room with four and five unmatched chairs scattered around them. "How about this one," he said as he pointed to the last booth against the wall.

"That's great, Randy. Thanks."

Randy hollered at the girl who was waiting on tables in that section. "Hey, Beverly, don't sit anybody in this booth," he added pointing to the booth next to the one I was sitting in.

"Randy, I appreciate that, but if you need to seat somebody there, you go ahead. I wouldn't want you to lose a customer."

"Nah. We're fine. You just keep us safe around here," he said, walking away, visiting a table of regulars who wanted to chat with him. This was another affirmation of how nice it was to live in a small town where you could be a big fish in a little pond. I laid my cell phone on the table. I'd set it to vibrate, so it wouldn't disturb other patrons in the restaurant. Cell phones ringing in businesses, churches, meetings, and public places in general pissed me off, so I kept my cell phone on vibrate most of the time. I picked up the menu, but I didn't even look at it. I wanted oysters.

The waitress was tall and skinny, wearing a red Hunt's tee shirt that was at least one size too large, which she had compensated for by pulling the loose material together and twisting a knot in the side of the shirt. She had bleached blonde hair that was crying out for a refresher application to the black roots along the part down the center of her head. She looked like she was trying to set a world record for chewing gum faster than any human had ever chewed before. "How you doin'?"

"I'm fine, thanks."

"What can I getcha?"

"Two dozen oysters and a Coke please."

She scribbled my order on her palm-sized order pad, and then dashed away from the table with a, "Thanks, sweetie," spoken over her shoulder between gum smacking. I was sure she called every customer sweetie, and I took comfort in knowing she meant nothing by it. She was back in less than five minutes, leaned down next to the table with a round serving tray and began to transfer items from the tray to my table. Hunt's was one of the few places left in America that still served Coca Cola in a bottle. Next came a row of saltine crackers sealed in wax paper, then some seafood cocktail sauce, and a bottle of hot sauce. She followed that delivery with some southern expressions that required five or more years of living deep in Dixie to comprehend. "I'm fixin' to brang yor oysters rat back." She darted towards the oyster bar and returned seconds later with a tray full of oysters on the half shell. "Kin I getcha anythang else?"

"No thanks. Just those wonderful Apalachicola oysters," I replied. I picked up the first one and slid it onto a cracker. I shook a little cocktail sauce on top of the oyster, topped that with a few drops of hot sauce and took a bite. There is something about the taste of oysters from this part of the world that always gave me a comfortable homey feeling. The clear waters of the Apalachicola River emptied into the Apalachicola Bay before funneling out into the Gulf of Mexico. This perfect blend of fresh and salt water provided the best oyster breeding region in America.

Sailboats, spinnakers billowing, cruised the bay. I watched them as I ate, my mind briefly diverted from the anticipated call from Sydney. That diversion ended when my cell phone dauntingly vibrated and bounced around on the tabletop. My heart rate raced as the cell phone chattered to the edge. Steadying myself, I pounced on the phone, flipped it open, and looked at the number in my caller ID window. It was my stockbroker. I didn't answer it, which sent it to my voicemail. John Johnson was a nice guy, but I didn't want to be in a conversation with him and possibly miss the call from the FBI. My waitress returned, and the speed of her chewing had slowed dramatically. Either all the sugar was gone, or her jaw finally became exhausted from moving so fast. I ordered another Coke. The Louisiana Hot Sauce tasted good going down, but when you'd had too much, Hunt's didn't have enough Cokes to put the fire out.

"Anythang else?"

"No, I'm great, thanks." She left me to my last dozen of the little gems. I lightened up on the hot sauce and finished them posthaste. Now when I was ready for the damn phone to jump all over the table and scare the hell out of me, I got nothing. Hindsight was twenty-twenty. I could have sat on my favorite stool, if I had only known. I paid my bill and headed to my car.

Plenty of time had elapsed since I'd left my message with the switchboard operator at the Bureau. Maybe Sydney wasn't going to call at all. Maybe she'd been told not to call.

I wasn't ready to give up on her. I'd give it a little more time.

I drove back to the sheriff's office and was walking into the lobby when Tom Garrett, a criminal investigator who was headed out, stopped me in the doorway. Tom was huge. He weighed nearly three hundred pounds, but at six five he wasn't heavy. His tie was always loosened and his collar always slightly opened. The rumor around the sheriff's office was he couldn't get any of his shirts to button all the way up to the collar button.

"The sheriff is looking for you," Tom said. "He bumped into me outside your office and asked if I'd seen you. I told him I hadn't. I think he went into your office and left you a note. Sounded serious."

"I've had my phone and radio turned on. He could have called me."

"Not sure why he didn't, but I'd drop by his office if I were you."

"Thanks, Tom." As he moved past me through the doorway, I grabbed the door and asked, "Hey how's that new baby?

"She's wonderful. Up to eleven and a half pounds and one week old yesterday. Thanks for asking."

I entered my office and dropped my briefcase on my desk. The sheriff had stuck a post it note on my phone. It said "Downing see me ASAP." He wasn't one to waste words. None of us ever procrastinated when it came to getting back to him. He had a temper that fired from a very short fuse.

I made my way down the long green corridor. There were sixteen large, framed pictures of previous sheriffs, going back to the year 1930, eight hanging on the right and eight on the left. A couple of those old guys whose images hung in that hallway had been removed from office by the Governor, so we nicknamed this the Hall of Shame.

Donna, the sheriff's secretary, asked me to have a seat. Her hair was pulled back in a bun as usual, and she was wearing a tailored business suit. She was very matter-of-fact and organized. People who met her for the first time usually thought she was a bitch. She didn't have the most outgoing personality, but the truth was, she was a consummate professional, dedicated to her job and her boss. She scribbled a quick note, rose from her seat, and reached for the sheriff's door. She turned and gave me a serious look that reminded me of the way a junior high teacher would look at you to warn you about your behavior. "I'll let him know you're here, Scott. I wouldn't take any phone calls, radio calls or anything else if I were you." She turned back around with her shoulders arched, her head held high, her nose in the air, and disappeared through the doorway, leaving it partially open. He kept talking on the phone when she handed him the note.

She retreated from the office and started to close the door when the sheriff shouted, "Downing, get in here." I knew this tone of voice. He was pissed.

He was sitting behind his huge mahogany desk that was always covered with files, stacks of reports from the various departments, and three to five newspapers. Today looked like a five newspaper day. Other than his high back, nail head leather executive chair, the two side chairs in front of his desk were the most comfortable chairs in the building. There was no doubt that his favorite color was sheriff's department uniform green, because that was his color selection for all of his office furnishings, accessories like paper weights, note pads, even the hallway walls.

"What the hell are you doing calling the FBI about the Gallatti case?" I was less than five feet away, but I was sure they could hear him at the other end of the building. His face was dark red and the veins in his forehead and neck were bulging. At six eight he was one of the few people I knew who was taller than me. Folding his arms, he laid them in the center of his desk and leaned his body towards me. He was a big man, and he was intimidating even sitting down.

"Sheriff, I needed to reach Agent Sloan, but the Bureau cell phone number she gave me when I was in DC isn't her number any longer."

"Why the hell do you need to talk with her about the Gallatti case?"

"Sheriff, I never said anything about the Gallatti case. I told the switchboard operator that Sloan and I had worked together on a case. I wasn't referring to the Gallatti case."

He unfolded his arms and reached all the way across his desk, grabbing the edge on the side I was sitting on. For a minute I thought he was going to pick up his desk and throw it out from between us. His nostrils flared and I could feel the warm air he was loudly exhaling. "Correct me if I'm wrong, Scott, but isn't the Gallatti case the only case you worked with Sloan?"

I squirmed back and forth in my seat like my butt cheeks were landing on tacks with every move. "She has some information about something I've been working on, and I was trying to reach her regarding that."

"You're working with the FBI on a case that the sheriff, and for that matter, no one in this entire damn department knows anything about. How do you think that makes me feel or look in the eyes of the people who've been calling me from Washington? They're asking me why my goddamn chief homicide investigator is calling the Bureau. Do you know what I've been telling them? I've been telling them I have no fucking idea why you'd be calling. Now, Mr. Downing, how stupid do you think I look in their eyes up there now?"

"I'm sorry, sir. All I can say is that it's personal, and I'll try not to do it on your time."

His knuckles were pale when he let go of the desk, rocked back in his chair, softening his voice, "Scott, I have never once worried about the time and effort to you give me. Hell, for that matter you probably have enough comp time and annual leave to retire five years early, so neither of us is going to worry about whose clock you're on. I'll back you up about whatever it is you're working on, but I can't help when you leave me in the dark." He was now reclining so far that he looked like he was in a dentist chair preparing for a cleaning.

"Thank you, sir. I appreciate that, and I apologize for making you look bad."

"I take it that means you're not offering any information."

"Sir, this is very personal." A long pause was followed by a facial color change from red to pink. He knew the story about my parents' murders. I didn't need to offer any additional explanation.

"If they call me again, I'll cover for you as best I can. If it gets to be political, I mean beyond my pay grade, and they start calling the county manager or county commissioners who approve our budget, I may not be able to back you up."

"I appreciate your understanding and your support, sir."

"That's all, Downing."

"Thank you, sir," I said as I stood and exited his office. I wished I could have told him everything, but there was no way I could put Sloan in that kind of spot. If the sheriff had promised someone at the Bureau that he'd look into this situation, and I had told him too much, he might give them some information without knowing the possible consequences. I didn't even know what those consequences were, but for the Bureau to have placed a call to the sheriff so soon after my call, it was very apparent that someone in DC was concerned about me speaking with Sloan. The question was why.

CHAPTER 7

I sat down at my desk and pulled out my day timer, searching my calendar for pending cases, trials, or anything urgent related to work. The next ten days looked incredibly clear. A business card tumbled out of the back of my day timer when I reached to put it in my briefcase. My eyes zeroed in on the FBI seal. "Shit." I snatched it up and flipped it over. I remembered Sydney had given me her card, but I'd totally forgotten that she written her personal cell phone and home phone number on the back. Why didn't I remember that? I thought about calling her right away, but opted to take the card with me and try her when I got home. The sheriff had agreed to back me up, but he reminded me that the Bureau could go political and complain to the county manager if they were concerned with my communications with one of their agents. For his sake, I needed to wait on making the call.

Jay Arthur, a rookie investigator, beeped me on the intercom while I was putting Sydney's card away. Arthur was the low man in seniority, so he was assigned most of our larceny and burglary cases. He asked if I'd come over and take a look at a case he was working on. I put my day timer in my briefcase, zipped it up, and placed it on the top of my desk.

His case file was open and the papers were scattered across the top of his metal desk. I moved around and stood next to his chair, looking over his shoulder, like a good old-fashioned schoolteacher would do.

"I know this isn't as glamorous as homicide, but I could sure use a fresh set of eyes looking at this."

"Jay, I'm always happy to help out on any case, but I need you to make me a promise."

"What kind of promise?"

"Never refer to a homicide case as glamorous."

"Sorry, I should have known better than that."

"Great, now let's have a look at what you've got."

"Lieutenant, this case started out as a few simple burglaries, but it's evolved into a complicated case." Jay had a look of frustration that cied out for a little help.

Thumbing through his reports, I felt like these burglaries were spontaneous, ill-conceived B&Es. These crimes were all over the board. "Probably kids," I said as I picked up one of the reports filled out by an officer who had worked the case in the field. Pros almost always presented patterns or similarities, such as the time they committed the burglaries, the type of neighborhood they hit and the type of items they stole. They were neat, cautious, and seldom left any sign that they had ever entered the home. "Don't get me wrong, Jay, these kids appear to have enough criminal savvy to keep from getting caught, temporarily anyway. You're sure none of the stolen merchandise has surfaced anywhere around the county in pawn shops or flea markets over the past three months?"

"Lieutenant, we've worked the pawn shops, consignment shops, classified ads in the paper, and our deputies have worked their asses off canvassing the area where the burglaries occurred, but we keep coming up empty." He rubbed his forehead with his right hand. He pinched his eyes between his index finger and his thumb, and for a second I thought he was going to get teary eyed.

"No prints?"

"Gloves."

"Footprints?"

"A couple."

"Make any molds?"

"Yeah, the lab made some, but we have nowhere to go with them right now."

"Sooner or later, they'll make a mistake. Hopefully they won't break into a home and discover a homeowner with a gun, prepared to protect his property at all costs. Then your case becomes mine."

"Let's hope it doesn't come to that."

"How about eBay, Jay?"

He was dumbfounded by that question. "eBay?"

I thought the younger guys were much more astute about the Internet, but it appeared Jay needed a little eBay 101. "You search until you find an item that matches one of your stolen items. Then you email the sellers offering to come pick that item up if they'll end the auction early. If you have a Panama City seller, you snag a search warrant to get a look at his or her shoes."

"Damn. The Internet. I should have already checked that. Thanks, Lieutenant."

"No problem. Let me know how you do with it."

I went back to my desk and pulled up the homicide cases on my computer to make sure the notes in my day timer were accurate. There were only two cases on the screen. One was an old case under an appeal that probably wouldn't be granted a trial date until much later in the year, and the other was the Wade case that the state attorney's office had plea-bargained. I entered the plea information next to that one. It looked like I had a decent opening for locating Sydney Sloan.

I picked up my briefcase and headed to my car. On the way home, I stopped at a local wine and cheese shop where I picked up a bottle of Antinori Tignanello. It was a blend of mostly Sangiovese, a little Cabernet Sauvignon and even less Cabernet Franc, and it was my favorite Italian wine. I had enough cappelletti stuffed with spinach and cheese left over from a recent dinner party to make myself a little leftover Italian.

The crème de la crème of tonight's meal would be a loaf of Aunt Maggie's freshly baked bread. Walking out of the wine shop I reached for my cell phone and called her. She was the wonderful woman who had cleaned our house one day a week since I was two years old. Maggie was like a surrogate mother to me. Although she would have never complained, I knew she wasn't up to the same kind of work she had taken on over thirty years ago, so I tried to keep my house as clean as possible.

About six years ago, she took in her grandson when her daughter, the boy's mother, was arrested for drug abuse. Maggie did a terrific job of raising Dion, and he was a good kid. Last year I created a fictitious trust, which had anonymously presented a college scholarship to Dion, provided he maintained a good grade point average and was a solid citizen. My accountant and investment counselor did everything they could to prevent Maggie from discovering where the scholarship originated.

I'd seen an ad in a Best Buy circular in last Sunday's paper showing phones for seniors with large numbers and a larger than normal ID display, so I bought her one and delivered it to her that same afternoon when she got home from church. Dion and I programmed it for her, and we promised her she would love this newfangled thing once she got used to it. My cell phone number was the first to appear in her caller memory.

She picked it up on the second ring, like she was expecting my call.

"Scottie, you smell that bread from the sheriff's department, don't you?"

"Maggie, I'm not at the sheriff's department right now, but I sure can smell your fresh bread."

"Well come on over, child, and get yourself some, before the preacher picks it up and hauls it to the church for the bake sale." Maggie's church sold baked goods as a fundraiser, and her bread was famous in our little town.

"I'll be right there. I'm just around the corner from you on Sixth Street."

"I'll get some ready for you, Scottie." She was the only human being on earth who I'd still allow to call me Scottie. Maggie could call me anything she wanted.

When I pulled up in front of her small beige stucco house, the aroma of fresh bread baking wafted all the way across the yard to my car. She knew if I came inside I'd find something that I wanted to repair or replace, that's why she always met me at the front door with my bread fresh from her oven. I had to smile when I saw her. She looked like a female version of the Pillsbury Doughboy with her large girth wrapped in a white apron. My mother had always told me that Maggie had to be that size to hold her huge heart.

Her pastor'd had her name embroidered across the top of her apron in three-inch tall, red letters. Patches of gray hair were peeking out from her white baker's hat. Her wire-rimmed spectacles had white flour around the edges, contrasting against her dark mocha skin. "You look tired, Scottie. You not working all day and all night are you?"

"No, ma'am. I'm working my usual hours."

"Scottie, I was there when you buried your mama and daddy, and I was with you the day you buried your grandmama. I know you promised to make them all proud, but you inherited twenty million dollars, Son, you don't need to be out chasing criminals all hours of the day and night."

"Maggie, I swore I would get my law degree from Georgetown and do something with it to help people. I feel like Mom, Dad, and Gram are all happy with me being a cop. Besides, Maggie, I like what I do."

"Your mama and daddy know what you're doing, Scottie. Those people are all in a special place, and they're keeping track of you. They're just as proud of you as I am." I gave her a hug and said goodbye. My parents had always treated Maggie like a member of our family and now that they were gone along with my grandmother, she was all I had left. Every time I threatened to move out to my beach condo, Maggie would admonish me and tell me I'd better stay in the Cove, so I'd be close enough to have hot bread by the time I drove home from her house. What she was really saying to me was please don't leave me, and I wasn't about to.

CHAPTER 8

I backed into my driveway, a law enforcement habit that allowed for a quick takeoff if necessary. The yellow bush daisies and allemandes I had planted around the sides and beneath the two bay windows were in full bloom, and the hanging baskets on either side of the front door were loaded with red geraniums and ivy. Opening the oversized red front door, I dropped my keys and cell phone on the table in the foyer and hung my shoulder holster and Glock 19 in the closet. Ten quick steps across the open living room, and I reached the green and gray speckled granite kitchen countertop, laid my briefcase on the counter, setting the bread next to it. I opened the wine to let it breathe, took the pasta out of the fridge and turned on the oven. I sat on a bar stool, checking my phone messages. There weren't any. I was so sure there'd be a message from Sydney.

I picked up the cordless phone and walked down the hall to my bedroom, where I took off my sport coat and tie before returning to the living room. The news junkie in me needed a fix, so I picked up the remote control and turned on MSNBC. The first ring of the phone sent my heart into my throat. Damn, I'd tossed the phone on the bed when I took off my coat, so I raced to get to it. My loafers were fairly new, and

I couldn't get any traction, so I slipped on the polished hardwood floor, causing me to bump into a very old box-like piece of furniture with an open lid containing a collection of ironstone pitchers. The early nineteenth century grain bin was next to the hallway, and I'd just crashed into the corner of it. That would be an ugly bruise tomorrow. I ricocheted off it and dashed towards the bedroom. On the fourth ring I picked up phone as I dove onto the bed.

"Downing."

"Lieutenant, this is Jay Arthur."

"Hello, Jay."

"I hate to bother you at home, but I wanted you to be the first to know that we found several matches on eBay, from a Panama City seller. I emailed the seller and asked if we could meet. The sellers were two juveniles. I called for a search warrant and discovered a good bit of the missing merchandise. One of the juveniles was as savvy as you gave them credit for. He was wearing tennis shoes that matched a shoe mold we'd made from under a window of the last house that was burglarized."

"Good work, Jay."

"I just did what you suggested. Thanks, Lieutenant."

"Good night, Jay." It wasn't the call I'd been waiting for, but it did make me feel good to have helped.

Lying on my back, I stared up at the six-foot by twelve-foot Turkish rug depicting the Tree of Life that I'd hung on the wall. I'd purchased the rug on a vacation to Greece. It wasn't as great a treasure as the original Monet, Salvador Dali, and a Georgia O'Keeffe that my grandmother had collected and displayed in the living room, but the rug was special purchase for me. My grandmother had lived in this house for over forty years, and although I'd completely renovated it, I tried to maintain it as close as possible to the way it was when she lived there.

Back in the kitchen, I wrapped Maggie's bread in foil, took the casserole dish with the pasta and shoved it all in the oven. Checking my wristwatch, it was nearly six o'clock central time where I was in the Florida panhandle, seven for Sydney in DC. She had to be home by now. Taking a deep breath, I listened to the ringing sound. Then I heard her voice. It was a recording, so I hung up without leaving a message. The card also had her cell phone on it, so I tried that number this time. After four rings I got another voicemail message. This time I left a message, giving her my home phone number and my personal cell phone number.

There was a gourmet meal waiting for me, albeit leftovers. Just as I clutched the casserole dish, the phone rang. It sounded like thunder booming through my house. I slid the dish back into the oven, brushing my left arm against the upper rack, getting a nasty little burn. "Shit."

Spinning around I swiftly reached for the phone.

"Hello." It was Ellen Gardner, who I'd been dating off and on for several months. Trying my best not to reveal my disappointment that she was on the line instead of Sydney, I told her I was expecting a call about a case. With an apology for cutting the conversation short and a promise to call her back as soon as possible, I ended the call and went back to my pasta and bread, this time getting it out of the oven without incident. My mother would have been appalled to witness my eating habits.

Proper etiquette was drilled into me as a young boy, because of my parent's work in the State Department. If I had been invited to dinner with the royal family in Buckingham Palace, I could have done so without dishonoring my mother or my country. However, when you're a cop and a bachelor to boot, etiquette is not always high on your list of priorities. I took a large spoon and a fork out of the silverware drawer and began eating directly out of the casserole dish. I poured myself another glass of wine, cut a piece of Maggie's bread and had a real Italian picnic. Sometimes, when I came home for lunch, I would stand over the sink and eat. I called those meals sinkies. I knew my dining habits must have had my parents regularly turning over in their graves.

Most of the pasta was gone when I decided to call it quits, throwing what was left down the disposal. A quick flip of the switch, a turn of the faucet, and the last of the noodles disappeared. I left the dishes in the sink for a later cleanup.

Night after night I'd reviewed my parent's murder case in hopes that I'd discover some tiny piece of evidence to justify reopening the case.

I kept the file under the cushion of my favorite chair. I don't know why I felt like it needed a secret hiding place, but I did. It wasn't a secret to Maggie, though. She never mentioned anything about reading the file, but on several occasions it was obvious the file had been moved. I pulled the file out from under the cushion and started reading. The cops' reports said they had dusted everywhere in my parents home for fingerprints, including the telephone, the toilet, light switches, door handles and their bodies. There was no ballistics report from the crime lab, and the medical examiner's report only mentioned that the bullet wounds were believed to be from a .22 caliber weapon.

The grandfather clock chimed seven times, so I got up and slid the file back under the cushion. It was time to talk to Sydney. I punched in her home number, and when I heard the first ring, I held my breath. A voicemail message picked up precisely on the fourth ring. It was the voice of the FBI Agent I had worked with at Panama City Beach. Her tone was confident, but not arrogant. The message on the recording was her law enforcement voice. I never knew anyone needed a different voice until I worked the Gallatti case with Sydney. An attractive female working as a cop, any kind of cop, was often forced to put up a ballsy front in order to be respected by her male counterparts. Ironically we men didn't have any expectations of each other.

I began recording my message, "Syd, this is—" and I was cut off. I looked down at my phone to see if the battery had died or if I had hit a button or anything that would have cut off the call. I hit redial, and this time the phone rang a half dozen times without any answer, not even including voicemail. That was strange. Maybe my redial was off somehow. I slowly punched in the number again. This time I let the phone ring fifteen times. No answer. What the hell was going on?

CHAPTER 9

I redialed twice. The first time I got a voice message after four rings and on the next try it rang fifteen times with no answer or no voicemail. How can you go from voicemail to no answer? I searched for the quickest distraction, so I turned on the TV and flipped through the cable new channels. It was no use. I stared at the chair across from me, knowing that the case file was under the cushion. Eerily, it felt like I could hear them asking me to make the call.

Dammit! Her voicemail picked up again after four rings. It was ten o'clock in DC, so my chances of speaking with her tonight had probably expired for the evening. If she hadn't answered by now, she probably wasn't going to. My next choice for a sedative was a hot shower.

I was lifting my shirt over my head when I heard my cell phone ring. I spun around to go answer my phone and before I could pull the shirt all the way off my head, I plowed into the doorjamb. Jesus, I was going to kill myself over this damn call. The phone was sitting next to my keys on the table in the foyer. I flipped it open.

"Hello."

"Scott, this is Sydney."

"What's going on with your phone? I called you earlier tonight and got your voicemail and then—" She cut me off in mid sentence.

"I hung up on you the first time before you said your name, and then I unplugged the phone, so it just rang after that and bypassed the recording."

"You Feds play espionage even with your telephones don't you?"

"Scott, I'm at a payphone inside a convenience store a couple of blocks from my townhouse. You can't call me, Scott. I'll have to call you."

"I don't understand, Syd. I tried your FBI cell phone from my office this morning, but I got a male voicemail and a male agent called me back. At least I assumed he was with the Bureau."

"He was. That phone number has been transferred to a special agent. I have a new number, but I can't give it to you."

"Sydney, what's going on? How's the Bureau involved in this?"

"Scott, I can't say right now, but I'll tell you everything soon. Right now I need to get back to my apartment."

"Why? Are you being followed?"

"Just do what I say, please. You need to buy a long distance phone card tomorrow. Call my cell from a pay phone and ask for Whittaker. I'll say you have the wrong number and then I'll get your number off my caller ID. Then I'll use my phone card to call you back from a pay phone."

"My mother's maiden name was Whittaker," I said.

"I know."

"What do you mean you know? How the hell could you know that?"

"Call me tomorrow at nine p.m. sharp. Good night, Scott." The phone went dead. I stared at it like I had just received a call from outer space. I knew an FBI agent could easily get information like my mother's maiden name, but what would cause her to look up something like that? It almost felt like I was a criminal or someone the FBI was chasing.

I realized I was standing by my front door stark naked. I turned the phone off and went back to the shower. The shower was invigorating. It was also a stimulating think tank for me. Sydney's behavior could mean a thousand different things. If I was going to guess, I would say the Bureau wants agents to strictly focus FBI business, and maybe Sydney was working on something for me on company time. But if that was the case, why was she so secretive and why'd she have to go to a convenience store to call me? I turned off the shower before any more thoughts filled my head.

Several good novels were sitting on my nightstand, but I was too uptight to read. I turned out the lights, hoping that tomorrow would be a day of answers instead of more questions.

CHAPTER 10

Thursday, April 8, 2004

The sun was barely above the surface of St. Andrew Bay, but high enough to shine into my bedroom through the double glass doors. The deck outside my door and the dock on the bayou were usually dull and dry. They both glistened in the sunshine this morning after being covered by a heavy dew. The eight posts on the end of my dock were all occupied; five with pelicans, two with white egrets and one with a great blue heron.

The walk-in closet presented my first decision of each day. The Bay County Sheriff's Department was not exactly a fashion show, but dressing professionally and wearing properly color coordinated suits, shirts, shoes and ties was something my father always prided himself in, and he must have passed that quirk on to me. Even though I had no court appearances, no sessions with any government officials, no significant reason to put on a coat and tie today, I was always aware that a homicide could occur at any time, which could thrust me into the local media spotlight. I went with a dark brown sport coat with tiny cream-colored flecks, and an eggshell colored long-sleeved shirt and dark brown silk tie. After a quick shave and shower, it was off to my second office—my car.

I let dispatch know I was in service. "Thirteen to Bay."

"Bay, go ahead, thirteen."

"Ten eight."

"Ten eight, thirteen." Although I was miles from my desk at the sheriff's office, I was now officially at work.

Detouring a few blocks out of my way, I stopped at a little bagel joint, parked out front, grabbed my handheld radio and cell phone, and followed the aroma of fresh bagels and coffee. Joel Miller and his wife Cathy had moved down here a few months ago from New Jersey, so I no longer had to order from H& H Bagels in New York and have them delivered by FedEx. Joel and Cathy were the closest thing to being there. Joel was usually in the kitchen and Cathy was managing the dining room. Through the large plate glass window, she waved as I exited my car. I raised my hand and returned her hello. Cathy was probably a size two, which seemed ironic for a restaurant entrepreneur. She had short dark hair, bright dark eyes, and a warm comforting smile, with which she always greeted me when I stepped through their door.

This couple had worked hard at making their little café succeed. Their special touches were evident from the hand-painted checkerboard border around the ceiling and above the chair railing. A whimsical mural of a male baker and his female assistant painted directly on the back wall appeared to be watching over the operation. The other interior walls were a soothing pale yellow.

"Table for one," I said, holding up an index finger.

"Good morning. How about this one, sir?" Cathy responded with a genuine laugh, since we went through this routine several times a week, and I always ended up at the same table.

Ushering me to my regular spot, the steam rose above the just-poured cup of vanilla bean decaf. I closed my eyes, and deeply inhaled, savoring the aroma. Today's edition of the *Panama City News Herald* was folded and lying next to my silverware on the left hand side of the table. When she saw me coming, as she did today, she tried to have my coffee poured and also share their copy of the local paper.

I picked up the *News Herald*, held it out to the side and tapped it a few times. This was a task I'd learned to do before opening the paper based on some earlier mishaps. Joel was a baker who enjoyed reading the paper while he worked. Without giving it a second thought, he'd turn the pages with floury fingers, thus the next person to open that paper and tilt it upright stood a very good chance of receiving a lap full of white flour. Cathy walked away to take someone else's order, and I started perusing the morning *Herald*. Our hometown paper was small, but they did a great job of filling in the details of what was on the late news. I scanned the A section and the sports before reading the local and state news.

"Mother of God," I accidentally said out loud, dropping all of the paper except for the page I was holding.

"You okay over here?" she asked, sitting the plate with the bagel and cream cheese in front of me.

"Sorry. I didn't mean to blurt that out. I saw something about an old case of mine that surprised me, that's all."

"Thank goodness. For a minute, I thought Joel made the decaf like he's been brewing the regular coffee lately, black as crude oil."

"No, the coffee's fine, thanks."

"How about a refill?"

"No thanks, Cathy." She strolled back behind the counter, scooped up a coffee pot, and headed over to refill her other patrons.

The local story was infuriating. Tyrone Montgomery, an African-American who had brutally murdered a friend of his when he was nineteen, about five and a half years ago, was being paroled. It was my first homicide case, and Montgomery had been convicted of second-degree murder. He never showed any remorse when he admitted the grisly details of what happened the night he went to a friend's house, got into an argument with that young man, spotted a .357 magnum revolver lying on a table, picked it up and fired from point-blank range. I remember wincing as he coldly described the way he watched his friend sweat for several minutes, crying and stuttering as he put the barrel of the gun against his friend's forehead. He described the blood splattering all over the room like he had blown open a watermelon. Montgomery was sick and should have been put away for a long time. He was sentenced to twenty-five years, but apparently the parole board must have believed his story that Jesus had appeared in his cell one night, and after a long chat with God, he was now a new man. The cons I'd met who'd spent five years or more in Raiford typically had become more callused and hardened, not kinder and gentler. If he was coming home to Bay County, I felt certain I'd have reason to deal with him again, but it wouldn't be in any church.

I finished my breakfast and the newspaper, paid my check, waved goodbye, and headed to the sheriff's office. Radio traffic was light this morning, which was always a good sign. The trick was keeping it this quiet all day. I glanced at the message light on my cell phone at every traffic light. Thank goodness I'd only had decaf coffee. Between Sydney and the news about Montgomery's release, my nerves were frazzled.

Following Sydney's instructions, I stopped in a convenience store and bought a twenty-dollar long-distance phone card. That should allow me to talk to Sydney for a good while—if she ever called.

Her concern about security inspired me to drop by our communications chief engineer when I got to work to see what he could tell me about the security of my cell phone, and my house for that matter. Not just my home phone, but bugs that could be planted in other places. It may have been nothing more than paranoia on my part, but when an FBI agent refuses to communicate with you unless you're using phone cards from pay phones, it's certainly disconcerting.

Not only was Ollie Horton more than a radio technician, he was a computer geek and an electronic spy aficionado. Every day he wore starched khaki slacks and an equally starched plaid shirt with a pocket holder filled with pens and electronic gages and such. Ollie was slim, about average height, with thinning black hair, and old-fashioned black horn-rimmed glasses that slipped down on his nose every time he lowered his head, so he was constantly pushing them back into place with his index finger. I knew there wasn't a single gadget in the spy world that Ollie didn't know about, so asking him to check my phones and my house for a bug would be like asking a seven-year-old to be a tester at Toys R Us. He took my cell phone and pried it open.

He picked up an eyepiece like the ones jewelers use, opened the back of the phone, and held the phone under a bright light. He angled it back and forth and then put the cover back on.

"This one's clear. Go get yourself a cup of coffee, and I'll check the one at your desk."

"Thanks, Ollie. If anyone asks you any questions, would you mind telling them you're just trouble-shooting my phone? You know I work with a bunch of snoopy people."

"Not at all, Lieutenant, seein' as though that's what I'm doin'."

"When can you drop by my house to take a look?"

"You don't have to tell me who you think might me bugging you, but tell me how good you think they might be."

"As good as anyone in this country, Ollie."

"Damn. Must be the FBI or CIA," he said.

"I didn't say that," I sternly replied.

"Didn't have to," he answered, walking away from me, collecting some gadgets, and putting them in a large black leather tote bag. "Give me a couple of hours to finish a few things up here, and I'll ride over there with you. I don't like going into anybody's house when they're not home."

"Ollie, if I didn't trust you, I wouldn't ask you to check, but I do understand how you feel about that. Call me when you're ready."

"Scott, you need to understand those boys play with some toys that are way out of my league. If you have even the slightest belief that the feds are listening to you, then I don't want to be the one who misses something I've never seen before, and you end up with a problem."

"Ollie, I appreciate that. I'll try not to say anything that pisses off the feds."

CHAPTER 11

Robert Ramer, my homicide investigations partner, was cussing loud enough to be heard halfway down the hall when I reached the door to my office. The department was comprised of eight cubicles to a row, two rows deep. In the center of the second row I saw a file folder fly up into the air, then rapidly falling out of sight. I heard papers landing on the floor followed by Robert's voice again, "Those son of a bitches."

"Ramer, got a minute?" I said.

"Yeah, Lieutenant," he answered like a school kid who'd just gotten caught misbehaving. He followed me into my office, and I closed the door behind him. His blond hair fell across his forehead, and he used his fingers to comb it back into place. Robert Ramer was built like a linebacker with broad shoulders and a narrow waist. He claimed to be vertically challenged at only five feet ten inches tall.

"Have a seat." He sat in a chair facing my desk, and I went around and sat in mine.

"Sorry about the language, Lieutenant. The fucking state's attorney's office is driving me nuts."

"Glad to see that you're calming down."

"You know I don't normally use this kind of language. Those assholes just kicked the Duane Washington case."

"Is that the case where the kid and his mother wrestled over a butcher knife?"

"That's the one."

"Robert, I told you back then that case probably wouldn't hold up, not even as a manslaughter."

"If it'd been me or you, they'd have prosecuted the hell out of us."

"What's that supposed to mean?"

"Those black kids in the Glenwood project can get away with anything, and you know it."

"Robert, that kid was respectful and remorseful, and it was an accident. His mother picked up the butcher knife to scare him because he skipped school. She waved it at him first."

"Then they should have tried for manslaughter."

"Robert, I know how you feel when you spend weeks working a case and the state attorney's office refuses to go to court. I really do. The larger problem we have this morning is the tone I'm hearing from you."

"What do you mean 'tone'?"

"I can't afford to have an investigator thinking that because a kid is black or he lives in the subsidized housing project that he's a criminal."

"I didn't mean it like that, Lieutenant. I'm not a racist."

"That's what I needed to hear. All we can do is work a case as professionally as possible, and after that the system has to take over. I'll go you one better."

"How's that?"

"Remember the Tyrone Montgomery case?"

"Wasn't that your first homicide?"

"Yeah. The parole board decided he's ready to be returned to society."

"No shit."

"The system ain't perfect, but it's all we've got."

"Jesus, if anyone's got a right to be losing it this morning, you do. Sorry about that, Lieutenant. I apologize for the way I acted." Ramer reached across the desk to shake my hand. I stood to accept his handshake and his apology.

"Is that all, Lieutenant?"

"You're a good cop Robert." Then I pointed towards his office. "That's all. That scene in there a few minutes ago was unprofessional, but it told me how much you care about your work."

"Thanks for understanding," he said as he opened the door. He even walked like a linebacker coming off the field after making a big tackle. His shoulders rocked from side to side and there was an athletic bounce in his step.

I opened my day timer to this week's calendar and sat it in the center of my desk. Today's date was highlighted in hot pink on my desk calendar. Pepto-Bismol pink was more appropriate. Today was the much-dreaded weekly department head meeting with the sheriff in the conference room at nine. Notes that I would take to the meeting from my department were already on my laptop, so I typed in the tidbit about Tyrone Montgomery getting paroled right under my last entry, which was about Duane Washington's case getting dropped. The printer clicked and crackled before feeding the paper and spitting out my talking points for today's staff meeting. I stuffed the papers in a file folder and put them next to my day timer. That calendar was how I kept my life organized. It contained significant dates, like court cases, swat training, and birthdays. The morning's emails contained BOLOs from other departments in North Florida and South Alabama. I printed those as well as two of the FBI's most wanted posters. The two I printed were persons from the southeastern US, and the most likely the ones on the list to be headed in our direction. I printed them because it was easier for me to access them sitting next to me in the front seat of my car than to scroll through my laptop. I forwarded the reminders from the sheriff about the blood drive, United Way pledges, and the Florida Fallen Officers Fund to my investigators. An email from the midnight shift watch commander informed us that Deputy Marty Suggs was beaten up badly during the early morning hours when he attempted to break up a bar fight before backup arrived. Fortunately he was treated and released from the ER.

Ollie Horton was standing in my doorway just as I was about to leave for the meeting in the conference room. "Ollie, thanks for taking a look around for me."

"No problem. I heard you were having phone trouble, so I thought I'd take a look," he said with a wink. It was time for the meeting, so I nodded and walked away. My watch read nine o'clock straight up, twelve hours until I called Sydney. This day was going to drag by very slowly, and there was nothing I could do but wait.

CHAPTER 12

The weekly meeting was the same old stuff, and the sheriff reminded us he was the co-chair of Bay County's United Way drive, so he wanted all of us to encourage the people who worked in our various departments to fill out their commitment forms. He was counting on a one hundred percent participation. Everyone was taken aback by the news I shared about Tyrone Montgomery being paroled and Duane Washington's case being dropped by the state attorney's office. I had to share the information, but I knew it would trigger the frustration levels of everyone in the department.

As soon as the meeting ended, I headed to my car and drove over to Lee Covington's mother's house. Lee was the boy who was killed by Tyrone Montgomery. I wanted to make sure that she had been notified that Tyrone had been paroled. That was the responsibility of the state attorney's office, but things like that had fallen through the cracks before, and this lady didn't need to hear it through the grapevine, or even worse bump into Tyrone on the street.

Mrs. Covington spoke to me through a front door she held slightly open. She was a polite, humble woman. I couldn't see her too well through the opening, but I recognized her voice from the day she identified her son's body, and the day she testified during Montgomery's trial. She was appreciative of my visit, but when she closed the door after thanking me, I sensed she was saddened by the news.

I radioed Ollie Horton and told him I was headed home. He said he could break away, and he'd meet me there.

Turning off Cove Boulevard onto Cherry Street, I entered the shadows of the Cove, my neighborhood. The shadows were caused by hundred-year-old live oaks that canopied across the roads, blocking out a great deal of daylight. I turned left onto Bunkers Cove Road, looking for Ollie's car. He wasn't there yet.

The driveway to my house welcomed me to the most comfortable retreat I had in this world. My garage door opener worked at the same speed every time, but today it seemed unusually slow. My first stop at home was the table in the foyer where I dropped my cell, badge and shoulder holster. This was a typical Florida floor plan. The great room opened into the kitchen, with windows and door across the back of the house, providing a wide view of the bayou. Stepping into the kitchen I reached across the counter, and fumbled for the TV remote control. Aiming it at the TV, I hit the power button and the channel selector. Lou Dobbs CNN News and Market Report was on. The clock on the microwave showed six forty-five.

Ollie arrived, and I let him in the front door. He was carrying a little green fishing tackle box. "Where are all your phones, Scott?"

I showed him around, and he checked each phone meticulously. After the phones he took the light bulbs out of every lamp in the house. He scrutinized light fixtures, switch plates, and wall plugs. He gave me Ollie's good housekeeping approval, and pitched a fit when I tried to give him some cash for coming by. I told him I'd see him at work tomorrow, and showed him out.

My grandfather clock showed it was nearly seven-thirty. Suddenly, I had a thought that made me break out in a cold sweat. Sydney had never confirmed whether or not she meant nine o'clock eastern or central time. She might not have even remembered there was an hour difference. I went to the table in the foyer, snatched up my badge and cell phone and hustled out to my car. The worst I could do was call her too early. I drove over to the Tarpon Dock Bridge, swerved into the first available space in the parking lot, and walked down to the dock of the marina to a pay phone that was seldom used by anyone except a few boaters. There was no visibility from the road, which was what I wanted. A guy who had two cells phones using a payphone might seem a little strange to someone who knew me.

I dialed the number she had given me last night. Checking my watch while holding the phone between my ear and my left shoulder, I noticed it was straight up at eight o'clock my time. The phone must have rung a dozen times. No answer. I waited five minutes and dialed again, still no answer. I went back to my car and drove off. She must have meant nine my time; I'd try again.

Pulling onto the road, I turned right instead of left, which was the way back towards my house. I had an hour to kill, so rather than hang around the house, I decided to take a drive out to the beach. Just over the Hathaway Bridge, I turned left on Thomas Drive, a U shaped road that connects with US Highway 98 on each end. My grandparents had homesteaded over two thousand feet of beachfront land and some sixty acres of land to the north of the beach. It had long since been sold, and being the only heir to a twenty-million-dollar estate was both humbling and stressful.

I was always so proud to tell people what visionaries my grandparents had been over fifty years ago when all of their friends thought they were wasting their time fooling around with land that wasn't suitable for any type of crop. Now the responsibility I faced was to be a good steward of their vision.

Habitat for Humanity was my favorite way of giving something back to the community that had been so good to my family. Fully funding one house a year for Habitat was my commitment, and so far I had built five. My grandparents and my parents had taught me that living a comfortable lifestyle meant that you had to be comfortable with how you felt about and treated your neighbor. The library and literacy programs in poor neighborhoods were also at the top of my list. They were all issues my grandmother and mother were passionate about.

Tonight the waves sounded like thunder each time they burst onto the shore, yet as noisy as they were, there was a calmness in the sound. I wasn't officially on duty, so I reached to turn down the volume on my sheriff's department radio. Before I could adjust the volume, dispatch called in a robbery that had just occurred at a convenience store a few blocks from me on Thomas Drive. "Shit!" I said out loud as I picked up my radio. There was no way I could avoid helping out on this call. I'd have to radio that I was in service and headed to the crime scene. "Bay, this is thirteen. I'm ten eight on Thomas Drive and ten fifty-one to the burglary."

"Ten four, thirteen. Be advised the suspect has left the store and ran to a brown Chevy Cavalier, Alabama license plate, no plate numbers available."

I plucked my magnetic blue light off the floorboard next to me, pushed the plug into the cigarette lighter, and reached up and attached it to the roof. Before picking up my radio mic, I flipped the switch to turn on the blue lights in my grill as well. "Bay, do we know which direction the suspect is headed?"

"Sorry, thirteen. The caller, who I believe was the store clerk, didn't have that information. She did advise there was another individual in the getaway vehicle."

A small brown car was headed in my direction, and even though I didn't have a radar gun, I knew the car was speeding. I made a u-turn just as it passed me, and I turned on my siren switch. There were two white males in the vehicle.

"Thirteen, Bay."

"Bay, go ahead."

"I'm in pursuit of a brown Chevy Cavalier, two white males, Alabama license plate alpha alpha bravo zero six two. We're headed east on Thomas Drive."

"Ten four, thirteen. Alabama alpha alpha bravo zero six two. Bay to all units, thirteen's in pursuit of a possible robbery suspects in a brown Chevy Cavalier eastbound on Thomas."

"Eighty-five to thirteen, tact two." A deputy whose ID number was eighty-five was asking me to leave the main frequency and go to a car-to-car frequency on the radio. This would allow us to carry on a conversation without interfering with the main radio traffic.

"Ten four, tact two, eighty-five." I reached down and switched the frequency on my radio to the next channel over.

"Ten twenty, Lieutenant?" eighty-five asked.

"Rounding the state park curve and now heading north," I answered as my siren yelped over and over and cars up ahead angled for the shoulder of the road.

Eight-five called me back. "Lieutenant, I'm southbound on Thomas Drive. I'm gonna try to toss the spikes at him."

"We're almost to the Grand Lagoon Bridge, eighty-five. You'll need to spike him on the other side of the bridge, because when the road widens to six lanes, he'll be able to swerve around them."

"Ten four, Lieutenant. I'll try to get there."

I was worried I might have encouraged the deputy to drive too dangerously. I had to slow this pursuit down. "Eighty-five, be careful. Let's not push it. If we miss this chance to throw the spikes here, we'll wait for another chance."

"Ten four, Lieutenant."

Coming off the bridge, I was chasing the little brown car at about eighty miles per hour in heavy traffic. My palms were clammy with sweat; I wiped them one at a time on my pants legs to get a better grip on the steering wheel. I had another thought about the spikes.

"Thirteen to eighty-five."

"Go 'head, Lieutenant."

"We're pushing eighty, let's hold off on using the spikes. If he loses control at this speed, somebody could get hurt."

"Ten four. I'll just fall into the pursuit northbound."

"Back to main frequency," I shouted as I reached to flip the radio switch so everyone else on duty could follow the pursuit.

I glanced down at the radio for a split second, and when I looked back up the suspect was turning. "All units, he's turning west on North Lagoon," I yelled into the mic.

Dispatch relayed my transmission, "Bay to all units. Thirteen advises suspect is turning west on North Lagoon." That was SOP. In case another officer had difficulty hearing my radio, dispatch repeated the transmissions over their powerful system.

I was braking hard, and I never saw a hint of a brake light from the Chevy. There was no way he could make that turn. The brown car lifted off the ground and traveled on the two right wheels. The two wheels on the driver's side were now at least five feet off the pavement. The little car seemed to balance itself for about a hundred yards. Then the tires on the ground hit the soft shoulder and the driver lost control. The car rolled over on its top and skidded along the ground, finally wrapping itself around a power pole. One of the wires instantly snapped from the pole and floated to the ground beside the pile of crumpled brown sheet metal.

I called in the accident. "Thirteen to Bay, we've got a single car signal four on North Lagoon. Advise Gulf Power we've got a line down and roll EMS."

"Ten four, thirteen." Eighty-five had been following us, so he was the first to arrive, although I could see blue lights coming at me in three directions. I noticed him in my rearview mirror opening his car door, so I threw the mic switch to PA and shouted, "Eighty-five, stay in your car. A power line just fell. It could be hot." At that instant I saw hands reaching through the open window of the overturned car. The passenger was pulling himself through the window. I called over my PA system again. "Stay in your vehicle. There's a power line down out here."

The kid must have decided he'd rather take a chance on being electrocuted than getting caught by us. He wiggled out of the window and stood up wobbly. His blond hair was spiked and disheveled, and blood streamed down his neck in at least two places. He ran west away from my car towards a cluster of pine trees in the next block. Another deputy who had just arrived shined his spotlight on the kid, and got out and chased him on foot. "Bay, seventy-two is in pursuit of the driver on foot." Eighty-five pulled out from behind me, driving towards the chase. When the kid turned to run away from the deputy chasing him on foot, he nearly ran into eighty-five's patrol car. For a second he was the proverbial "deer in the headlights" until seventy-two swept him out of my view with a flying tackle.

"Eighty-five, Bay."

"Go ahead, eighty-five."

"Seventy-two has the suspect in custody."

"Ten four, eighty-five." I maneuvered my car to within five feet of the wrecked Cavalier, directing my headlights through the windows of the overturned vehicle. The other person in the car on the driver's side started screaming for help. I knew the power company would arrive soon, but those screams didn't sound like I should wait. I grabbed a pair of latex gloves out of a box lying next to me. The screaming faded and the passenger stopped moving. The downed power line was about ten feet from the passenger's side of the car. I moved toward the wreck, got down on my knees and stuck my upper body through the driver's side window of the overturned car. The kid looked like he might have been around eighteen or nineteen years old. I called to him. "Hey, can you hear me?" There was no answer. I asked again, louder this time, "Can you hear me?" Still no answer. I crawled farther into the car.

The car seat he'd been sitting in moments ago was hanging over his head, and he was dangling in midair, held in place only by his seat belt. Slithering close enough to the kid to reach out and put two fingers on the side of his neck, I checked for a pulse.

"My neck," he faintly mumbled. There was a pulse, albeit a weak one. I had come through a front window and I needed to get behind him to stabilize his head and neck. Snaking my way back out of the car, I dragged my body through the backseat window, crawling across the roof of the vehicle until I was behind the driver. Lying on my stomach, my legs and feet protruding out the window, I propped my arms against the top of the upside down seat and put my hands on the sides of the kid's head, preventing him from moving his neck.

"Don't hurt me, Officer."

"Stay calm. I'm not here to hurt you. I don't want you to move your neck, so I'm going to hold you in something called inline stabilization. Do you understand?"

"Yes, sir. It hurts so bad."

"I know, son. An ambulance is on the way."

Sergeant Billy Lark approached the car from where my feet were dangling out through the window and said, "Let me come around and give you a hand."

"No, Billy," I shouted. "There's a power line down right on the other side of the car."

"Every business in that strip center and the motel next door have their lights on. Everybody around here has their lights on, Lieutenant. I don't think that's a power line. It must be cable or telephone."

"Sarge, I've got this kid stabilized and there's nothing else in here you can do, so to be safe, why don't you stay on that side?" I was supporting the weight of my body on my elbows while attempting to keep a firm grip on this kid's head. It was close quarters, there was no air flow, and the engine heat filled the inside of the car. My forehead beaded with sweat and it dripped down into my eyes, into the corners of my mouth, and drop after drop rolled down my nose, paused a second or two and then plunged off the end to make way for the one coming behind it.

"Lieutenant, what about the gas?"

"What gas?"

"I smell gasoline, and there's a puddle of something at the back of this heap."

"Christ. That's all I need. Tell the smokers to stay the hell away from here."

I'm going to call for a fire truck, Lieutenant. Twenty-six to Bay."

"Bay. Go 'head."

"Have Thomas Drive Fire Department get a truck here ten eighteen."

"Twenty-six is the car ablaze?"

"Bay we've got gasoline pouring out onto the ground, and Lieutenant Downing is inside the car holding a victim in inline stabilization, and we have some kind of line down next to the car."

"Ten four, Sarge. We've got Thomas Drive Fire Department on the line now."

"Bay can you get us an ETA on EMS? If it's going to be a while, I'm gonna drag Lieutenant Downing out of this thing. Cancel the ETA check, Bay, I see 'em now."

The paramedics pulled up, and a female entered through the front window and crawled in parallel to me.

"What do we have?" she asked me.

"He's complaining of neck pains. Couldn't get him completely in inline from this angle, but I stabilized his movement as best I could."

The other paramedic had joined us, kneeling and looking through the driver's side window.

The female paramedic contorted her body across the roof of the car, lining herself up with the kid who was suspended from the driver's seat. She groaned and told her partner, "I need a C collar and a backboard." Then she made eye contact with me. "I'm going to crawl under him and put my legs past him into the back seat. When I get in place, I'll take his head and you can slide back out."

As difficult as this situation was, I felt compelled to tell her about the gasoline. "They tell me we may have gasoline on the ground, so the quicker you can get him out of here the better."

"Lieutenant, I'll move as fast as I can, but I'm not going to jeopardize damaging this kid's neck over the possibility of a fire," she said as she slithered underneath him, reached up and pushed her hands into place, forcing mine off the back of the kid's head.

"Want me to stay with you?" I asked.

"Thanks, Lieutenant, but we're already kind of cramped for space in here." Her partner arrived with the C collar, so I crawled backwards out of the window, stood, and hurried away from the upside down vehicle. Leaning against the trunk of my car, I wiped my arm across my forehead, which was still soaked with sweat. My light blue shirt was smeared with brown and black splotches of dirt. Brushing the dirt off the sleeves of my shirt, my hand bumped into my wristwatch. Dammit. I'd forgotten about the time. I slid my sleeve up to check. It was five after nine.

"Sarge, where's the closest pay phone?" His eyes narrowed and his brow wrinkled. He was obviously puzzled by my question

"You need my cell, Lieutenant?"

"No, I need the closest pay phone."

The puzzled look wasn't dissipating. "You okay, Lieutenant?"

"Fine. I just need a pay phone."

"Front side of that little shopping center I suppose."

I jumped back in my car, wheeled around to the front of the center, parked, and ran to the pay phone. I tore the long distance phone card from my pocket, scrolled to the last number dialed and hit send. It rang and rang, and no one answered. I looked at my watch. It was twelve after nine. She must have given up on me. I tried it again to make certain I had dialed the right number. Once again it rang without an answer. I started to hang up and was reaching to put the phone on hook when I heard a male voice. I snatched the phone back and said, "Hello."

"Whatsup," the voice replied.

"Sorry, wrong number," I said. I hung up the phone, climbed back in my car, sitting with my head slumped against the steering wheel, exhausted, and exasperated. I was soaking wet with sweat. I'd been so busy being a cop, I'd missed one of the most important calls of my life. My radio went off again.

"Nine to thirteen."

"Go ahead, Captain." Captain Simpson, the man in charge of this patrol shift, was calling me over the radio.

"Lieutenant, you gave us a helluva lotta help tonight, and I hate to ask you, but would you mind writing us a report?"

"Sure, Cap. I'll go into my office and knock one out on the computer."

I drove to my office, trying to calm myself down. It wasn't working. Every time I thought about missing that call, I smashed the palm of my right hand into the steering wheel. I was so frustrated I couldn't control myself. The muscles in my body stiffened, I ached all over. I was physically and emotionally spent.

Entering the investigations wing of the sheriff's department, I turned on the lights, went into my office and began working on the report. When it was finished, I proofread it and dropped it off with the dispatcher.

"Been in a mud wrestling contest, Lieutenant?" she asked.

"I feel like it, Sally. I guess I look like it too, huh?"

"If it hadn't been for you, Lieutenant, we might not have caught that kid. You were something tonight."

"Thanks, Sally."

She was right. I was a good cop tonight. I should at least be proud of the help I had given to the patrol shift. When I slid into the driver's seat of my car, the phone card was lying next to me. The pride of being a good cop dissipated and the pain of missing that call consumed my body. I put the key in the ignition, but didn't start the engine. My hand drifted down to the phone card, my fingers gently touching it. I wondered if I'd ever get a chance to use it to call Sydney.

CHAPTER 13

One single chime tolled from my grandfather clock as I toweled off after a hot shower. A new Stuart Woods' Stone Barrington novel was on my nightstand. Climbing into bed, I scooped it up immersing myself in the story. In a little over ten minutes I was in the middle of the third chapter reading about a phone ringing. My concentration on the book was suddenly shot. All I could think about was Sydney's phone ringing and ringing without an answer.

If only I'd gone back home and waited after Sydney failed to answer my first call, I would have been at the pay phone at nine o'clock. But I had to stop dwelling on the past and start thinking positive thoughts. Tomorrow I'd start fresh. I'd get in touch with Sydney and everything could be worked out. I opened the book again and found the place where I'd left off. Two chapters later it fell onto my chest and I tossed it onto the nightstand. I drifted off a few times, but I never fell into a deep sleep.

A little after six the next morning, I awoke even more committed to getting in touch with Sydney Sloan. I would talk to her today even if it meant getting on a plane and flying to DC. I reached into my closet and put on a yellow long-sleeved dress shirt, and an eggshell colored pair of

Dege and Skinner slacks. I tied a yellow and brown silk necktie around my neck and carried a dark brown Dege and Skinner bespoke sport coat in my hand. I was off to my office by six forty-five thinking about payphones along the route.

A few minutes before seven, I turned left onto Twenty-Third Street and parked next to a pay phone in the back of Krispy Kreme Doughnuts. I dialed Sydney's number feeling as nervous as a boy in junior high calling his girlfriend for the first time. What if she refused to talk to me? A Panama City Police officer drove around the building. I turned my back to the parking lot like I didn't notice him, hoping that he didn't notice me as well. The last thing I needed was for Sydney to answer while a local cop stood next to me waiting for a chance to chat. On the third ring she said, "Hello," answering in two syllables like she was dumbfounded to get this call on her personal cell.

"This is Whittaker. Your caller ID has my number…. I'm waiting." I hung up and stood next to the phone. I checked my watch every minute or so. Ten minutes went by, but I still waited. I made a commitment to myself to wait at least another five minutes. No matter how bad the traffic was on the beltway, she should have been able to get off and get to a pay phone by now.

Seven minutes later I checked my watch one more time, gave up, and headed inside to buy some doughnuts for the staff at the office. The door had almost closed behind me when the pay phone rang. I spun around, banging into the door with my forehead and right shoulder, but hitting it hard enough to open it without the use of my hands. I pounced on the phone. "Hello."

"You have to follow my directions in this thing, Scott. You don't understand how important it is that we communicate unnoticed."

"Sydney, are you afraid your phone is tapped?"

"I'm not afraid of anything."

"Last night I was in a pursuit of a robbery suspect who overturned in front of me a few minutes before nine. I'm sorry I don't have the luxury of sitting in an office all day staring at a computer screen and waiting to make a phone call. I can only talk to you when I get the chance."

"I thought you worked homicides."

"I head up the homicide investigations unit, but bottom line, Sydney, I'm a cop."

"Scott, it has to be my time or no time."

"How about now. How about making time right now, or else I'll head to the airport and get on a plane to DC and track your ass down."

"You don't want to do that. This is a lot more complicated than you realize, Scott, a lot more."

"Sydney, the only thing that's complicated is that my parents' murder case has been unsolved for three years. How the hell do you think I felt when you said what you did in the airport the other day?"

"Scott, this isn't the time. I'm late for a meeting at the Bureau."

"Dammit, Sydney, I can't wait any longer to find out what you know!" I shouted into the phone and then looked around to make sure that no doughnut shop customers heard me lose my cool. She didn't answer. "Sydney, are you still there?"

"I'm here, Scott." There was another long pause. "Scott, I know what happened, I know who killed them, but we can't do this over the phone.

"I can be on a plane within an hour."

"Okay, fly into Dulles and check in at the Ritz-Carlton Tyson's Corner. The address is 1700 Tyson's Boulevard, McLean, Virginia. Check in under my name. I'll have the reservation all set."

"Sure, that shouldn't be a problem. Should I call back and give you my flight information?"

"Absolutely not. No more calls. Get up here, check in and wait. I'll contact you at the hotel."

She hung up before I could tell her I'd have to clear my days off with the sheriff, and make sure there was an available seat on a flight out of Panama City. It wasn't like we had an unlimited number of flights going in and out of our small town.

I bought the doughnuts and delivered them to the radio operators' desk. I wrapped a napkin around a chocolate covered glazed and headed for my office. I sat at my desk and looked through my Rolodex for the number of Delta Airlines. Their ad campaign said, "Delta is ready when you are." I was hoping they were going to live up to that today. While I was on hold, I typed a leave request. The beginning date was today, but in the space for the ending date I typed the letters TBD or to be determined. I knew that would not go over well.

A bubbly voice came on the phone, and I booked a one-way flight to Washington, DC, leaving at two forty-five that afternoon. I printed my leave request, poured myself a cup of coffee and took the request to the sheriff. He saw me right away and offered me a chair.

"Downing, before we get started with whatever it is you're here for, I want to thank you for the job you did last night on that robbery and fleeing and eluding case. Damn good report too."

"Thank you, sir. Sheriff, I need to take some personal leave, sir."

"I thought that might be what you wanted to see me about." He leaned his bulky frame back in his tall leather chair. "Any loose ends in your department?"

"No loose ends that I'm aware of, sir." With that answer, I handed him my leave request.

He glanced at it, turned it around so I could see what he was pointing at and asked, "What do you mean by TBD, Downing?"

"Sir, I'm not certain how long this might take. I didn't want to put down a date that wasn't realistic. The last thing you need around here is people shuffling assignments based on my return and then discovering I'm not going to be able to return on the anticipated date."

"Do you need anything?" He asked as he tossed my paperwork on his desk.

"Sir?"

"Introductory letter, reference from me, anything I can do to help."

"I appreciate your understanding and allowing me to try to work this out," I said.

"Stay in touch. If you need anything, anything at all, you call me. My cell phone is turned on twenty-four hours a day."

"Sir, I-I-I uh—"

He cut me off, stood and offered me his hand. I shook it and looked him squarely in the eyes. He gave me a fiery look of encouragement and then said, "Get out of here. You go get this thing done, Downing."

"Thank you, sir." I left his office and hurried down the hallway, relieved that had gone so well.

Back at my office I called Ramer on the intercom. "Robert, got a minute?"

"Be right there, Scott." The first thing that appeared in my view was the point of an elbow, and as it continued moving into the opening of the doorway I saw the last bite of a Krispy Kreme doughnut being forced into Robert's mouth. I directed my outstretched arm to a chair in front of my desk.

"Thanks for the doughnuts this morning, Lieutenant."

"I was in the neighborhood, and the 'hot now' sign was on. I couldn't resist. Must be a cop thing."

"Must be," he said with a smile. "What can I do for you?"

"I'm going to be taking some personal leave, and I want you to keep an eye on things for me."

"Sure. How long you gonna be gone?"

"I don't know yet." He was looking at me the way I'd taught him to read a suspect.

"Body language, or vocal cadence?"

"You taught me that shit."

"Well?"

"Just curious, Lieutenant."

"Like I said, it's personal. Keep things under control from me."

He watched me zip my briefcase closed, taking that as his cue to leave. When he reached my office door, he stopped, looking over his shoulder at me.

"Something else on your mind, Robert?"

"If this is…" There was a long pause. An anguished look shrouded his face as if he was in some kind of pain.

"Robert?"

"I've have some extra leave time, and—"

"Thanks, but this is something I have to do." I picked up my briefcase, walked to the doorway and shook his hand. "Take good care of this place." Before turning out my lights I looked back at my office as if it were the last time I'd ever see it. A brief stop at my house to pack some clothes, and then it was on to the Panama City Airport. Four hours from now, I'd be in our nation's capital.

CHAPTER 14

The arrivals and departures board showed a fifteen-minute delay. The agent who printed my boarding passes said there was heavy traffic in Atlanta. Fifteen minutes turned out to be thirty-five. The commuter flights were all coach class and it seemed like they were late more than not from our airport. I didn't care about any of that, because I was on my way to Washington, DC, to meet with Sydney— the one person who might really know who killed my parents.

Once we were in the air, I took out my briefcase and removed the case file of my parent's murders. I clicked on my light and flipped through the pages. There was a copy of every piece of paperwork generated from their case in the file.

I studied it as carefully as if I were reading it for the first time. The ballistics report, the coroner's report, and the detective's report were all in there. The only thing I had removed were the photos from the scene. I could still vividly recall all of that without the help of photographs.

By the time I'd reached the last page, I had a driving pain in my stomach. It was the page that simply read, "Thomas and Elizabeth Downing murders—CASE UNSOLVED."

An hour and five minutes after takeoff, our plane touched down in Atlanta and taxied to gate C-34, conveniently, the same terminal where I would be boarding my flight to Washington. By the time I entered the terminal and rushed to C-8, my departure gate, passengers had already begun boarding.

Buckling my seat belt, I stretched out my six-four frame into the aisle. The only available seats today were in the cramped quarters of coach, so I'd have to make do. At least the aisle seat allowed me to extend my legs, provided the flight attendants didn't roll their serving cart into me when I wasn't paying attention.

An hour and a half later at twenty minutes past seven, we landed at Dulles International Airport in the Virginia suburbs of DC. The last time I'd been in an airport in Washington, Sydney shouted the revelation about my parent's murder case. Tonight I caught myself looking for her with every step I took, even looking behind me occasionally. Even though she had told me to go straight to the hotel, there was something chilling and unnerving about being back in the city where I'd first learned from an FBI agent that she knew something about the murder of my parents.

Getting a rental car in DC without a reservation was usually impossible, but tonight Hertz had a Ford Explorer available. After doing the paperwork and locating the vehicle, I headed for the Ritz-Carlton Hotel at Tyson's Corner.

Two sixty-seven was a toll road, and I took it to exit seventeen where I turned right on Springhill Road, which became International Drive. A few blocks up International, I spotted Tyson's Boulevard and turned left. The Tyson's area was a shopping Mecca, with every well-known department store located in the two huge malls.

I cautiously entered the lobby, checking out every person in the room in case Sydney had set me up. At first glance, nothing looked unusual. There was a young woman behind the front desk. She took my credit card and swiped it before handing it back to me. "Here you are, Mr. Downing."

I read her nametag and responded, "Thanks, Gabrielle."

"I gave you a special government rate, Mr. Downing."

"Thanks again, Gabrielle."

"My pleasure." This had to be Sydney's handiwork. Gabrielle handed me my room key and directed me to the elevators.

Before I left the front desk I asked, "Gabrielle, is there a room adjoining this one?"

"Yes, Mr. Downing, but I wouldn't think you'd be needing that, since you already have a suite."

"Oh I wasn't aware I had reserved a suite."

"It's an upgrade, but you're not being charged for it."

"That's very nice, thank you, but I'd like to have the adjoining room as well. I sometimes get claustrophobic in small spaces."

"Certainly, would you like that on the same credit card?"

"That'll be fine, Gabrielle."

"Would you like a separate key for the extra room?"

"Yes, please." Gabrielle looked at me like I was crazy while she made the second key. I had no idea what the FBI might be up to, and a backdoor, so to speak, gave me a real comfort level. It wasn't that I didn't trust Sydney. Hell yes it was. I didn't trust anyone in this town.

"Oh, I almost forgot. I have an envelope for you, Mr. Downing." I took the envelope, thanked her again, and rolled my luggage to the elevators.

The suite was spacious with a full kitchen and dining room, a large TV in front of an attractive red and gray-striped sofa and love seat. The bedroom opened from the combination living room and dining room. I threw my bag on the bed, tore into the envelope and pulled out the letter. Sydney wanted me to meet her downstairs at Maestro's Restaurant at nine. I hadn't eaten much that day, but it wasn't food I was hungry for.

It was barely eight thirty, but I was too antsy to wait in the suite, so I took the elevator down and picked up a *USA Today* in the lobby. A comfortable settee gave me a good vantage point of most of the room. There were more people leaving the hotel than arriving, and no one even closely resembled the attractive FBI agent I was eager to see.

At nine sharp I made my way into the Maestro. Italian music played in the background and an arrangement of fresh cut flowers flanked by a pair of candles provided the centerpiece for each table.

"Table for two please."

"Very good, sir. Follow me," the maitre d' said, ushering me to a table in the center of the dining room.

I noticed the place was at about half capacity, so before he attempted to seat me, I asked, "Pardon me, but would it be too terribly much of an inconvenience if we sat at that table in the far corner?"

"Not at all, sir." We moved to the other table and I chose a seat facing the door, putting my back to the wall. Not having to worry about who or what was behind me was an old security measure I'd learned from law enforcement. It also allowed me to spot my dinner date when she arrived.

He handed me a menu and a wine list. "Would you care for something before your other party arrives, sir?"

"No thanks, I'll just look over your wine selections while I wait."

"Your waiter's name is Ernesto. I'll have him check on you momentarily." The maitre d' strolled back towards his perch at the entrance, and I mused at my waiter's name. Chances were very good that Ernesto was just plain Ernest until he took the job here.

The wine list was outstanding with selections from some wonderful French and Italian vineyards. I had no idea what kind of wine Sydney liked, if any, so I passed the time perusing the list the sommelier had put together. The ambiance of this restaurant and the unusual Italian choices brought back wonderful memories of two trips I'd taken to Italy with my parents. I checked my watch to see how tardy Sydney was. Fifteen minutes wasn't bad in a city like DC. Between traffic and work, she probably had a dozen good reasons for not being on time. At twenty after, I started thinking about calling her cell phone.

It was nine twenty-seven when she walked through the door. She was as lovely as I had remembered. She approached my table with the deportment of someone of royalty or very blue blood. She was wearing a camel-colored tight fitting turtleneck sweater over tailored walnut brown silk slacks. She had large loop gold earrings hanging next to diamond studs. Around her neck was a gold chain with a bulky gold round pendant lying just above her breasts. Sydney Sloan was the kind of woman you couldn't look at only once.

I stood, greeted her with a gentle hug, and pulled the chair out for her. I had forgotten how tall she was. Not many women came this close to seeing eye-to-eye to a man who was six four. I checked out her shoes. The dark brown stilettos might have added four inches of height, which turned her five-ten to six-two, and her body was firm and tight. Her blonde hair had changed since I had last seen her. It was shoulder length and appeared to be slightly darker than I recalled, but perfectly coiffed and in place. Her eyes looked like two blue sapphires that had been dropped in freshly fallen snow, and her smiled showed off her perfect china-white teeth.

"Sydney, I don't want to seem rude or abrupt, but my nerves have been riddled for the past three days. What the hell did you mean when you said my parents weren't killed by a burglar?"

"I'm sorry about the way that happened in the airport that day. I wanted so desperately to give you all of the information I had, and I couldn't stop myself from blurting that out. My timing was awful. I know it was a terrible way to leave you. Please forgive me."

"You can say that again, but I do forgive you."

"Scott, I didn't mean to..." She stopped speaking as our waiter returned. He asked if I had decided on a wine, which prompted me to ask Sydney if she cared for any.

"They have a wonderful wine selection here," I told her.

"I'm a Italian red kind of girl. The chef has some contemporary pasta dishes that are out of this world if you'd like to pick something to go with one of those."

"Good choice." Apparently, we had more in common than being tall and in law enforcement. "How about the Avignonesi Toscana Desiderio ?" I asked.

"Scott, are you a wine aficionado?"

"If you're calling me a wine snob, I hate to disappoint you. I don't smell corks, and I don't play all those show-off wine snob games. I just know what I like."

"Fair enough," she replied.

"I assume you wanted to meet in the restaurant so we could talk in a safe room."

"I did, but now I'm not as comfortable talking here as I thought I'd be."

"Sydney, for God sakes."

"Take it easy, Scott. You're here, I'm here, we'll get this done."

Our waiter returned, presented the bottle, and Sydney and I broke out in laughter as he offered the cork.

I held up my hand to stop him from going any further. "It'll be fine," I said. With the glasses poured, and the waiter gone, we toasted our friendship. "Sydney, you know how long I've waited—"

"He's back," she replied cutting me off from any further conversation as the waiter returned. For an appetizer I ordered the pan-fried Cape Cod scallops wrapped in crisp focaccia with Nova Scotia chanterelle mushrooms and salsa verde. Sydney chose a liquid-center ravioli with organic egg yolk and monkfish liver with a periwinkle-brown-butter glaze and a Champagne sabayon.

She must have heard a voice that sounded familiar, because she was certainly distracted by someone speaking at the table behind her. When the waiter returned with our appetizers, Sydney asked if we could turn our table slightly, so she didn't have to face the wall. He and I turned the table to provide both us with a view of the room. I knew she was trying to put a face with the voice. The man sitting behind Sydney spoke again, but the distraction seemed to have disappeared.

We shared our selections with each other, and they were both superb. The assistant waiter refilled our water and wine glasses and cleared our appetizer dishes.

"Why don't we ask them to deliver the rest of our meal via room service?"

"Let's enjoy our meal, and afterwards, we'll go up to your room. I promise, I'll tell you everything I know." I let out a sigh of relief.

My coastal roots nearly always sent me in search of fish, so I ordered the wild Brittany Coast sea bass dusted with fennel pollen cooked en cocotte with sautéed fennel confit in a fennel-anise sauce Sydney had raved about. She opted for red meat, ordering the Australian pasture-fed beef tenderloin Rossini. So much for the contemporary pasta dishes.

When the waiter left our table, I tried again. "Sydney, I don't know if I can wait any longer."

"I'm really not comfortable talking about this in here. The restaurant was a bad idea on my part. I thought the public area would be a safe place to talk, but it isn't. Can we just finish our meal and talk in your room?"

"I've waited three years, I guess another hour isn't too much to ask, but how about a few of the basics of the case before we go up."

"I'll see. Tonight in your room, I promise," she said just our waiter and his assistant returned with our food. The waiter must have overheard Sydney, because he gave me a sly wink, thinking tonight in the room had another meaning altogether.

"Will there be anything else?" he asked.

"Not from the kitchen," I answered returning his wink. With that line I felt certain the wait staff would leave us alone, thinking we were having an intimate conversation.

"Bon appetite," I said to Sydney.

She smiled, took her first taste and said, "Mmm, delicioso."

After allowing the time for each of us to enjoy a few bites, I couldn't resist one quick question. "You said it wasn't a burglar. How'd you know that?"

"Scott, you said you could wait until we finish."

"But I just realized that I can't wait for the answer to that question. At least tell me that."

"You really aren't going to allow me to wait until we go to your room, are you?"

"Sydney, I can't wait."

"What I know was by way of an accident, Scott"

"What the hell do you mean 'accident'?"

"The information was classified. Very classified."

"My parents worked for the State Department. Their work was public relations, not classified stuff."

"Scott, this was classified well beyond my bounds."

"How could that have anything to do with my parents?"

She frowned, took a deep breath, and exhaled slowly. "I was given the clearance to do some research, and stumbled on the file. That's what I meant by accident."

"The file. Am I supposed to guess what file that would be?"

She ate another bite of her beef and then answered, "The Thomas Downing file."

"A file with my father's name on it. Why would the FBI have a file with information about my father, who was basically a glad-hander for the government? And why would it be highly classified?"

"Scott, I want you to promise not to cop an attitude about the Bureau, but I was doing a little background research on you."

"I already have an attitude about the Bureau, and it's not a good one. What kind of background research?"

"Just don't jump to conclusions before I'm finished. I want you to hear me out and understand that the Bureau gets shot at by politicians all the time. Sometimes we have to do whatever it takes to defend ourselves and our work."

"Fair enough," I said.

"When you were coming up to testify about the Bureau before the Senate Subcommittee on Criminal Justice, the director asked me to use his security clearance and get any dirt I could on you from the National Security Agency's database."

"Dirt? Who the hell do you people think you are, and what right does the Bureau have…"

She took another deep breath and held both hands up in front of her, motioning for me to stop. "I asked you to be understanding and not to cop an attitude until I finished. For God's sakes, Scott, we don't need everyone in this room to hear this."

I was furious and I couldn't hold back. "How dare you."

"Scott," she said loudly, scowling back at me.

"I'm sorry, but this is so bizarre."

"Scott, do you know who your parents' employer was?"

"What kind of question is that? Certainly I do. They worked for the State Department my entire life. My family was very close. We shared everything together. I traveled with them to sixteen different countries. Yes, I am quite aware of who my parents worked for."

"Scott, this isn't easy for me."

"Goddamn it, Sydney, you think it's been easy for me?" My fork fell back to the plate, making a disturbingly loud noise. Eyes shifted as heads turned subtly at several tables nearby. Sydney lifted her napkin and dabbed it across her mouth, allowing some time to pass before she spoke again and for the people sitting around us to turn their attention away from us.

When it was clear, she continued. "Since the day I discovered the file, I've been torn by whether or not to say anything at all. A loyal agent would have just let it drop. I couldn't do that. I'm sorry I did such a poor job that day at the airport. I was trying so hard to not let you get on that plane and leave without knowing what I knew. I should have never let you go inside the terminal without talking to you."

"But you did, and that's over with. Sydney, if it wasn't a burglar, who the hell was it?"

Sydney had clearly told me she wanted to hold off on this conversation until we went to my room. I had forced her to say more than she's wanted to already, so when our waiter returned to ask if we had room for dessert, I asked for the check.

A moment later we were in the lobby in front of the elevator. When the doors closed Sydney hit the call button for the twelfth floor. My room was on the fifteenth floor, but I didn't ask questions. I merely followed her lead. We took the stairs and walked up the last three floors. Agent Sydney Sloan was a cautious professional. The amount of concern about being followed, or overheard indicated there was a lot more to the story than the bomb she had just dropped on me in the restaurant.

CHAPTER 15

Without saying a word, Sydney placed her purse on a table in the kitchen area and went straight into her FBI mode, searching my suite. I stood next to the picture window, soaking in the spectacular view of DC at night, while Sydney continued her task. She was diligent and thorough, checking in light fixtures, electrical outlets, and every nook and cranny that might contain a hidden camera or microphone. My eyes drifted back into the room to follow Sydney into the open bathroom. She checked behind doors, in cabinets, in the shower, before coming back out to look under my bed, under the sofa pillows, and in the closet. She even examined the clothes hangers.

"Sydney, did you tell anyone why I was coming to Washington, or where I'd be staying?" An index finger held in front of her lips stopped me from asking another question.

She snatched her purse off the table and went back into the bathroom. My curiosity was piqued. Having left the door open, I assumed she wasn't doing things you'd normally do in a bathroom, so I stepped over and sat in a chair to get a better view. Sydney placed her purse on the counter, reached for the faucet, and turned it on full blast into the sink. She walked out, closed the door behind her, and nonchalantly sat across from me on the sofa.

"Sydney, I didn't bug this place, if that's what you were thinking."

"I wasn't looking for anything you might have put here."

"Comforting to know you trust me. At least I suppose that's what that meant."

"I do trust you, Scott. If I didn't, I wouldn't be here."

"Good point. By the way, I think you left the water running."

"I also left my purse in there, so if anyone dropped a listening device in my cell phone or my bag, it'll be harder for them to eavesdrop."

"You mean the water is supposed to drown out the sound of our voices?"

"Believe it or not, it helps."

"What about downstairs?"

"I hadn't counted on us having as much of a conversation there as we did. If you recall, I did hang my purse on the back of the chair," she replied, pantomiming the actions she had just described. "Hopefully the extraneous sounds of the restaurant helped to muffle things a little."

"You carry a weapon in that purse?"

"Why else would I carry a purse? Scott, can we start over?"

"Sure."

"I don't know where to begin," Sydney said.

"How about from the beginning."

"Okay. Let's see. When you were coming to testify before the Senate Subcommittee on Criminal Justice, my director wanted to know if there was anything we needed to know about your background."

"You told me that. He wanted you dig up some dirt on me, in case I said something negative about the agency."

"I don't think that's what I said."

"Yes it was."

"Can I finish?" She stood up from the sofa, stepped to the window, and took in the view.

"Sorry, Sydney, I didn't mean to interrupt."

"That's okay. This is difficult for both of us." She faced away from me towards the window and began again. "Since I had worked with you on the Gallatti case, the director asked me to do the background research, giving me his security code to get past any glitches I might run into. I did a root search of the name Downing. Your name didn't come up, but Thomas and Elizabeth Downing did. They had an Alexandria, Virginia, home address, so I started to scroll down past their names when I saw the words Panama City Beach, Florida."

She wrung her hands and peered toward the heavens as if she was searching for divine intervention. "Scott, I'll probably lose my job for sharing this with you." Her voice cracked repeatedly. I waited anxiously.

A couple of minutes passed before she turned back to face me. She looked more afraid than the prospect of losing her job should have made her. An investigator has to read people's expressions and body language, and try to determine what those looks and movements are saying to you. Sydney was terrified.

"Scott, your mother and father worked for the government, but not the State Department." I smiled at her comment, already making up my mind that she was wrong.

"So who the hell did they work for all my life? Sydney, you either have very bad information, which is entirely possible, or you're a liar," I said that to her with conviction, but inside I was scared to death of the possibility that I hadn't really known some vital information about my very own parents.

"The information isn't bad, Scott, and I'm not a liar. Your parents were CIA."

"You're telling me that for twenty-one years, I had no idea who my own goddamn parents were! You go to hell, Sydney Sloan!" If she'd been a man, I would have pinned her against the window and forced her to tell me the truth. There was no way that could be true.

"Scott, I know this is difficult."

"It's not difficult. It's fucking ridiculous."

"Scott, please."

"Please my ass, Sydney. You think the Bureau can contrive shit about other people and then make the rest of the world believe it. Well it isn't happening. I won't let you or the goddamn Federal Bureau of Investigation do this to my parents."

"Scott, lower your voice, or I'm out of here. I mean it."

I was gritting my teeth so hard I felt a headache coming on.

"Scott, I highlighted your parents' names and hit enter on the NSA database. Their background information came up including the name of their son, Scott. I scrolled down and found a file titled *The Osprey's Nest*."

"What the hell was *The Osprey's Nest*?"

"The plan that outlined the murder of your parents." I bent over and buried my face in my hands. "Do you want to take a break?"

I jerked my head back up and hollered at Sydney. "Don't even think about taking a break. Not now."

"Okay. The file had been on the servers of the Bureau and the Defense Department. It should have been deleted on all of those servers, but it was what we call a dangling file. It was still on the NSA server with the words *access denied* posted in bold letters across the cover page.

"So someone failed to delete the file."

"The Bureau and the Defense Department have separate servers, but they're networked to the National Security Administration's server. When you delete a file from the NSA server, you still have to delete that same file from each of the other servers it appears on. In this case, someone deleted *The Osprey's Nest* from the Defense Department and FBI servers, but not the NSA server."

"How could that happen?"

"Because the men involved are high-ranking powerful men who normally have people like me doing their computer work. In this case they couldn't afford to have anyone else know what they were doing, so they used their secure password-protected servers to communicate. They knew it was safer than using the telephone, and there were very few people in America who could breach their security levels. They actually thought they knew enough about the computer system to be safe, but they didn't understand the backup at NSA.

"Your parents had been spies for the CIA for twenty-six years, even though most people thought they were envoys with the US State Department. In late December 2001, a man named Calev Heber summoned your father to secretly meet with him at the Israeli Embassy in Tel Aviv. Heber was a spy for the Israeli Mossad. The meeting apparently took place without the knowledge of the CIA Director. That's a big no-no in the Agency."

"My father operated by the book."

"Heber must have convinced him somehow to violate agency policy. He picked up your dad at the embassy and took him to a secluded spot along the Mediterranean Sea near the town of Ashod, about thirty minutes from Tel Aviv. Heber informed your father about a diabolical plot by two Americans to overthrow several Middle Eastern countries in order to take over their oil production and also award billions of dollars worth of contracts to an American company called Halburson for the rebuilding of the overthrown countries."

I must have looked stunned. I felt my jaw drop. "Where did all that information come from? Was someone tailing my father?"

"No, someone was tailing Heber. The people he worked for, the Mossad. They had learned that he had some information he was sharing with a spy from the US, so they tailed him and had him under surveillance."

"Who were the two Americans?" She either wasn't going to tell me, or she wasn't ready to tell me. I'd allow her to move for now, but sooner or later I'd come back to that question. I had to know.

She stood and paced the length of the room. "The name of the conspiracy that Heber told your father about was *Operation Freedom Flows*. It was a plan to stage terrorist activities by paid operatives of the US government around the world. Notes or Internet posts would claim responsibility on behalf of extremist Arab groups. They knew that after 9-11, terrorist activities like car bombings, blowing up hotels, kidnapping and beheading civilians would incite most Americans to rally in support of any invasion into Arab territories. As soon as America had invaded a Middle East nation, our two conspirators knew they could easily persuade the President to take over the invaded country's oil operations. It would take billions of US tax dollars to occupy a country like Iraq, so using Iraqi oil revenues in order to repay the cost of rebuilding the infrastructure would almost be demanded by the American public. When the American oil companies took over the oil production in a country like Iraq, they would never relinquish their control.

"So the President wasn't one of the two men?" I asked trying to bring her back to the question of who were the two Americans involved.

Her chin dropped towards her chest. Muscles were contracting in her neck, and she struggled to swallow. She turned and looked directly at me. "It was the Secretary of Defense and the FBI director," Sydney said, losing her ability to look me in the eyes, staring at the floor again.

"Director Fisher and Secretary Young."

"Director Fisher and Secretary Runnels, before Runnels resigned from his post and took a teaching and speaking job in the UK."

"You've got to be kidding. I thought they were patriots; true public servants who bled red, white, and blue. I guess the power of greed can bring about dramatic change in anyone."

"Billions of dollars can bring about dramatic change."

"I would have never dreamed men like Runnels and Fisher would have been behind murdering two American citizens, or invading a country without due cause."

She looked out the window again. This time she placed her fingers on her temples and rubbed in a circular motion.

"Sydney, what you're saying is my parents were killed because my father was going to tell the President about a conspiracy dreamed up the Secretary of Defense and the director of the FBI to invade Middle East countries for their oil." There was another long pause before she continued.

"Fisher and Runnels felt it would be almost painless to convince the President to invade Iraq after 9-11. Groups like al-Qaida, the PLO, Hizballah, Abu Midal, and Hamas all wanted to take credit for nearly every terrorist activity that happened around the world. Even when US operatives orchestrated the terrorist activities, responsibility was almost always claimed by one of those groups."

This was fiendish. It was the most despicable act I'd ever heard of. My palms were sweating, and my body felt like it was on fire. I'd maintained my temper up until now, but I felt like a teakettle left on the stove too long.

"For Christ sakes! Those low life sons of bitches. I'm going to fry their asses." I'd lost my temper a few times, and I'd been mad before, but this was the first time in my life I'd felt rage.

"So the blood of my parents, American soldiers, and God only knows who else is on the hands of Fisher and Runnels. Those bastards. Are they still actively behind *Freedom Flows*?"

"Well, we still have troops in the Middle East, but my guess is that's just because we can't find a way out. I think the plan blew up on them when we failed to find any weapons of mass destruction or control the insurgents. "They probably thought it would be like Kuwait. We'd breeze in, take over, and with little loss of life, it would all be over in less than a week," Sydney said, sounding like she was basing that theory on speculation.

I attempted to create a timeline in my mind. My parents were murdered in December of 2001. The war in Irag started March 19, 2003, my second year of law school. That was over a year ago. Runnels and Fisher were still in their high-ranking positions, America was deeply divided over the war, and now I had a greater appreciation for the fear and trepidation Sydney was dealing with. Solving my parents' murders would also expose *The Osprey's Nest* and *Operation Freedom Flows* as well. Runnels and Fisher, two of the most powerful men in the world, would ultimately be charged with murder, recklessly invading another country for the purpose of getting rich, and America's reputation and her trading opportunities would probably drop to an all-time low in modern history.

"Scott, these two guys and our government have a lot to lose if any of this information gets out. You understand the global ramifications don't you?"

"I'm outraged, but I still have some logical brain function, Sydney. I was just thinking about how this could impact the country. Who else knows about this?"

"You, me, Runnels, and Fisher."

"So if we make a case against Runnels and Fisher, what do you think happens with our allies, and countries we trade with?"

The color in Sydney's face dissolved with that question. She closed her eyes again before she spoke. "Members of the United Nations, allies, countries American companies do business with would all surely look at us as a rogue nation. I think they have to take some kind of action against us to renounce the conduct of our leaders."

"I was thinking the same thing, Sydney, only what happens to American jobs if those other countries stop trading with us, even for a few months?"

"We don't know any of that for sure, but it's the risk you'd take if you pursued Fisher and Runnels."

"I have no intention of ruining the economy of this country, but I have every intention of finding the man who came into my house and murdered my parents."

"Scott, I understand how you must feel."

I stood directly in front of her, and lifted her chin with my hand until we were nose to nose. "I appreciate what you've done for me. I can't imagine what it must have been like to struggle with the internal debate between doing what's right or maintaining the code of the Bureau."

She simply nodded slightly.

"Do you know how Runnels and Fisher were getting paid?"

"Heber did. He apparently told your father about some offshore bank accounts Director Fisher and Secretary Runnels called their payroll accounts. The money that was used to pay the mercenary who killed your parents came from their payroll accounts."

"Was the killer paid in cash?"

"Wire transfers."

"Aren't those transactions traceable?"

"In the computer file, I found where Fisher and Runnels transferred money from accounts in two Caribbean Island banks. The day before you testified in front of the senate committee, I asked a friend to do some unofficial looking for me. Sure enough, Fisher and Runnels have joint accounts, one in the Caymans and on the French side of the island of Saint Martin. My friend told me that over a three-day period just before your parents were killed, there were two transfers of one hundred thousand dollars each out of those accounts to another offshore account."

"Why was there a break between the bank transfers? Why not do it all at once?"

"Good question. I'll get to that."

"You found that out without a subpoena?"

"Scott, we find a lot of things out without subpoenas."

"What's the name on the account the money was transferred to?"

"Lee Oswald."

"As in the Lee Harvey Oswald who killed President Kennedy, and was later killed by Jack Ruby?"

"You didn't think he'd use his real name, did you?" I was stunned as I heard about the brutal plans my government had instigated with little or no concern for human life. I felt like I was part of spy novel.

"After my father was killed, why didn't Heber try to do something else to expose the conspiracy?"

"Heber was on his own when he shared the information with your father, but unfortunately the Mossad had Heber under surveillance. His driver used a listening device to pick up the conversation between Heber and your father. The Israeli government traded the information to Secretary of Defense Runnels for some state-of-the-art tanks and helicopters. The equipment was delivered within five months after the murder of your parents."

"Any idea why this Heber chose my father to share the information with?"

"Trust. He felt like your father would be able to bring the details of the conspiracy to a halt before it got out of hand. Heber was a smart man. He knew your father was connected all the way to the President, and he also knew it would be best for America and the rest of the free world for us to stay out of the Middle East."

Sydney leaned her shoulders against the window and folded her arms across her chest. "The Israelis contacted Secretary Runnels, who called Director Fisher, who hired the mercenary to carry out *The*

Osprey's Nest. They called your father an osprey or shore bird who frequently returned to his nest, meaning his house at Panama City Beach."

"So this mercenary followed my father all the way back to Panama City Beach?"

"Eventually. He thought he was following your father to Panama City Beach, when your father detoured to the home of a close friend and confidant."

"Would that have been David Collins?"

"Exactly. The killer reported your father's stop to Director Fisher, and that's when the second payment was wired into the killer's offshore account. I'm sure you're aware that Collins was an editor at *The Washington Post*, so Runnels and Fisher couldn't afford to have Collins investigating anything your father might have told him."

"What if my father hadn't told him anything?"

"The killer was on the same flight as your father. My guess would be that he stuck a microphone somewhere on your father's carryon luggage. It's easy to do. You wait until the luggage is stored in an overhead bin, then you put your bag next to it. While you're shuffling the bags around you stick a listening device on the bottom of the other bag. The killer overheard the conversation between you Collins and your father, and he knew that Collins agreed to wait until after Christmas when your father returned from Florida.

"So my father led the killer to Mr. Collins' home in Alexandria, then the killer followed him to Panama City Beach, where he kills my mother and father. Then he goes straight back to Washington and kills Collins."

"You got it. Director Fisher emailed the killer a new plan called *The Burning Post*, which detailed how he wanted Collins killed while making it look like an accident."

I walked back to the window, mesmerized by the information Sydney had told me so far. About two blocks away a young man was filling the gas tank of his Jeep at a convenience store. The gasoline streaming into the tank more than likely originated from the Middle East, the very reason my parents were dead. I couldn't read the numbers on the pump, but I could see them rolling over and over in a constant blur. That gasoline fueled more than cars. It fueled the greed that led to my parents' murders. I slammed the palm of my hand into the metal brace that divided the glass window. The thrust of the blow rattled the length of the window.

"The fucking United States of America hired someone to kill my parents. Who is he, Sydney?"

"I don't know."

"Please don't lie to me."

"Scott, surely you don't think I'm holding anything back."

"I don't know. I have no idea what to think."

I pointed towards the District. "Those monuments over there are supposed to represent freedom and everything that is good. Now all I can think of is how sleazy this whole goddamn place is." I turned to face Sydney, stepping close enough to her to feel the warmth of her breath. "I want that guy, Sydney."

"I'd give you a name if I had one, honest, Scott. Around the Bureau or the Agency, mercenaries' names are almost as secret as the code to launch a nuclear missile."

I gritted my teeth; I could feel the muscles in my neck tighten until they started vibrating under the stress.

"I'm going to find him, Sydney. If I have to tell this story to every Congressman or Senator on Capitol Hill, or our dumb ass President, who allowed those guys to influence him into going to war with Iraq, I'm going to find the son of a bitch who killed my parents."

"Scott, if I were you I would have already gone ballistic. But I hope that before you do anything like what you just said, you'll think about the circumstances. What these men did was terribly wrong, but to expose them puts the reputation of our country, not to mention the stabilization of the Middle East and the entire free world in dire jeopardy. Fisher and Runnels successfully carried out *The Burning Post* and *The Osprey's Nest*, but when things went bad in Iraq and soldiers started dying in unacceptable numbers, *Operation Freedom Flows* appeared to be shut down. All of the attention of those men right now is focused on covering everything up and keeping it covered up.

The minute Fisher, Runnels, or their mercenary discover that you're in town asking questions, there will be another plot, and this time you'll be the target."

"I know how much power they have in this town, but I'm not afraid of them, Sydney. I want the men who killed my parents to be brought before the bar of justice, one way or another. "

"What about the fate of America's stature in the world? What about the possibility of having millions of citizens from friendly and not-so-friendly nations protesting in their streets, asking their governments not do business with a country like America whose leaders kill their own citizens, and invade defenseless nations in order to take over their oil production? Restoring our global reputation could take years and years." Sydney was almost in tears. I could see the pain she was suffering between wanting to help me seek justice for what happened to my parents and preventing her nation from suffering irreparable harm.

I paced in front of the window. The lights from the capitol dome were glaring back at me. I pressed my forehead against the glass. It was wonderfully cool to the touch, especially since my rage had increased my body temperature. Then two gentle hands slid up on my shoulders. Her left hand rested on my left shoulder and her right hand began to lightly rub the middle of my back. Under any other circumstances, her touch would have felt sensual. Tonight it just felt comforting.

I might not be able to find the mercenary who had pulled the trigger, but I knew who had hired him. I knew where to find Runnels and Fisher. Sydney's concern over what would happen to America had me thinking about those consequences. What would happen to our soldiers who were still patrolling in the Middle East if I exposed this whole mess? They were still fighting insurgents, and this news would turn the rest of the people of the Middle East against them. There would be so much pressure on our allies, they'd drop us like a hot potato. Sydney was probably also right about our trading partners around the world. But where was the justice for my parents?

"Sydney, I'm going to have to think about what I should do next. Is there anything else I need to know?"

"Yes there is. I printed the entire contents of the *Operation Freedom Flows* file before I destroyed it online."

"What do you mean by the entire contents?"

"Every piece of communication, email, notes, details of the efforts to persuade the President to invade Iraq, as well as all of the information regarding *The Burning Post* and *The Osprey's Nest.* It had been dangling on the server for over three years until I came across it on the Downing search."

"Is there any way that file could be traced to you?"

"Director Fisher gets a report from the IT people every week. Part of that report is a listing of secure information that's been deleted. When that happens, there's always a memo or directive explaining the deletion."

"So he must suspect that somebody knows about the conspiracies."

"They can do keystroke analysis. If he asked the IT people to look into the deletion, the keystrokes would lead them to the time I logged on searching for information about you."

"Oh Christ, Sydney. What have I gotten you into?"

"You haven't gotten me into anything, Scott. I did all of this on my own."

"Where's the file? You don't have it with you, do you?"

"That'd be like painting a target on my forehead. I rented a mailbox at one of those postal and shipping stores near where I live. It's in there."

"Could we go get it? I'd like to study it."

She picked up pen and paper off the dresser. "I'll write the directions and the box number on this hotel notepad." She tore a sheet of paper off the pad and placed it on the dresser before she wrote the directions.

"Protecting yourself from the note fairy, I see."

Sydney paused from writing long enough to give me a smile. She appreciated that I'd picked up on the fact that she'd torn the first sheet off the pad and laid it on the hard surface of the dresser before writing. It would have been simple for someone to come into this room, put a piece of tracing tissue over the sheet of paper directly behind the one she wrote on and rub a pencil over it, picking up an impression of every word that Sydney had written.

"You're less likely to be noticed if you go by this place during the morning or around noon when they're busy."

I wanted to go right away, but her advice made sense. "What are the chances you're being followed tonight?" I asked.

"Hard to tell for sure. The day after you came to DC to testify, I was given a new Bureau cell phone, an office assignment and I've had an unfounded, but spooky feeling I was being watched."

"Well as of tonight, you're out of this."

"How can you say that? I'm in this thing as deep as you are, maybe deeper. I'm the keystroke kid, remember."

"Okay, tomorrow I'll rent a couple of cell phones and give you one of them. At least we won't have to worry about those being bugged. I'll only call if I need some information that I can't get anywhere else."

"Scott, there's no doubt in my mind that Fisher and Runnels know what I've already discovered, and they probably know that you're in town too. I know you have a law degree, and I've seen your work in law enforcement. You're very bright and your work is superior, but the FBI, CIA, and Department of Defense are all in the spy business. Runnels and Fisher will do whatever is necessary to prevent the details of these conspiracies from reaching the public. You have to assume they want us dead."

"So how do you feel about going to work tomorrow?"

"I'll be watching my back, if that's what you mean." Sydney's reply was firm and convincing. She went back into the bathroom and picked up her purse before heading across the room to the door. "Call me from a pay phone when you have the new cellulars." I'll try to come up with a safe place to meet," she said.

"Sydney, tomorrow's Saturday. Federal government employees don't work weekends do they?"

She grimaced before she answered. "With the war going on, a lot of us are pulling weekend duty."

I followed her to the door. She said goodnight, gave me a gentle kiss on the cheek, looked through the peephole and reached for the doorknob.

"Sydney, wait a second." She took her hand off the door, turned and faced me.

"Thank you isn't nearly enough. I owe you for all that you've done for me, Sydney Sloan."

"You saved my life in a shootout at the beach when we worked the Gallatti case together. I'd say we were about even." She opened the door, walked to the stairwell and headed down.

I lay awake thinking about my options. I wanted to track down the man who killed my parents, but I didn't want to destroy the reputation of my country. Diplomatic and military decisions had been made based on the bullshit of two conniving American public servants. American soldiers and civilians as well as thousands of Iraqis had been killed as a result of our occupation of their Iraq. If I exposed the conspiracies these assholes were responsible for, it could hurl our country into financial chaos that could take years if not decades to recover from. There were plenty of members of the EU who already didn't like the US, and if this news got out it could easily ignite them into calling for a vote to drop America as a trading partner. That action could put millions of Americans out of work. Terrorist activities directed at the US could become more commonplace. I'd heard an expression once about having the weight of the world on your shoulders. Tonight I felt like I did. I had to choose between possibly ruining the economy of the United States of America and alienating our nation from the rest of the world, or bringing the person who killed my parents to justice. I hadn't slept in three nights. Tonight would be number four.

CHAPTER 16

All night long I tossed and turned. I doubled the pillow over, threw it on the floor, curled up and stretched out. Finally the morning sun peeked into my room between the window curtains. I was torn about what to do. I'd actually considered getting on a plane and going home, but I could never let my parents down like that. On the other hand, they wouldn't want me to do anything to decimate this country.

I showered, dressed and headed downstairs. The smell of fresh brewed coffee brought me to a halt in the lobby. I poured myself a cup, picked up *The Washington Post*, and sat at one end of a long sofa, checking out my companions around me. Everyone appeared to be business types, or "suits" as they were affectionately called. I was trying to see if any of them might have been in the restaurant the night before, or checked in about the same time I did. It could always be coincidence, but it could also be a tail.

After I finished my coffee and scanned *The Post*, I strolled out to the parking lot to my rental Ford Explorer, got in, and drove south on the Beltway towards Alexandria. This drive reminded me of my days at Georgetown and all the wonderful times I had with my parents up here. I took the Old Town Alexandria exit and headed up King Street to the intersection of West Avenue. The Mail Boxes store was right on the corner.

There was a space right in front, so I pulled in, but stayed in my seat. The debate was still raging in my mind. If I went inside that store I was going ahead with the investigation. If not, I would drive around the block, turn back towards Washington Reagan National and never look back. I laid my head back against the headrest and continued soul-searching. I reached for the door handle, but I couldn't open it. Finally I took a deep breath and lifted the handle. The door opened and I stepped out. That was it. I was committed to continue until I resolved this.

Last night I had promised Sydney a couple of phones that we could be positive were secure. It made sense to get that out of the way before going after the file, because I didn't want to have to carry a file into the phone store, and I sure as hell wasn't about to leave a file like that on the front seat of my car. There was a Radio Shack a couple of blocks away, so I walked down the sidewalk past the Mail Boxes store. I picked out the phones, signed up for one year of service plan, and charged it all on my credit card. The home address I used for the cell phone form was 1700 Tyson's Boulevard, which looked a little suspicious to me, but apparently not to the young man who had signed me up.

Ten minutes after I had walked into the store, Scott and Mrs. Sydney Downing were now officially cell phone subscribers. I carried my bag of phones to the car, tossed them in the passenger's seat, and locked the doors.

I leaned against the Explorer and stared at the store. I had never been a fanatic about religion, but I always believed that a higher power would provide a sign in times of indecision like this. Several minutes passed, but there was no divine intervention. Hundreds of people scurried along the sidewalk in both directions. They were all a blur. I totally focused on the wall of mailboxes visible through the plate glass window. A chill raced through me, and I shivered. To my right a small bell banged into a door and the bell rang, catching my attention. A neatly dressed little old man was descending the steps from an antique shop. Probably the storekeeper I thought as he approached the edge of the sidewalk and unfolded an American flag. He reverently raised the flag, looked up at *Old Glory*, saluted, and went back into his shop. That was the answer I'd been looking for. I was definitely going to find my parents' killer, but not at the expense of my country.

Inside the Mail Boxes store I located Sydney's mailbox, I inserted the key and opened the door. There was nothing inside. Surely Sydney wasn't lying to me. I looked around and noticed a young man behind the counter with short black hair and silver wire-rimmed glasses who was observing my every move. I ran my index finger over each of the numbers stamped into the face of the box. The number was correct, and there was no doubt I was at the right store. Maybe Sydney had just forgotten to pay the bill, or changed her mind and picked the file up last night after she left the hotel.

I started to ask for the manager, but my better judgment told me to pick up the manager's business card at the counter and call later. If the FBI or CIA had confiscated the file, they probably also had a standing order for the staff to call them if someone came in asking about that particular box.

A telephone hanging on the wall behind the counter rang, and when the clerk turned to pick it up, I walked briskly to my car. The Explorer was right out front. Very seldom do you wish that you hadn't gotten such a convenient parking space. Maybe it was paranoia, but I sure wanted to get away unnoticed.

I had to talk to Sydney, so I drove over to G Street and parked next to the Williams Law Library. There were several pay phones there, which were used mostly by students. Even though I had a secure new cell phone, I'd promised Sydney last night that I would call her from a pay phone after I picked up the cell phones and the file. At least I'd accomplished one of those tasks. She answered on the second ring. "Hello."

"Ms. Whittaker," I said and then I hung up. I leaned against the blue box that housed the payphone and waited for her return call. Five minutes later, the payphone started ringing. "Hello."

"I was going to call you at the hotel later this afternoon," she said.

"I hope you were going to call to tell me that you decided to swing by the Mail Boxes store last night and pick up the file?"

"No, that wasn't why I was going to call you. Are you telling me the file wasn't there?" There was no quiver in her voice. I felt sure she was being honest with me.

"Sydney, it wasn't there."

"Maybe you went to the wrong Mail Box store?"

"Yeah, and your key opens the door to a mail box at multiple locations."

"Right. It was a stupid thought."

"I have your new cell phone. Hopefully now we can eliminate some of this pay phone hassle."

"I'll meet you at Clyde's at one. Do you know Clyde's?"

"Isn't it a little past the Tyson's Corner Mall?"

"You got it. I'll see you there."

It was almost eleven a.m. I wanted to check my emails, so I drove to the hotel, carried the bag with the two new phones up to my room, laid them next to my laptop, and logged on. Robert Ramer, my partner from the Bay County Sheriff's Office, had sent me an email, letting me know that everything was okay at home. I wrote a short reply to Robert and cleared a few other insignificant emails before signing off.

After four restless nights in a row, I couldn't resist lifting my feet up on the bed and laying my head on the pillows. I grabbed the remote control and flipped on CNN. It seemed like a repeat of the last time I had watched, whenever that was. Unless something really big was happening in the world, cable news always seemed to look and sound the same. The producers of all of those twenty-four hour cable news channels would probably have orgasms if they were to learn any of the details of *Operation Freedom Flows, The Burning Post,* or *The Osprey's Nest.* I was going to be damned careful to make sure that didn't happen. I simply wanted to quietly find my parent's killer.

A quick look at my watch indicated I had thirty minutes before I was to meet Sydney, so I took out the new cell phones, saved my number on Sydney's phone and her number on mine. At a quarter 'til one I left for Clyde's.

It was late in the lunch hour, but the parking lot was packed. Sydney had beaten me there and raised her hand to get my attention. Sitting down, I handed her the phone I'd bought for her and told her my number was already saved on it. She flipped it open and punched several buttons. "Did you save it under Downing or Scott?"

"Try the W's."

"W's?"

"Whittaker," I said with a smile.

We both ordered salads; Sydney chose a Cobb, I went for the Caesar. I wasn't sure if I should ask Sydney about her day at work. Against my better judgment I asked.

"How did work go?"

"It was okay, nothing unusual happened."

"Any thoughts about the file?" I asked as I observed her body language to try to determine if she was being honest with me. She put both hands on the table, leaned in my direction and stared into my eyes.

"Scott, I put the file in that mail box right after I printed it, and I never opened that box again."

"Well somebody did."

Our salads were delivered and we spoke very little as we ate. I was pondering what could have been behind the missing file. Sydney must have been doing the same thing because she stopped eating and rolled her fork around in the salad over and over without taking a bite. When she did look up it was very distant.

I had a thought that might frighten her, but it had to be said. "Someone must have followed you to that mailbox. Any ideas?"

"None. Scott, I've been checking every day to see if I had a tail, but I never picked up on anyone who might have been following me. I'm not comfortable talking about this in a public place."

"I keep forgetting that. When can we talk?"

"How about tonight? I'll come to the hotel, and we'll go over everything."

"Sure, what time?"

"Why don't I come by when I leave work—say sixish?"

"Sixish is good for me." I finished my salad, but Sydney didn't eat more than a few bites before she picked up the check and excused herself. This was a tough, confident woman whom I had worked alongside when she was pursuing members of an organized crime family. The lack of appetite, the stressed expression, the hesitation in her stride as she walked appeared to be signs of a meltdown. Anyone in her shoes would be scared as hell right now, me included. Looking through the window, I watched her get in her car and drive away. Three cars followed her out of the parking lot. Coincidence, I hoped.

Fumbling through my wallet, I found the business card from the Mail Boxes store. The young man at Radio Shack had showed me the sequence to hit to block my number from being displayed on the caller ID of anyone I might call. I followed his instructions before dialing the Mail Boxes store. I introduced myself as Mr. Sloan and inquired about the missing file. She asked to put me on hold, but I begged her not to do that because I was borrowing someone else's cell phone and I had promised to not use up his minutes. She told me I'd have to come into the store to fill out the paperwork necessary to track down anything lost from a mailbox. I thanked her and hung up.

There was a feeling in my gut that the manager was already dialing whoever had the file. If that was what the manager was doing, then I had just officially put them on notice that I was in town. I called Sydney on her new cell phone. She didn't answer, so I left her a message about my phone call to the mail store.

I had a sinking feeling. Why didn't she answer her phone? Why didn't I get a better look at the people who followed her out of Clyde's parking lot? That was sloppy police work today.

CHAPTER 17

Sydney called at six-fifteen to tell me she was stuck in heavy traffic, but she was on her way.

"Did you get my message?" I asked.

"Yeah, I got it."

"Do you think anyone's following you?"

"I've been checking and double checking, but you know how that goes. Sometimes you miss things."

"I remember your undercover work, Sydney. You don't miss anything."

"Thanks, Scott. See you shortly." I took the elevator down to the lobby and waited. When she entered the hotel, she walked past me. She pushed the elevator call button, and I followed her inside. A huge man in a brown suit followed both of us inside. He must have weighed three hundred pounds standing six-six or maybe six-seven. He reached first to select his floor. He pushed the button for the fourth floor as the doors closed. Sydney then reached forward and pushed five.

She hadn't acknowledged me, so I followed her lead and ignored her as well, pushing eight. The big man stepped off on the fourth floor and when the doors closed Sydney said, "Hi, Scott."

"I wasn't sure you remembered who I was for a minute."

The elevator bumped and slowly adjusted itself before the doors opened on the fifth floor. I continued to follow Sydney's lead, getting off and turning to face the elevator as it headed back down. When the next elevator came up, it didn't stop on the fifth floor. Sydney exhaled a sigh of relief. She pushed the call button and when the elevator arrived, it was empty. We took it to the fifteenth floor. I opened the door to the room, she entered, and I checked the hallway one last time before closing it. She came out of the bathroom and checked the closet. "Room's clear," she said.

She sat on the corner of the bed while I paced in my usual spot in front of the window. Sydney sprang to her feet, walked over to the curtains and closed them. In one motion she spun around and landed back on the corner of the bed.

"Have you been taking the elevator directly to this floor?" she asked.

"Other than my first time up to the room, I've gotten off on a different floor every time. Not even close to this floor when I rode with strangers."

"Why not the first time?" she asked.

"I'm more skeptical now—about every man, woman, child, car, phone call."

"Sounds like someone trained by the Bureau," she said.

"I was."

"Oh yeah. I forgot. Scott, you asked me more than once about checking for a tail. Are you uncomfortable with me coming here to the hotel?"

"I'm not uncomfortable with anything you do. I'm only concerned about who's out there with that file and what he plans to do to next. Sydney, I don't think there's any way they can let either one of us live."

"Well, that sure as hell makes me feel better."

"Sorry, Sydney. I got you in the middle of this. If there was any way for you to get out of it right now, that would be what I would want more than anything."

"Scott, you didn't get me into this. I'm the one who found the file, and I contacted you." She was right. She took the initiative to follow up on that file. She could have simply read it and deleted it or forgotten about it. There had to have been no doubt in her mind that sharing this information with me would put her directly in the crosshairs of the men behind the conspiracies.

I let out a deep sigh before continuing. "For the past three years I prayed I'd discover some little shred of evidence that the detectives who had worked on my parent's case had missed. Now the only way for me to get the justice I want might mean exposing *Operation Freedom Flows*. That could bring this entire country to its knees. Thank God the Secretary of Defense is out of government, but your boss is still the director of one of the two most powerful spy agencies in the world. I want to make him pay for this too, but I don't want anything to happen to you. Weighing your safety and the good of the country against bringing all of those slimebags to justice is a helluva quandary. We really don't know if they might still be trying to take over the Iraqi oil production."

"With Runnels retired, I think Director Fisher has all he can do to keep the conspiracies covered up. Think about all the media that's focused on the Middle East right now. I can't imagine that the US oil companies would risk being connected with a takeover of Iraq's oil production, then or now."

"You're probably right."

"Your parents were killed because they knew about *Freedom Flows*. That makes us just as much of a target as they were, and we can't call time out or decide that we don't want to play anymore. The game is on, Scott."

"Is there anyone at the Bureau or anywhere in government we could take this to?"

"I have a former boss whom I trust, but I can't see any way of prosecuting the killer, the Secretary of Defense, and the FBI Director in secret."

"How about just the killer?" I asked.

"Possible, but a stretch." Then she pulled down the bedspread, grabbed a pillow, put it against her chest, and lay across the bed. I pulled a chair up next to the bed.

"Do you have any vacation or leave time you can take, Sydney?"

"Why do you ask?"

"We need a plan to go after the killer, and if we're in this together, it needs to be a full-time effort."

"Just remember that Runnels and Fisher manipulated a president, his cabinet, and the Congress of the United States. I feel certain they can hide one of their mercenaries," she said.

"I think if those two believe we're about to expose them, they're going to send their shooter after us. We see that he gets charged with attempted murder and receives the maximum sentence. Then there'll be no reason to bring up any of the old charges. As far as I'm concerned, it'll be over."

"As long as we get him for attempted murder."

"What do you mean by that, Sydney?"

"I believe they'll send him too. In fact, most mercenaries would take your investigation personally, and he'd come after you without anyone sending him."

"You said it earlier, the game is on."

"You know, Scott, this could be worse. Runnels and Fisher could turn this problem over to the oil companies."

"How could that be worse than a killer who works for the CIA and FBI?"

Sydney sat up, still cuddling her pillow against her chest. "The oil companies use mercenaries to protect executives when they travel in foreign countries. Those guys have no limits and no boundaries. Consultants who work for the US government can be ruthless, but the oil company security types usually were booted out of Special Forces because they got out of control."

"Great."

"Don't you know some people in Congress from Florida?" she asked.

"You mean to take this mess to?"

"Just a thought."

"I know my Senators and the Congressman from my local district."

"What do you think about contacting one of them to see if they could establish a safe house?"

"Sydney, I think you know that they'd need more information than we'd be willing to give them. That's not an option."

She didn't reply. Her eyes were dilated, and her head looked like a bobble head doll. I suddenly felt dizzy and lightheaded. Fear gripped Sydney's face. Sitting on the edge of the bed, she was trying to stand, but couldn't. I fell back against the dresser and steadied myself. Sydney finally pushed herself up and stood next to the bed. She wobbled around like a heavyweight boxer who'd just taken a knockout punch. I suspected we'd either been poisoned or gassed. We needed to breathe some air from outside this room. I stumbled towards the door, banging into the wall next to it. The doorknob turned, but it wouldn't open. I put my foot against the wall and tugged on the door. It didn't budge.

Sydney was watching me, but she didn't react. I yelled to her, "Can you give me a hand over here?" Sydney tried to get up, but when she did, she fell to the floor. I kicked at the doorknob, still nothing.

Stumbling sideways and leaning on the bed to keep myself upright, I staggered to the door of the adjoining room. I had rented the adjoining room as a backup plan, because I wasn't sure whether or not I could trust Sydney when I'd checked in. I had actually thought of this room as a safe room from bugs, not as an escape. Regardless, I was glad it was there.

I opened the adjoining room's door, grabbed Sydney under her arms, and pulled her inside. Sydney was lying in a heap at my feet and staring at me with a look of bewilderment. She'd taken in more of the gas than I had. I closed the door, ripped the bedspread off the bed, stuffing it under the bottom of the door. I fell onto the floor next to her. Two deep breaths and I was able to muster the energy to lift Sydney onto the bed. I stared at the door to the corridor. It was fuzzy. It almost appeared as if there were double doors. There was no telling how potent the gas was. The bedspread was no guarantee to keep it out of this room either, which meant we had to get into the corridor.

Stumbling across the room, I fell face first into the carpet five feet from the door. I crawled the rest of the way, pulling myself up by the handle, opening the door, and falling into the hallway. Two men dressed in khaki shirts and slacks stood at the end of the hallway. It looked like they had names embroidered on the front pockets. When they saw me, one of them took a step in my direction, but the other one grabbed the back of his shirt, spun him around and snatched the stairwell door open. I got a glimpse of the lettering on the backs of their shirts as they disappeared down the stairs. It said hotel something. They were moving faster than my eyes were focusing. I took a deep breath of what I hoped was cleaner air.

Sydney was still groggy when I got back to her, but not quite as lethargic as she'd been in my suite. I helped her to the door and down the hall. The farther away we got from the dirty room, the better the air seemed. I wanted to get her into some fresh air outside the building.

We must have looked like a couple of drunks leaving a bar at closing time because we had to lean against each other to keep from falling. I pushed the call button for the elevator, it arrived and a man stepped out. Sydney and I banged into the right hand side of the door and it rattled like thunder. I saw the man who'd just stepped out turn to observe us. "Too much to drink again," I said to him just as the elevator doors closed. He shook his head, probably thinking we were too old to be acting like spring breakers.

On the ride down to the lobby, I reflected on what had just happened. I was at a total loss. Those guys were amateurs. Highly trained mercenaries would have been in that room and taken us out. We would have never gotten a look at them. These guys were sloppy. So who the hell were they and why did they want to gas us?

When I got her through the lobby and out the front door into the fresh air, she slowly began to regain her composure and her equilibrium. A bulky gentleman approached us from the lobby. He had black curly hair, graying on the ends and down his temples where it contrasted with his dark skin. He was wearing a gray suit with a red tie, and the pursing of his lips along with the angry scowl on his face was a clear giveaway that he was not from the concierge desk. The only people I'd ever known with his kind of flat-footed walk had either been a high school band director or a cop who'd pounded a beat in a big city for years. I knew a lot of cops lately who had reached retirement age, only to discover that their retirement fund or 401 K had gone south for their golden years, which meant another job after retirement.

"Frank Harkness, chief of security for the hotel," he said. "Can either of you tell me what's going on?"

"I apologize, Mr. Harkness. We were celebrating tonight, and I guess we had a little too much wine," I said.

"Sir, I've picked up more winos on the streets of this town than you have hairs on your head. This lady's eyes aren't red; they're teary. Neither of you smell of alcohol or marijuana, so why don't you tell me what's going on?"

"What do you mean by 'going on'?" I asked.

He held out his huge hand, palm up and said, "I think it's time I take a look at some ID?" I knew that was coming sooner or later. Once he confirmed our identity, we would need to cooperate more than we had thus far in order to keep him from making calls to our bosses.

"Her name is Sydney Sloan and she's a federal agent. My name is Scott Downing and I'm in law enforcement from Florida."

"Florida, huh? Well I don't care if you're Mickey Mouse from Walt Disney World—you have no authority in Virginia. What's your room number, Mr. Downing?"

CHAPTER 18

Harkness led us into a narrow claustrophobic space he called his office. Sydney's ghostly look had finally given way to a little color, and I was concerned that she might have a relapse in the close quarters we found ourselves in. Harness unstacked two plastic chairs and separated them in front of his desk. We sat and watched as he squeezed past his desk that covered the width of the room save about six inches. This security office had to have been an afterthought, probably a closet in its former life.

I felt like a criminal who had been caught shoplifting. "Mr. Harkness, we certainly didn't want to cause you all this trouble. If we haven't broken any laws, we'll go back to our room now and stay inside the rest of the night," I said raising up from my chair.

He stuck his arm out in front of him, palm down, and lowered it while telling us, "Keep your seats a few minutes longer if you don't mind."

Sydney had rallied enough to talk. "We just got a little light headed, that's all."

"Your name is Ms. Sloan, right?"

"Yes it is."

"Ms. Sloan, do you abuse drugs or alcohol?"

"Absolutely not!"

"You really don't expect me to believe that the two of you got in this shape from drinking a little wine do you?"

"Mr. Harkness, anything's possible," Sydney said.

"Well, Ms. Sloan who is with the FBI, I was with the lowly Metropolitan Police Department in Washington, DC, for thirty-five years. Now I know that only makes me a dumb beat cop, but I'm smart enough to know that when all the surveillance cameras go out on a single floor and that floor happens to be the same one you two are staying on, I start suspecting that something unusual might be going on."

Sydney and I looked at each other. I knew we weren't going to be able to bullshit our way out of this. I sure didn't want him to call the local police, because I was afraid Director Fisher might have already set us up with the local cops as some sort of federal criminals.

There was a knock on his door. "Come in," Harkness shouted. A young man wearing a starched white shirt and green and blue-striped tie squeezed by us to Harkness' side of the desk. He leaned over and whispered something.

"Excuse me for just a second, folks," Harkness said, prodding the young man past us and out the door.

They were having a discussion on the other side of the door. Sydney and I both turned and attempted to overhear their conversation, but it was muffled.

"Do you think they discovered the gas?" I asked Sydney, who was still trying to overhear the conversation.

"I heard them say something about the cameras," Sydney responded.

The door opened, and Frank Harkness stood over us. "Folks, I'm sorry but I'm going to have to contact the local police and have their Haz Mat team come secure the building."

"Haz Mat?" I asked.

"No more games, Mr. Downing," he said, giving me stern look of frustration.

"Frank, if you'll let me take a look, I can probably tell you what it is without calling the police and having to evacuate your entire hotel, which will also bring out the local media," Sydney said in a most convincing voice.

"What makes you the expert on hazardous materials, and why should I trust you?" he asked.

"I've had some training on gases and hazardous materials."

"Did I say anything about gas, Ms. Sloan?"

"You're a good cop, Frank, but you don't want to face management tomorrow and tell them about a building evacuation do you?"

"You pretty good yourself, Ms. Sloan. No, I don't want to have to explain an evacuation to management, but before we go any further, could I see some ID?"

Sydney's head swung frantically from side to side, obviously searching for her purse. She bounced up from her chair, looking in her seat. Genuine fear gripped her face. "My purse has my ID and my weapon in it. I've got to go get it. I've never left my ID and my gun in an open room before."

"I have a man in your hallway. I can assure you no one will take your weapon or your credentials if they really exist," Harkness said.

I reached for my wallet, opened it to my sheriff's department ID and badge, and held it up in front of him. "Mr. Harkness, here's my ID, and if you don't mind, I'd like you and me to go back up and retrieve Agent Sloan's possessions and mine from that suite." He took a long, close look at my ID.

Sydney got aggressive, "Frank, I'm the only one here who's qualified to check out that room. Follow us back to the room, I'll show my Bureau ID, and see if I can come up with some answers about the gas."

"Okay, Ms. Sloan, we'll all go." He moved around from behind his desk and held the door. The trio followed the young man who had interrupted into the elevator. The doors closed and Harkness punched fifteen.

My curiosity was driving me nuts, so on the way up I said, "Our door was jammed shut from the hallway. Any way to lock one of those card swipe hotel entry systems from the outside?"

"Never heard of it before, but I suppose there might be a way to reverse the program. You'd have to know how to manipulate the computer chip in the locks. If you could do that, I guess you might be able to lock the door from the outside."

Harkness' forehead wrinkled and his eyes narrowed. I wasn't sure if he was mad or perplexed. "Now, I have a question for you," he said.

"What's your question?"

"Mr. Downing, you're the only one checked into that suite, right?"

"Right."

"Well, even if it's the two of you staying there, what made you rent the adjoining room?"

"A Southern expression explains it best, Mr. Harkness: This ain't my first rodeo."

He nodded as his frown turned to a wide grin. "I guess not," he responded.

"You rented the adjoining room?" Sydney asked.

"I did."

"Were you concerned that I was setting you up?"

"Let's just say I'm the overly cautious type."

"Fair enough," she said with a smile of approval.

Harkness's assistant stood outside the elevators, standing watch over who was coming and going on the fifteenth floor. We returned to our suite and saw a "do not disturb" sign hanging on the door, only this was not the same door hanger used by this hotel. This door hanger was attached to some sort of box. Sydney entered through the adjoining room and returned clutching her purse in her left hand and holding up her credentials with her right. Harkness looked closely and then pointed towards the strange door hanger. This had to be the tool used to disburse the gas. It was a thin box bearing the "do not disturb" sign. There was a clear tube attached, running from the box to the card slot in the door lock.

Sydney knelt down, held the box in her left hand and studied it. "Pen," she said to Harkness, wiggling her free hand like a surgeon in the operating room. He handed her his pen. She used it to pry the box open. She opened the box to examine the gas and the mechanism that had forced it through the door lock. She moved the contents of the box around and picked up a pair of CO_2 cartridges, turning them in her hand to fully examine them.

Sydney placed the CO_2 cartridges back inside the box settled it gently back against the door. She wiped her hand across the key slot and tasted the residue. "What the hell is this thing?" Frank asked.

"You don't have to evacuate the building. It's a relatively harmless gas. The CO_2 cartridges forced the gas from this box through this tube, which was wedged into the card slot opening of the lock. Then the gas escaped into the room. This gas is like an anesthetic. It expands and fills the room, knocking anyone in the room out for a brief period of time, depending on their size."

"Are you telling me these were high-tech thieves?" Harkness asked.

"I'm telling you they didn't want to kill anyone. Beyond that I don't know what their intentions were," she said.

"Well, Mr. Harkness, we've caused you enough trouble for one night. We'll be getting our things and checking out of your hotel," I offered.

"Not a bad idea," he responded. He stood in the doorway, waiting for us to get all of my belongings. I tossed my clothes into my only piece of luggage and zipped it closed while Sydney folded my laptop's power and phone cords. She handed them to me and I put them in my briefcase.

We started toward the door. Harkness was still standing in the doorway.

Sydney pointed toward the door hanger. "Mr. Harkness, you'll want to have your people place that in a plastic bag that can be sealed. There should be very little residual gas left in that box, but to be on the safe side, have them seal it." She was walking towards the elevator and talking over her shoulder. "You can dispose of it outside in a dumpster. It's not a haz mat threat." At the elevator she hit the call button, and two minutes later we stepped inside. Right before the doors closed, we saw Harkness barking instructions to his staff.

A bell rang, signifying the passing of each of fourteen floors and the arrival at the lobby. We felt a slight hesitation under our feet, before the doors gradually opened. I slowed as we strolled past the registration desk, tossing my key cards into the express checkout box. Sydney never broke stride and had gotten several steps ahead, so I jogged to catch up to her.

"Where are you headed now?" she asked.

"I'm not sure. Any ideas?"

"How about my place? It's not the Ritz," she said with a wide smile, pointing her thumb over her shoulder at the hotel, "but I feel more comfortable there right now. I've got a spare bedroom."

"Fine," I said. "I'll follow you."

Sydney was driving a four- or five-year-old Toyota Camry. It was the same car she had driven me to the airport in nearly a week ago. I was surprised that she didn't have a government issued vehicle. It seemed curious that the Bureau would want her driving around in that clunker when she was on government business.

Back on the Beltway we were headed towards Alexandria again. Sydney had not only put herself at risk by sharing this information with me, now she was offering me a secure place to stay at her house.

Her right turn signal blinked, so I turned on mine as well. A green, wooden routed sign with tall white letters spelling out Bell Haven marked the entrance to her complex. We were behind the Bell Haven Country Club off the Mount Vernon Parkway. She pulled in, but there wasn't a space nearby, so I parked farther down. I grabbed my briefcase containing my laptop and my gun, and hustled to catch up with her.

Sydney approached her front door, glanced in the direction of a window, and did a double take. She drew her Glock from her purse.

"Something wrong, Sydney?"

She looked at me with wide eyes, expressing caution. "Scott, I left some of my lights on," she whispered, pointing at the window that was filled with darkness. I scrambled to unzip my case and snatch out my gun as well. I laid the case on the sidewalk and stood across from her at the opposite side of the door. If she was correct about the lights, someone had either been in, or was still in her apartment.

She pushed the door open, gun extended in front of her searching the darkness. Stepping inside, she moved around like a cat in the dark.

There was an advantage to knowing where everything was in the house. I heard a crunching sound, and ten seconds later, Sydney backed all the way to the door still aiming her weapon inside her apartment. She reached to her left and flipped on the light. The apartment was in shambles. Someone had tossed it.

Sydney was in shock, so I hurried in and began checking room by room, looking in closets, behind shower curtains, and under beds. My search had brought me back to the living room. "It's clear," I hollered. She moved into the doorway, and her eyes welled up as she scanned the possessions that had been recklessly tossed about.

"Sydney, I'm so sorry." She was frozen in place, and this time it was my turn to offer a hug. I joined her in the doorway. This was all my fault. I felt so bad for her. Sydney turned and hugged me, laying her head on my shoulder. I wasn't about to ask her to move until she was ready, although the doorway wasn't the most secure place for us to be standing.

It took another couple of minutes before Sydney was ready to reenter. She took baby steps, apprehensive about seeing the inside of her apartment. I pushed the door closed and dead bolted it behind us. A small elegant lamp was crushed under a marble top walnut Victorian table overturned in the foyer. The door of a tall grandfather clock was ripped off, lying on the floor. A two-tiered mirror backed étagère had been thrown onto an American Renaissance rosewood sofa. We moved into the bedroom and bathroom where we found more of her belongings from clothing to towels and linens strewn all over the floor.

It took until two in the morning to put her apartment back together again. My stomach was churning with sympathy. I tried to tell her I would replace anything that an antique refinisher couldn't repair, but she ignored me as if she didn't hear me.

Finally she looked at me and spoke. "They can't be replaced, Scott." She pointed to the pile of broken and destroyed antiques. "Most of those things belonged to my great grandmother." I knew exactly how Sydney was feeling. It was incomprehensible that someone could violate your space and your life like this. The things we had in common were uncanny.

"I'm going to my car to get my bag," I said, unlocking the dead bolt on the door before going outside. I scanned the parking lot and the woods next door as I briskly made my way to my car. I picked up my luggage and walked backwards continuing the surveillance until I was inside. I locked the door with the dead bolt before putting my bag under the end table next to the sofa.

Sydney had picked up a pillow and blanket off the floor in her bedroom and placed them on the couch for me.

"You want to take the first watch?" she asked.

"I'll take the first and the second watch."

"Scott, I'm sorry I acted the way I did, but I'm okay now. I just wasn't prepared for that."

"Believe me, Sydney, I understand completely."

I put my Glock G19 on the end table, took off my shoes, and lay down.

"You go to your bedroom and get some rest. You've had a helluva day," I said as I propped myself up against the arm of the sofa and covered myself with the blanket.

"Thanks," Sydney said. She went back to her bedroom and turned out her light, and immediately flipped it back on. I jumped up and reached for my gun as Sydney gingerly stepped out of her bedroom, her hands pressing against the sides of her face. She made her way over to the pile of antiques that we had placed in a corner of her living room and picked up every piece of a little lamp.

"Can I help you?" I asked

"No, but thanks for asking. This lamp was in my room at my grandmother's house. When I was little she used to read me bedtime stories by its light." She clutched it against her chest and headed back to her bedroom.

The chances of these guys coming back tonight were probably slim to none, but I was determined to be ready for them in case they hadn't found what they were looking for the first time. I checked my Glock to make sure the clip was full, then I laid it back down and doubled my pillow over so I was almost sitting straight up. There was no way I was going to close my eyes tonight. I owed her this watch.

We were in a scary situation for sure, and there probably wasn't a good place to hide. In the morning, I'd have to put on my game face for Sydney. The last thing she needed now was to think her new partner was a sissy, but Sydney was also the kind of cop who knew that anyone in our line of work who never admitted to being afraid from time to time was either a liar or an idiot.

CHAPTER 19

The first signs of daylight were showing around the edge of the blinds on her windows. I heard some movement from Sydney's bedroom, so I gave her a few minutes to open her eyes and get oriented before coming out. It seemed like it was taking too long for her to appear, so I knocked on her door to see if she was okay.

"Good morning, Scott. Can you give me a sec?" I could see her empty bed from the partially opened door and the muffled sound led me to believe she was either in a walk-in closet or the bathroom.

"Good morning, Syd. I have a cloak and dagger question for you."

"Cloak and dagger?" she asked quizzically.

"Mercenaries don't gas people unless the gas is deadly. A professional killer wouldn't break in here and toss the place and just leave. If he didn't find what he was looking for, he'd wait and get you to show him where it was, then kill you. I thought about that all night. Whoever visited us at the hotel and here at your apartment wasn't a professional killer."

Sydney came out of her bathroom and walked towards me wearing a white FBI tee shirt. She opened the door all the way, and I struggled to hold eye contact. Her nipples were erect and it was clear that she hadn't yet put on a bra. I wasn't sure if she was wearing panties, because her tee shirt covered her long body to the tops of her thighs. She was one of those fortunate people who looked fabulous from the minute she rolled out of bed.

"You're right, Scott. I thought about that last night too. But if this isn't the work of a government operative, who do you think is doing this?"

"You work up here with all these spies. I was hoping you'd have an idea. Did you ever talk about the file with anyone at the FBI?"

"Of course not, Scott. The truth is, I was so afraid of what I had found that I'd made up my mind not to tell anyone, including you."

"So why'd you tell me?"

"I knew how important it was to you. I tried to imagine how you would have handled it if our roles had been reversed."

"Sydney, if someone had killed your parents and I had discovered some information about it, I would have told you, too."

"That's what I thought," she answered with a look of justification.

"Nothing personal, Sydney, but I also would have done the same thing for anyone that had happened to."

"I don't take that personally. I assumed you would have done that for anyone else as well."

"So can we positively rule out a colleague of yours from the Bureau?"

"We can and I already have."

"Can you try to recall out loud what was in that file while I type it all onto my laptop?"

"All I remember is just what I've already told you. Besides, what does it matter if it's in my head or on your laptop?"

I went back to the sofa and picked up my notebook computer before answering.

"Sydney, if anything happened to your pretty little head, I might need the correct information to continue the investigation."

Sydney put both hands on her hips like she was taken aback. "Thanks for the vote of confidence. I didn't think you were burying me so soon."

"That's not what I meant, and you know it, Sydney. Besides, this file could also be our insurance."

"What kind of insurance?" she asked.

I patted the case. "We at least would have the option of emailing the recreated file to someone if we got into trouble."

"Who would you email it to?"

"I have no idea. We'll have to work on that." Sydney followed me to the kitchen and started a pot of coffee brewing while I opened my laptop, turned it on, and waited for it to boot up. I couldn't take my eyes off of her as she moved around the kitchen.

She opened several cabinets, but they were all empty. The intruder had destroyed most of her glassware. Then she checked the dishwasher and found a coffee cup and a short glass. She placed them next to the coffee maker and sat on a stool across the counter of the breakfast bar from me.

"How do you want to do this?" Sydney asked.

"You just blurt out whatever you remember as chronologically correct as possible, and I'll pretend to be a court reporter."

"Okay, let's see, the overview to the file was written by the Secretary of Defense and it dated back to December 2001 when your father first spoke with Calev Heber about the plot to overthrow Iraq, Iran, and Syria in order to turn their oil production over to American oil companies. Your father was told that Runnels and Fisher were going to receive hundreds of millions of dollars from the oil companies. They'd also negotiated some kickback money from the corporations they were planning to award the contracts to for rebuilding of the infrastructure of those countries."

Sydney fidgeted on the stool and appeared to have difficulty forming the words of the next portion of the story. "When the Mossad contacted Fisher with the information about the meeting between your father and Heber, he shared the news with Runnels, and they developed *The Osprey's Nest*."

"So the Israeli government probably knows about the conspiracies, and if they got their hands on your file, they could hold America hostage for military equipment, support in their war against the Palestinians or practically anything they wanted."

"That's an interesting thought. If the Mossad knew I'd printed a file, there's a possibility they'd come after it."

"Exactly, Sydney, like with the gas in the hotel and even here at your house. Those incidents didn't have the feel of something a mercenary would have done."

"Scott, I wish Mossad and mercenaries were all we had to worry about."

"What do you mean by that?"

"The list of consultants the Bureau and the Agency uses for things like this is the baddest of the bad boys."

"Sydney, did anything in the file specifically identify who the killer was?"

"There was never any mention of who officially gave the order or the name of the killer, but I've certainly seen the consultant list."

"Then you know the names of those people, right, Sydney?"

"I took an oath not to answer a question like that from a civilian."

"Contract killing and oath don't seem to fit in the same sentence," I angrily replied. "Sydney, maybe killing my parents wasn't a big deal to Fisher or Runnels, but what about the soldiers?"

"Like I said earlier, I think they thought it would be another Kuwait. You know, a walk in the park."

"But damn, Sydney, when the death toll of our soldiers went from hundreds to over a thousand, why didn't they call the whole thing off and use their influence to persuade the President to get us out of there?"

"The only way for our country to save face was to make it look like we were fighting terrorism and assisting Iraq in building a democracy. I'd bet they got a handsome payout from the oil companies to make sure the whole thing was covered up, and from Halburson for the contracts they were awarded for rebuilding work."

"Sydney, do you mind if review the timeline again? I'd like to save those thoughts in a separate Word file."

"I can try to list each of the timelines,"

"Timelines as in plural."

"Remember there were actually three separate conspiracies. There was a must-complete date for *Osprey* and *The Burning Post*. The end-by date for *Operation Freedom Flows* was changed several times."

"Do you remember any of the dates?" I asked.

"Operation *Osprey's Nest* and *The Burning Post* both had deadlines of Christmas Day 2001."

"So that was my Christmas present from the United States government in 2001?"

She held out a cup of coffee in a tall cup with an FBI logo on it. No wonder the cup had survived yesterday's destructive search of her townhouse; it was plastic.

"Coffee smells great. Any chance of getting a little sugar? Never could handle this stuff black."

She opened the refrigerator and looked inside. "You're in luck, he left the sugar bowl." She dropped a spoon in it, and reached across the counter to hand it to me. When I held out my hand to take the sugar bowl, I accidentally knocked the spoon to the floor by her feet.

"Sorry, Sydney."

"It's okay." She bent over to retrieve the spoon. The instant she bent down I heard a cracking sound and glass breaking. There was a smell of friction in the air, and the powdery dust of sheet rock exploded from the wall next to where Sydney was standing.

"SHOT, SYDNEY, SHOT! STAY DOWN!"

"Where'd it come from?" she yelled, dropping to the floor, landing on her butt.

"Through there," I said, pointing to the window to the left of the backdoor. I crouched like a baseball catcher and duck-walked to the living room, grabbed my Glock, and stayed bent over scurrying to the back door. The bottom half of the door was solid wood; the top half was mostly glass. I looked at the broken window, then over to the bullet hole in the wall. Then I followed the line of flight in reverse, peeking through the window towards the rear of the house. There was a thick stand of trees behind her apartment that covered an area about fifty yards back to one of the fairways on the Bell Haven Country Club. That had to be where the shot was fired.

I unlocked the two locks and slowly opened the door using the solid wooden lower half for my cover. With the door about a quarter of the way open, I peeked around the edge. Maybe forty feet of grass divided the apartment and a thick stand of river birch, Virginia pine, and sycamore trees. If the shooter was still running through the woods, I'd hoped to hear the sounds of cracking limbs or leaves. Nothing. Not a sound. I shoved the door all the way open and ran as fast as I could to the largest tree nearest the apartment. I walked all the way through the woods, but there wasn't even an early Sunday morning golfer anywhere in sight.

Stomping through the woods toward the apartment I noticed the sun reflecting off something shiny that flashed in my eyes. I took cover behind a birch tree, slowly leaned around the side, leading with my gun.

"Scott, it's me," Sydney hollered from about thirty yards away. She must have put on some clothes, picked up her gun, and gone out the front of the building, then around the side. We held our ground for several minutes. I waved to her to go back to the apartment. She acknowledged and started walking backwards, still scanning. We met at the backdoor and went inside.

"You want to call the local cops this time?" I asked.

"Not hardly. Can you imagine the talk at the Bureau if they read a story in *The Post* about a sniper taking a shot at an agent?

"Sydney, these guys want to destroy the file and both of us. The only way for Director Fisher and Secretary Runnels to avoid being charged with accessory to murder, war crimes, and maybe even treason is to make sure we're dead. Every time another American soldier dies in Iraq or Afghanistan, it makes it more critical for them to bury this nightmare, and that means burying us with it."

"Scott, the war is a debacle, you don't suppose those two think they can revive *Operation Freedom Flows* if they can kill us, do you?"

I pointed to the television and said, "The media has had embedded reporters since the war began. My guess is once it started going bad Fisher and Runnels bailed out of the oil takeover. They needed a fast clean occupation of the country for a takeover of the oil production to be seamless and less noticeable. The oil for food scandal at the UN and the talk of corruption between the companies who received contracts to rebuild Iraq and the President created even more media attention. Even with us out of the picture, I can't see them getting away with the takeover."

"This guy killed your parents, and this morning he tried to kill me. I guess it doesn't matter if Runnels and Fisher are still after the oil or not, they're sure as hell after us. So much for starting the day with a cup of coffee and *The Post*. I'd love to go hunt this bastard down right now if we only had a place to start."

"Sydney, you just gave us a starting place."

"You want to share it with me, because I have no idea what I said that could have anything to do with a starting place."

"*The Burning Post*. David Collins' wife wasn't home at the time of the explosion. She's still alive, and we're going to pay her a visit and see what she knows."

"Don't you think if she knew anything, she would have already told the authorities and the information would already be public knowledge?"

"We're going to find out. First, why don't you pack some things. We're going to a safer safe house for a few days."

"I'm not sure there is such a thing as a safe house," Sydney said, heading to her bedroom. She tossed some clothes into a bag while I gathered my belongings.

We drove to the car rental agency across from the airport. I took my luggage and briefcase out of the Explorer and went inside, leaving Sydney waiting for me outside.

When I returned, Sydney followed me from the office over to a white Ford Taurus, not the sexiest car on the road, but one that would blend in commuter traffic. I opened the trunk and stored my luggage as I surveyed the endless rows of rental cars parked across the huge lot, wondering if the killer had followed us.

"Scott, this young man is trying to check your rental agreement," Sydney said in a louder than normal tone.

"Sorry," I said. "I let myself get distracted by all these beautiful cars." I handed him the folder, and he checked it and returned it to me.

"Thanks, Mr. Downing," the young man said, handing the paperwork back to me and opening my door.

Sydney waited until he closed the door to ask, "You sure were staring at these cars. Did you see anything out there?"

"No I didn't, and not seeing is even more disconcerting."

CHAPTER 20

Sydney's jaw dropped when I pulled into the valet parking for the Swissotel Watergate. This famous hotel was located smack in the middle of the United States government on Virginia Avenue, within walking distance of the White House, the monuments, and the capital building. I rented a room with a parlor suite, which provided us with two separate sleeping areas. The room was filled with antique furniture, and it felt more like a museum than a hotel room.

Sydney sat on the sofa, cupped her hands over her face, and her body drooped like something inside her that was holding her posture in place had just let go. She was trying to hold back the tears and muffle the sound, but she couldn't. This tough FBI agent was finally releasing her emotions. I sat beside her and put my arm around her shoulder. She'd been through a so much in the past twenty-four hours.

"Scott, I've screwed up my career, my apartment's ruined, my great grandmother's antiques have been destroyed, and now somebody's trying to kill us." She looked up at me and tried to smile through the tears. "Other than that, I'm having a good day."

"Maybe you should go back to the Bureau tomorrow and let me deal with this. You've already done more than enough for me."

"Thanks, but it's probably too late to go back. If you don't mind I'm going to make a call to confirm some leave time, just in case something were to work out."

"Who do you call on a Sunday?"

"I'm going to leave my supervisor a voicemail message. If I get lucky, I might still have a job when this over." She took the cell phone out of her purse, stepped into the parlor room, and closed the door. A few minutes later she emerged with the positive stride I had become accustomed to seeing. Sydney had pulled herself together.

She tossed the phone on top of her bag and said, "Okay, let's hear your game plan."

"Are you sure you're up to that right now?"

"Yeah, let's go to work. I do have a question though."

"Fire away," I said.

"Bad choice of words again," she shot back with another smile.

"I knew when I said it, but I couldn't stop myself."

"Why the Watergate?"

"It's the home of the most famous political screw-up in the history of our country. It's not the kind of place that anyone in government would want to risk another bad publicity episode. They also have pretty good security these days."

"What a strange mind you have," she said.

"I'll take that as a compliment. I'm going to call *The Post* and see if I can convince someone there to give me a phone number of David Collins' widow," I said.

"While you do that I'm going to unpack. Any preferences?"

"You take the big room, and I'll take the parlor room."

"Thanks," she said as she opened her bag and placed her clothes in stacks on the king-sized bed.

I took out the phone book and looked up the main number of *The Post*. I explained to the switchboard operator that David Collins was a friend of my father's, and at the time of his death I was away at college and never had the opportunity to offer my condolences to Mrs. Collins.

My call was transferred to a woman named Larsen. I explained that David had been a family friend. She asked me who I was, so I gave her my name.

"Scott, I don't think I ever met you, but your mother and father attended several dinner parties hosted by our publisher. I was so sorry to hear about what happened to them. I guess it's as dangerous in Florida as it is around the District."

"Not usually," I said, wanting so badly to tell her that it was only dangerous in Florida when people from Washington had our citizens assassinated. Instead I opted to continue seeking information about Mrs. Collins. "Ms. Larsen, David Collins was a close friend of my dad's. I wanted to apologize to her for not getting in touch sooner and extending my condolences." Sydney was placing her clothes in the dresser drawers, and she turned to face me, nodding her head as if she was impressed that I appeared to be having some success.

"Like father, like son," Ms. Larsen said, "But I'm so sorry I have to tell you that our policy won't allow any of us to give out personal information about our personnel or their families." I told her I understood and I thanked her for her time.

Sydney said, "Sounds like you have some contacts at *The Post*?"

"Not enough. They don't give out names or addresses."

"Most companies don't," Sydney said. "I could probably try a source at the Bureau, but that might be a little iffy."

"That would be more than a little iffy. I wouldn't want the Bureau knocking on her door before we did."

She folded the last piece of clothing in her bag, placed it in the drawer, turned and leaned against the dresser. "My first boss at the Bureau left me a voice message on my cell yesterday, asking if I was okay. I don't think he knows what's going on, but I'm sure he's sincere about my welfare."

"What makes you think he doesn't know what's going on? Is he close to Fisher?"

"He's loyal to the Bureau, but believe me, he's not supportive of Fisher. He was my mentor, and we talk every week, every week but this one."

"Right now I don't trust anybody at the Bureau."

She took umbrage at that statement, pushing off the dresser, placing her hands on her hips. "What do you want to do, call home to see if someone with the Bay County Sheriff's Department can help us?"

"Go ahead. Make fun of the lowly local cops. At least no one in our law enforcement agency ever tried to kill one of their own."

"Touché," she said. "But my old boss would be on our side. We could at least call him and try to find out if he's heard anything about us at the Bureau."

"He probably did. Don't you think that's why he called you?"

"Scott, he called me because we're close and it's unusual for him to not hear from me."

"I can't believe you're suggesting we put our lives in the hands of anyone at the Bureau."

She pointed her finger at me and her body became rigid. " James Markham isn't like Fisher," she said, separating each word emphatically.

"Okay, you think about what public place we could meet him in, and I'll think about whether I'm ready to play a hand of all-in poker. In the meantime, I'm still going to try to contact David Collins' wife."

"Change your mind about having someone at the Bureau locate her?"

"Not at all. We'll meet your guy, whoever he is, and by the time we finish meeting with him, my partner should have the information we need to contact Ms. Collins."

"Scott, come on. My old boss is for real. He hired me, trained me, and I was like a daughter to him. James Markham is one of the most respected people at the Bureau by everyone who ever worked with him. Five years ago there were very few females who worked in the law enforcement division, especially right out of law school. Mark gave me that chance."

"What was his position?"

"He was the ADIC in Washington, DC."

"Which means what?"

"Smaller cities have Special Agents in Charge, larger cities have Assistant Directors in Charge.

"So is he in charge of the DC office now?"

"About three and a half years ago, Fisher played a lot of politics and got himself promoted to the top job. Mark graciously stepped aside. Last month he put in his retirement papers. He's consulting to the director for the next eleven months, mostly on agent training. Fisher is a power broker; Markham doesn't think much of him."

"So you no longer report to Markham?"

"No, Deputy Director Tillman."

"Northwest gate of the White House." I said.

"Scott, what does that mean?"

"That's where I'd like to meet him. The secret service patrols the gate, they have snipers on the roof who can spot a weapon a half-mile away. Not even the FBI or the CIA would risk doing anything stupid in front of the White House. It's way too public and secure."

"So, I'll give him a call?"

"Not with our phones. They're only for talking to each other."

"Markham isn't going to try to trace my call."

"Sydney, if Fisher knows how close you are to Markham, he might suspect that you'd try to call him and be listening to his calls. It'd be simple to locate the nearest tower you're transmitting from and pinpoint your location.

"Just to be on the safe side, let's call him from a pay phone," I said.

"When do you want to call?"

I stood and walked to the picture window, pointed to the front of the John F. Kennedy Center for the Performing Arts, and tapped my finger on the glass. "As soon as we get to those phones down there,"

"Let's go," she said. This was my kind of woman and my kind of partner.

"Hang on. I want to get my partner in Florida started on finding Ms. Collins."

"We still don't know where she lives, or if her name is still Collins. There's a good chance she's remarried," she reminded me.

"Ms. Collins worked for some trade association that was headquartered in the northern Virginia, DC area. She was a native of Virginia, so I'd be willing to bet she's still around here somewhere."

"I'm impressed, Lieutenant."

"You'd better hold those accolades in abeyance until I have the address."

I called Ramer and gave him the information about David Collins and his former wife. He started to ask questions, so I stopped him with, "Robert, I'll fill you in as much as I can as soon as I can." He promised to find out what he could and call me back.

I hung up, turned to Sydney, and said, "Robert's a good partner. He's home with his family tonight, but he'll have something for us by tomorrow."

We left the room and headed to the Kennedy Center, walking briskly as if we were on our way to a highly anticipated performance. In reality I guess we were.

CHAPTER 21

A box containing Washington Post newspapers stood at the end of the bank of pay phones on the corner near the Kennedy Center. I glanced at the box while Sydney dialed the number. Today's date was displayed on the top paper. Sunday, April eleventh, only eleven days since Sydney had broken the news to me about my parents in National Airport.

Sydney held the phone at a forty-five degree angle to her ear, and I put my head close to hers, wedging the phone between us. James Markham answered on the third ring.

"Markham."

"Mark, this is Syd. I hate to bother you at home on a Sunday."

"I always enjoy hearing from my girl no matter what day it is. How are you?"

"Not so good. Somebody ransacked my house yesterday, and took at shot at me in the kitchen this morning."

"Oh my God, Syd, what's going on?"

"Mark, you haven't heard anything around the office?"

"What's that supposed to mean?"

"Never mind that question, I'll explain later."

"Sydney, I'm lost. Tell me what the hell is going on. Where are you?"

"I'd rather not say right now, but I need your help."

"I'll tell Sara to get the guest room ready. Can you get here?"

"Thanks, Mark, but I don't need a place to stay. I have a friend with me, so I'm not in this alone."

"Dammit, Sydney, in what? There's nothing illegal going on is there?"

"Mark, come on, I think you know better than that."

"Well I know you, but I don't know your friend."

"Can you meet me at the northwest gate of the White House?"

"Are you serious?"

"Dead serious."

"You're really afraid aren't you?"

"Why'd you ask that?"

"I've known you since the day you graduated, and I've never known you to be afraid of anything, but your voice sounds a little shaky to me."

"I've seen slugs in plenty of walls, but this was the first time I'd seen one in mine."

"Well, you've still got your wits about you."

"How's that, Mark?"

"The northwest gate of the White House is a hell of a cover. If you're concerned about a shooter, you picked a damn good spot. By the way, tell your friend who's listening in, I'm not bringing a shooter."

"Who says he's listening in?"

"I heard two sets of breathing. Christ, Sydney, I didn't even ask, you didn't get hit this morning did you?"

"No, I'm fine. Two sets of breathing. You never cease to amaze me."

"Okay, northwest gate in an hour," he said. I flashed my right hand open and closed twice showing five fingers followed by five fingers. She looked quizzically at me so I mouthed the words fifty-five minutes.

"Fifty-five minutes, Mark."

"Damn, Sydney. Let me hang up so I can get there. Don't leave until I see you."

"Fifty-four minutes, Mark." I heard the dial tone. He'd hung up.

Sydney glared into my eyes. Her face was tight with tension. "What's with your countdown?"

"I know you trust him, but other people at the Bureau may be following him or listening to his calls because of your connection to him. We can't afford to give them a minute longer than necessary to set anything up."

"You're an investigator, you heard his voice and his answers— what's your read?"

"He did talk to you like you were his daughter. I definitely detected a note of genuine concern."

"I guess we'll know in fifty minutes, won't we?" she said, watching me hail a passing cab.

"What about our rental car?" she asked.

"Markham doesn't need to know what we're driving or where we're staying."

"More trust."

"Sydney, if this guy were your father, I wouldn't trust him right now." She shook her head in disbelief.

"Northwest gate of the White House," I told the driver.

"I can't get you all the way to Pennsylvania Avenue," the driver said in an accent that sounded Indian or Pakistani. "I take you to Seventeenth Street. You will walk one block from there," he added.

"We understand. That's fine," I said. Sydney and I were already nervous. This cab driver didn't help matters by constantly glancing at his rearview mirror. I couldn't tell if he was looking at us, or another vehicle behind us. While I paid the driver, Sydney stayed seated, searching the area for anything or anyone that didn't feel right.

Sydney and I stepped out of the cab. I grabbed her arm and told her if shots were fired to try to show her badge to the Secret Service Agents on the fence line. That should put them on our team, at least temporarily.

The eclectic crowd that moved along the White House fence line on this Sunday afternoon would put any law enforcement officer on edge. A group of teenagers wearing Nike sneakers and Dallas Cowboy caps were arguing over where the Rose Garden was, while three scruffy downtrodden homeless men panhandled the passersby. A group of men and women who appeared Middle Eastern strolled the fence line in the opposite direction from the teenagers. The women were wearing hijabs scarves on their heads, and jilbabs gowns. The men walking ahead of them wore small turban hats called kufis, and galabiyyas gowns. One of them noticed the secret service snipers on the roof of the White House and pointed them out to the rest of his group.

"You're not comfortable mentioning where we're staying, right?" Sydney asked me, trying to verify how much or how little I wanted to share with James Markham.

"Not until we feel more comfortable about him."

"What do you mean we?"

"Sydney, you need to keep an open mind as well. You know this guy, I don't. If he acts even the slightest bit different or you notice anything unusual, you have to be prepared to identify it and dissect it on the spot. If that happens or if you notice anyone you're worried about around us anywhere, just use our old cell phone code word, Whittaker."

"Scott, don't get trigger happy on me."

"I think you know I'll give him a chance."

"Good, because here he comes."

James Markham must have parked somewhere east of us, the direction we were walking in. Markham either had a scruffy beard and a long red pony tail or he was a distinguished older gentleman who looked like he might have once played offensive line for the Redskins. I ruled out the ponytail in the wheelchair and went with the big guy hobbling as he walked in our direction. He was a little over six feet tall with a thick build. He had big arms and legs and a broad chest. He wore a medium-priced dark gray suit that fit him okay. He had on black wing tips, the kind of unfashionable, uncomfortable shoes he'd probably worn all of his adult life. His hair was thinning and closer to white than gray.

He hugged Sydney before he spoke. "Sorry, Syd, I parked next to the northeast gate and had to walk around."

"James Markham, this is Scott Downing."

"How do you do, sir," I said. He had a perplexed look on his face as though he was trying to place me.

"Hello, Scott," he said, shaking my hand like a preacher after church on Sunday, not wanting to let go until he was sure I had tithed properly. "Old age sucks. I know you, but I can't remember from where."

"Ever come to Florida?" I asked.

"No, that's not it. The last time I was there, Disney World was an orange grove."

"Mark, he's the guy who testified up here not too long ago about local law enforcement working with the Bureau."

"Oh yeah, that's it. Thanks for that testimony. I read the full transcript. We all appreciate your support."

"I just told the truth."

"Now, what's this about someone taking a shot at you?"

I pointed in the direction where Markham had come from before asking, "Do you guys mind if we walk while we talk?"

"Good idea, Scott," Markham said, putting his arm on Sydney's shoulder and turning her in the right direction.

"It happened this morning. The bullet was fired from the country club through my back door. I think it was an FBI shooter."

Markham took a deep breath and blew out hard. He wagged his finger at Sydney, and his voice became gruffer. "Sydney, what the hell are you on? Why are we having this conversation out here on a sidewalk in front of the White House?"

"We have good reason to believe the Bureau is involved," I said.

"Sydney, tell me about the shooting. Any possibility that Scott was the target?

"Mark, if I hadn't bent over to pick up a spoon, I'd be in a box right now."

Markham gave me stern look; I knew he was trying to read my eyes, facial expressions, and body language. "Let me get this straight. Neither of you saw anyone, and you have no idea why someone would pop off a round at you?"

Sydney checked the sidewalk, both behind and ahead of us. There was no one coming in our direction. She stopped and took Markham's hand and held it both of hers. Her voice cracked slightly as she spoke. "Mark, I'd never ask you to get in the middle of something like this, but I have nowhere else to turn."

"You know I'll help you. Whatever you need, you have my full support."

"Can I call you Mark?" I asked.

"Most people do."

"Mark, my parents were killed by someone who worked for our government, and Sydney found the file that brought that to light."

He winced like he was in pain. "Jesus Christ! Who were your parents?"

"Thomas and Elizabeth Downing. They were CIA."

"You can find them listed in the NSA database, Mark," Sydney said.

"My parents discovered a conspiracy called *Operation Freedom Flows*, which was basically a plot to invade Iraq, Iran and Syria, turning over each country's oil production to American-owned oil companies."

Markham threw his hands up and landed them on top of his head. "Holy shit! This involves the President," he said.

Sydney spoke up. "Only indirectly, Mark. The two government employees duped the President into the invasion. Then they hired a mercenary to kill Scott's parents and a friend named Collins who worked for *The Washington Post* to keep them quiet. The code name for killing his parents was *The Osprey's Nest*. Collins' murder was called *The Burning Post*."

I interrupted, "Now Sydney and I have that information, and we're the targets. The shooter was probably hired to eliminate us to bring the story to an end."

"On top of that he's probably trying to protect his own identity as well," Sydney added.

"We hadn't planned to share this much information with you, because the more you know, the more dangerous it gets," I told Markham.

"Scott, I worry about slipping on a grape in the produce section of the Safeway, falling, and breaking my hip. I don't worry much about a shooter these days. Let me see what I can uncover. You're not still staying at your place are you, Syd?"

"No, a hotel."

"Which hotel?"

I jumped in. "Mark, I've already told you more than Sydney and I agreed to share. We're probably all better off if you don't know which hotel."

He gazed into Sydney's eyes with the look of a parent sending a child off to war. "Sydney, I don't want anything to happen to you. Hell, I feel like I've raised you from the first day you came to work at the Bureau. If you get in a tight spot any time of the day or night, you call me...understand?"

"I understand, Mark. We appreciate anything you can find out around the Bureau."

"I'd like to take a look at something in your apartment. Do you still cook out?"

Sydney let out a loud laugh. "You bet your hibachi," she answered. I was dumbfounded, totally lost.

"Cookout?" I asked.

"Tell you later," Sydney answered.

"Scott, you take good care of her, and I'll see what I can find out. I'll try to get a lead on the shooter. Who's calling who?"

"We'll call you, unless you have something urgent," Sydney said. "Let me see your cell phone. She held out her hand while he took his phone off his belt clip and handed it to her. "Not the Bureau phone, your phone." This time he reached in his pocket and took out an even smaller cellular phone. Sydney punched her new cell number in, hit the save button, and said, "You can call this number anytime."

"Sydney and I are the only people who have that number, so be careful when and how you call it."

He smiled at my instructions. "I'll do my best to be careful with your numbers."

I shook my head in disgust for giving a man with over thirty years experience in the FBI such elementary instructions. "Sorry, Mark, I know you know what you're doing."

"No problem. I'd be cautious too if I were you," he said, handing me his business card. "This is the old-fashioned way of remembering someone's phone numbers. Sydney knows them all, but this is a little courtesy for you, Mr. Downing. I'm giving you the same offer. Call me if you need me. I've only heard of something like this happening once in my thirty-two years and that situation was very ugly. You two be damn careful." With that comment, Markham turned and headed back in the direction he'd approached us from a few minutes earlier.

Darkness had fallen over the capital as we walked to Seventeenth Street, hailed a cab, and went straight back to the Watergate.

Inside the lobby I pointed to the stairwell. We opened the door and hoofed it up the first four floors, then rang for the elevator. When it arrived there were four men in suits on board. I hit five instead of eleven, which was our floor. We got off on the fifth floor. Sydney checked both ends of the hallway before pushing the call button for another elevator. This time we were alone, so we took it all the way to the eleventh floor and entered the room, checking it as we went.

"Markham wasn't involved with anything that's happened in the past couple of days. You agree?" she asked as she lay on the bed.

"He's either very sincere, or he's a great actor."

"He's very sincere. If he was involved, he could have gotten into my apartment and killed us during the night."

"What makes you so sure about that?" I asked.

"He and Sara helped me move into that apartment, and I cooked steaks that night. We talked about a place for me to hide a spare key for Sara to come over and water my plants or check on my apartment when I was at the Bureau's training facility. Mark went out to his car and came back with a black metal magnetic key hider. He stuck it on the bottom of the hibachi grill and told me to put a key in the box when I got a spare one made. I did it the next day, and he and Sara used that key to check on my place several times."

"What a clandestine hiding place. Must be a secret FBI thing," I said unable to hold back my laughter.

"Never had a problem with anyone getting in until you came along," she said.

"Wow, that hurt."

"Scott, you feel like a burger?"

"You mean room service?"

"Let's go out and get something. This is a big city, and my guess is that they don't have a clue where we are," Sydney said with the first real smile I'd seen on her face in a couple of days.

"Mark was right about you," I said nodding my head in the affirmative.

"How's that?"

"You're not afraid of anything, are you?"

"Actually, I am. I'm afraid of hotel room service food."

"Do I need a sport coat, tie or anything like that?" I asked.

"Not where we're going."

CHAPTER 22

Sydney called down to have our rental car waiting for us. I tipped the attendant, and we were off with Sydney behind the wheel. We entered a roundabout and exited onto Pennsylvania Avenue. As we approached the White House, I asked, "We're not dining with the first family, are we?" I was grinning enough to catch Sydney's peripheral vision.

"More fun than eating with them," she said, turning onto Massachusetts Avenue. I could see Union Station approaching, but I couldn't recall any great restaurants there. We parked and headed towards a narrow restaurant with red neon letters that spelled the words *Johnny Rockets*. The next thing I knew, my sense of smell was engulfed by greasy, fat burgers frying on a grill. "Ain't Too Proud to Beg" by the Temptations rained down from the speakers and had everyone in the burger joint tapping their feet and bobbing their bodies to the beat of the music. We slipped into a booth with shiny red vinyl seats. Sydney ordered two originals with fries and chocolate shakes from a young woman wearing a white apron, white shirt, black bow tie, and a paper soda jerk hat. The order was delivered within five minutes. Sydney lathered her burger with ketchup and mustard and poured a huge amount of ketchup on her fries.

"How do you maintain a body like yours, eating like this?"

"It's nerves. When I get nervous, I eat junk, and I eat it often."

"This is scary," I said.

"What is?" she asked looking around the restaurant thinking I had been referring to something other than her last comment.

"I do the same thing."

"Then I should ask you the same question. There's a lot of bone and tone on that body too."

"Thanks," I said, wondering if my face had turned the same shade as the bottle of Heinz on the table.

"Now that we've exchanged all this adulation, let's get back to the case," she said, taking a big bite out of her burger and snatching up a napkin to wipe her mouth. I couldn't believe we were both eating a juicy burger with fries and sipping a rich chocolate shake through a straw, knowing that someone was out there who wanted us dead. Maybe he was watching and thinking all he had to do was wait awhile and our cholesterol would do the job for him.

"The Tracks of My Tears" started playing and it brought the entire wait staff out in front of the long counter. They began to lip sync the song and perform a crudely choreographed but cute dance. The instant the song ended everyone went back to bussing and wiping tables, taking orders, and seating newly arriving patrons. Choosing this place told me a lot about Sydney. We could have easily taken the safest and most conservative direction by ordering room service tonight. But coming here instead was the right thing for us to do. We needed this kind of outing to ease the tension that had us both wrapped too tight.

We were close to finishing our burgers when we leaped into a discussion about who we thought had sent a killer in our direction. My guess was that he was acting on his own to keep his record clean. Sydney thought Fisher had sent him. The one issue we now agreed on was how much better we felt knowing that Markham was going to be helping us from the inside of the Bureau. We also were feeling more comfortable with each other now. I wasn't sure what Sydney was thinking, but in the last three days I'd had feelings for her that went way beyond our work together.

She motioned for me to lean closer, so I did. We were nearly nose-to-nose across the table, and she lowered her voice to a whisper and said, "I've never seen the director of the FBI or the Secretary of Defense in this place."

"Damn, Sydney, I thought you had something profound to tell me."

She gave me one of her beautiful smiles that practically caused me to melt, before reaching across the table and grabbing my hands to keep me leaning into the center of the table. I was close enough to kiss her, and I thought about it for a instant, but my better judgment convinced me to change the subject back to the case.

"How could men in those kinds of power positions be dumb enough to leave a file floating around?" I asked.

"Humans make mistakes, even powerful humans," she said. "But how could those bastards have been so arrogant to think they could have pulled off something like the invasion of a country and the take over of their oil?"

"Sydney, your boss and Secretary Runnels must have been confident that they could lead the President wherever they wanted him to go. After 9-11, the President wanted desperately to get some revenge on behalf of America; Runnels and Fisher seized on that emotion."

"Then if we were out of the way, what's to stop them from pulling off *Operation Freedom Flows*?"

"Runnels has resigned, but I'm sure he's still in contact with Fisher, and he probably still has the ear of the President. There's a possibility that could happen."

I looked across the table at her, deep into her eyes. I held her hands tight. Her mouth opened like she was going to say something else, but she stopped herself.

"Go ahead, Sydney. We haven't held anything back from each other up until now."

"You're right. Okay here goes. What if we get lucky and capture the man who killed your parents? You can't bring him to justice without explaining the conspiracy can you? I'm counting on someone in our government to provide the justice for me. What about you?"

"What does that mean? They hired some to kill my parents. Surely you don't think they'll let him have a public trial."

"You think someone in our government would have him killed?"

"Sydney, I don't really know what to think about our government anymore."

"At least that tells me a lot about you, Scott."

"Meaning what?"

"Most people I know would have responded that they were going to implement their own justice on the killer of their parents."

"Sometimes I wish I was like that, but I'm not."

"I'm ready whenever you are," Sydney said.

I paid the bill, left the tip, and we headed back. This time we agreed to take the stairs all the way to the eleventh floor to try and walk off some of what we had just consumed. We checked the hallway carefully, and then the room. Sydney tossed her body onto the bed. She was exhausted.

I lay on the bed beside her, clicking the remote control to turn on the television. We watched cable news to get reacquainted with what was going on in the rest of the world. The lead story was about five American soldiers killed by a car bomb in Iraq. The next story was about the terror threat level being elevated to orange. Most of the news had something to do with the American intrusion into Iraq. I couldn't watch it anymore.

"Do you mind if I turn this off?" I asked.

"I'd actually appreciate that," Sydney said. I clicked off the TV and rolled over, putting my face down in the pillow. I felt a comforting hand stroking my back again. I wanted to roll over, grab her and make passionate love to her, but I knew I had to remain professional. Talk about arrogant. I was assuming she was lusting for me, too. But we were in a deadly precarious situation together and we needed to maintain confidence in and respect for each other, or we'd never succeed—or survive.

CHAPTER 23

My cell phone rang at ten minutes after five the next morning. My bleary eyes couldn't focus. I fumbled for the phone, finally corralled it off the floor, and hoarsely mumbled, "Hello."

"Morning partner," Robert replied in a wide-awake tone. It was ten minutes after four where he was.

"Up a little early this Monday morning aren't you?" I pushed my right hand through my hair, still trying to get my bearings.

He told me that he couldn't sleep, worried about what I was involved in up here.

I'd guessed he would wait until morning to begin to track down the name of David Collins' wife. I should have known better. He must have worked on it most of the night. The address he gave me was twenty minutes away in Arlington.

Sydney approached me from the other room rubbing her eyes. She was wearing a pair of white baggy chef's pants with black polka dots and a Mickey Mouse tee shirt.

"Morning, Scott."

"Morning, Sydney. That was Ramer. He called to give me Connie Collins' address."

"He's already at work."

"He's a little worried about what's going on up here. Said he couldn't sleep."

"Sounds like a good partner. Why don't I take the first shower and finish getting ready out here?" She pointed towards the dresser.

"Sure go ahead. Hey, I'm going to order room service. What would you like?"

"A bagel and a cup of coffee, thanks."

The more I was around Sydney, the more I discovered how much we were alike, almost to the point of being uncanny. I picked up my laptop from my bag, plugged it in and logged onto the Internet. I went to Mapquest to get directions from the hotel to Connie Collins' house. I typed in the required info and it gave me driving directions and a map. Without a printer, I just studied the map carefully, so I could recall the details as I drove.

She came out with a head full of wet blonde hair and a towel wrapped around her body. "Next!" she shouted. I carried my clothes on hangers and hung them on the hook behind the door. Then I turned the shower head to pulsate and let the warm water massage my body. It was very relaxing. I stepped out and was drying off when I heard her voice through the door.

"What do you think she's going to tell us?"

"Ms. Collins? I don't know. She may not know anything about what her husband and my father discussed, but at least it's a place to start." The more I talked about meeting Connie Collins, the more nervous I got. "I'm willing to bet that she knows her husband's death wasn't an accident."

"If she thought it wasn't an accident and the authorities didn't do anything about it, wouldn't she have taken her story to *The Post*?" Sydney asked.

"You're probably right. Maybe she did think it was an accident. Maybe she believed the police. If we can we convince her that we're putting a case together that might bring to light the real truth, I think she'll help," I said confidently.

Room service arrived with our breakfast and the attendant placed it on the table in front of the window while Sydney signed for it. As soon as he was gone, I heard her blow dryer whirring. Seconds later I heard a spoon stirring a coffee cup. "Two sugars okay?" Sydney asked reaching her hand through the door offering me the coffee.

"Wow, thank you. I'm not used to this kind of treatment," I said, reaching for the cup and taking a sip, before putting placing it on the counter.

I put on a long-sleeve yellow polo shirt over dark brown double pleated dress slacks. I came out of the bathroom holding a pair of brown socks, sat on the edge of the bed and slipped on my loafers.

Sydney was sitting at the table putting cream cheese on her bagel, so I sat down and joined her. "I'm having second thoughts about going to see Connie Collins," I said.

"You are kidding, aren't you?" Sydney fired back.

"I guess I feel a little funny bringing this woman into this mess. What if she doesn't know anything? We could inadvertently make her a target too."

Sydney held up her coffee cup and contemplated her next statement. "If she does know something that means she probably struck a deal with the government to remain silent."

"Damn, Sydney, I never thought of that. We'd better be careful how we approach the conspiracy with her. She could have agreed to some sort of settlement with annual payments, which would make her loyal to the government. I hope that's not the case."

We finished breakfast and headed for our rental car. It was only six-thirty, early enough to miss most of the morning rush traffic, plus we were headed out of DC. The line of cars coming into the District stretched for miles.

We found her house in a neighborhood of large executive homes that backed up to a beautiful wooded park along Donaldson Run. A thick morning dew blanketed the grass and shrubs. I called Connie Collins from her driveway.

"Ms. Collins, this is Scott Downing, I'm Thomas and Elizabeth Downing's son."

"Oh, yes, hello, Scott. I remember you."

"I'm parked in your driveway with a friend of mine who works in law enforcement up here, and we'd love to come in and talk to you for a minute."

"Scott, it's seven o'clock. I have to get ready for work."

"I promise we'll only take a few minutes of your time." She reluctantly agreed. By the time we reached the steps, the front door was partially opened. She stood in her foyer wearing a peach-colored robe drawn tight by a sash.

I held out my hand and she shook it. "This is Sydney Sloan, she's with the FBI."

"What's this about, Scott?"

"It's about your husband's death."

"I told the police everything I knew. By the way, do you have some identification?" she asked, looking directly at Sydney. We both reached for our IDs, but she told me that she recognized me and my ID wasn't necessary. Sydney flashed her credentials before Connie Collins invited us inside, leading us to her living room. Her home was very colonial, which related to her Virginia heritage.

"David and I never had any children, so the fire took away the only person I ever loved in my adult life. It's not easy for me to talk about it, Scott."

"Do you believe the fire was an accident?" I asked.

"Scott, the Arlington Police, the State Fire Marshall, and the FBI investigated. They all determined the fire was an accident. That's the end of it, Scott."

"What if we told you that David might have known something my father confidentially shared with him, which may have been the reason your fireplace exploded?"

Connie Collins folded her arms in front of her and pursed her lips. "David was a helluva reporter, and a lot of people placed their confidence in him, but no one ever threatened to kill him over anything he was writing or had written. It's been nearly three years, Scott. It's time to let it go. David's gone, and your parents are gone. Nothing is going to bring them back."

"Connie, I loved my parents as much as you loved David, and I can't and I won't let it go until I know the truth."

Her looked of frustration shifted to anger. Her facial muscles tightened and her eyes had a wicked look about them. "I'm sorry, but I have to get ready for work now."

Sydney stood and said, "Thank you for your time, Ms. Collins."

I was too irritated to be that polite. "Goodbye, Connie." I was furious that Connie Collins refused to tell us anything she might have known. She didn't seem interested in finding out any new information about her husband's death either. If she loved him as much as she said she did, why wouldn't she be grateful that we were still working on the case?

We made our way down the sidewalk to the driveway. Sydney started to get in on the passenger's side while I walked around to the driver's side.

"STOP!" Sydney shouted as I had reached to open the door.

"What?" I asked.

"Don't touch the car. There was dew on this concrete when I got out a few minutes ago."

"And it still is," I said pointing to the moisture all over the driveway.

"Not right here, it's not. This looks dry like a body slid underneath the car. "

"We were only in there for ten minutes, fifteen tops," I said.

"That's all it takes to attach most devices today, Scott."

Circling around behind the car to where Sydney was standing, I saw it. A dry spot the width of a person's body marked the concrete. We knelt down and warily looked under the car. At first I didn't see anything.

"See that gray wire?" she said pointing to a wire dangling from the driver's side.

"I do now." The wire stretched from each door to a square red block. We both stood and looked at each other. "That red thing is not something installed by the manufacturer is it?" I asked.

"Not unless they installed it in the last ten minutes."

"What now?" I asked looking around the neighborhood as if I were expecting to see the person who had put that device under our car. I noticed Connie's outline in the window through the narrowly opened plantation blinds.

Sydney lay on her back and slid her body under the car from the driver's side. I stepped back, intimidated by standing next to the car.

Connie continued to observe us from the window. "She's watching us," I said to Sydney as she slid her body out from under the car.

Flat on her back she said, "We can call the cops, or you can go back up there and ask her for a pair of wire cutters."

"I'll take the second option. What do you propose to do after I get the cutters?"

"Clip that gray wire where it goes into the box," she said.

"You're not killing yourself on my watch," I said.

"Your watch?"

"Sorry. That sounded a little arrogant, didn't it. What I mean to say was, I don't want anything to happen to you on my account."

"It's basic demolition, Scott. This thing isn't very sophisticated, but I need to clip it; I can't pull it."

I reluctantly forced myself back up and rang the doorbell. Connie opened the door, I told her we were having a little car trouble. We needed to borrow some wire cutters.

"Just a second," she said closing the door and walking away. She didn't invite me in this time. She returned with two wire cutters, a large and small pair. "Just leave them on the sidewalk by the garage door. Goodbye, Scott." The door closed literally and figuratively. I gave Sydney the tools; she picked the smaller one and handed me back the larger pair. She climbed underneath the car again.

"Do I need to wait in the backyard?" I asked, trying to lighten things up. I heard a snip, and she slid out from under the car.

"Don't drop this, okay," she said handing me the red box. I took it and stood frozen in place waiting for my next instructions.

"Put it on the floor of the backseat, and let's get out of here."

"Do you mind if I put it on your side?" I jokingly replied.

"Scott, that baby is large enough so it wouldn't matter whose side it was on."

"Thanks. That's certainly more comforting," I responded in the most sarcastic voice I could muster. "Am I supposed to put this in one of those garbage cans at the next fast food restaurant we come to?" I asked.

"No, I'm going to call Mark. He'll take it from us, and we'll see if my suspicion is right."

"What suspicion is that?"

"I think this was made by the Agency or by someone who used to work for the Agency."

"Jesus Christ. Car bombs. It's hard to believe our tax dollars go towards teaching federal employees how to make these things."

"You ought to be glad they do. Part of that education is teaching us to dismantle them as well."

The bullet in Sydney's wall and the little red box on the floor of the car made it clear this was a winner-take-all event.

CHAPTER 24

If I had been alone this morning at Connie Collins' house, I would have been blown to pieces. Sydney was not only very intelligent she was unbelievably courageous. I wiggled my butt around in my seat refusing to sit all the way back for fear of setting off the bomb. My palms were damp as I gripped the steering wheel, yet Sydney seemed oblivious to the deadly cargo behind my seat.

"Aren't you nervous?" I asked.

"Not now," she replied.

"Damn, Sydney, I'm as nervous as a rabbit in a pen full of greyhounds."

She smiled and dialed a number on her cell phone. "The red box is a connection pull device. The insulation's cut off part of the gray wire inside the box. If either door had been opened, pulling the wire, the bare wire would have made contact with the ignitor, setting off the charge. As long as no one pulls on that little gray wire, we're safe.

"Good morning, Mark, do you remember the shopping center where we used to meet Sara for lunch in Arlington?" She waited for his answer and then asked him to meet us there.

Markham was already there when we arrived. His car was parked alone in the outer reaches of the parking lot well away from the shopping complex. Sydney unbuckled her seat belt and stretched over the console, reaching for the bomb on the floor behind me. She instructed me to pull as close as I could along the driver's side of his car, so she could hand it to him through the window. I got within easy reach, and she passed the device to Markham. He took it and laid it on the seat next to him.

"Any news around the Bureau?" she asked.

"Nothing yet, but I'm still working on it." He opened his console and took out a white hand towel. Wrapping the bomb in the towel, he said, "I'll let you know about this as soon as the lab gives me an answer." Then without any further comment, he rolled up his window and drove away as nonchalantly as if he'd picked up a quarter-pounder at a drive through widow.

"Where to now?" she asked. I clutched the steering wheel, laid my head on the top of it, and exhaled. She was right not to dwell on what had just happened, but I was still a wreck.

"You okay?" she asked leaning in my direction trying to get a look at my face.

"Sydney, I have to tell you this is a lot faster pace than I'm used to in Florida."

"I know what you mean. This isn't exactly a normal day at the office for me either."

"What do you say we go back for a visit at the Mail Boxes store?"

"Scott, haven't we already fought that battle and lost?"

"I've got an instinct I'd like to follow up on, unless you have a better idea."

"No, I'm a big believer in instincts. The Mail Boxes store works for me. We don't have a lot of other clues to follow up on." She settled back in her seat, buckling her seat belt again. The ride back to King Street was as completely silent as if someone had put our car on mute. I was processing the events that had occurred over the past seventy-two hours. At practically every intersection Sydney glanced in the side mirror. I had been doing the same thing.

"I haven't picked up on a tail, have you?" I asked.

"I've been looking, but I haven't seen anything unusual." I turned on King Street. I parked about two store fronts down from the Mail Boxes store.

I handed her the key. "Maybe you'll have better luck than I did."

"I'll do my best." She took the key, slid out of the car and headed inside the store. I followed her in, but didn't acknowledge her. I picked up a label and a pen from a freestanding counter in the center of the store and pretended to be filling out a mailing label.

Sydney approached the counter and asked for the manager. The young girl turned and went through a doorway leading to a storage area behind the counter. She returned followed by a middle-aged, slightly overweight woman with short very red hair. There was no doubt her hair color was from a bottle and probably from misreading the instructions because God would have never come up with this shade of red. She had a pair of black-framed eyeglasses dangling from her neck attached to a gold chain. She asked how she could help her, and Sydney explained. A document she had placed in her box was missing. She'd asked the young man who was working in the store that day to make sure that the box would lock with the legal length file in it.

"He took it to the back and locked it in from back there," she said. "I didn't bother to check to make sure it was really in there."

The manager took the key. I noticed she had a slight limp as she walked over to the box at the end nearest to us. She reached for her glasses and put them on. The box opened perfectly but remained empty. Her steps were like someone walking with one shoe on and one off as she went around behind the wall where they inserted the mail into the boxes. I could just see her as she reached down her cleavage and withdrew a small key that was tied around her neck. It must have been a master key that opened all the boxes. She moved out of sight and I could hear three more boxes opening and closing. I assumed she was checking the boxes around Sydney's in case the file had been misplaced.

She leaned her head around the boxes and asked, "What did this file look like?"

"It was a long manila folder with a rubber band around it. The word classified and the letters FBI were stamped in red ink on both sides."

"That's been awhile hasn't it?"

"Yes it has."

"I can tell you what happened. The clerk on duty the day you came in must have put it in the slot just above yours. The owner of that box discovered the file and returned it to us. When I saw classified and FBI on that file, I called them, and they came right over and picked it up."

"You called the FBI?"

A female employee not more than eighteen years old was leaning idly against the counter and had apparently been voyeuristically following the conversation. She couldn't refrain from jumping into the dialogue. "They pulled up in a long black SUV. I think it was a Ford Excursion. Double-parked that baby right out front, but they had blue lights blinking on and off in the grill, so they wouldn't get a parking ticket. Man that was impressive," the girl said before picking up some papers on the counter and stacking them neatly.

"Did you give the file to an agent?" Sydney asked.

The manager responded, "Not an agent, sweetie. I'd seen that guy on the news plenty of times. He was the head man. Anyway, honey, it's in good hands." If she only knew, I thought to myself.

I turned and walked out first. Sydney thanked her and followed me out of the store. I stayed in front of her until we reached the car. I got in first, then she sat in the passenger's seat. She was quiet and tense.

Sydney called James Markham to tell him what we had learned. She told him we were going back to the hotel to regroup, and he promised to get us some answers as expeditiously as possible.

We decided to take a chance on using my laptop to access the National Security Agency server. Sydney still had the director's pass code, although we both felt there was little chance of that pass code still being valid. When she hit the first firewall, she typed in the code. It was rejected. She carefully typed it again, but the result was the same. She reverted to her pass code, but when she typed the search words *The Osprey's Nest* and *The Burning Post*, she got nothing. She tried again and again, and came up with the same empty results. Sydney's printed file was gone, and so were all the files on the NSA server. We had no evidence to back up what we knew about the case.

Before she could log off the site, her cell phone rang. My heart throttled.

Sydney checked the caller ID. "I don't recognize this number." I hustled over and sat close to her. Sydney held the phone so I could hear the conversation as well.

"Hello," Sydney answered.

"I just got a call from the director," James Markham said.

"What'd he want?"

"He said he wanted to do a little catching up with me. A few minutes into the conversation he excused himself, and put me on hold. When he returned he said he had to go because there had been a breach of the NSA server."

"Where are you calling from, Mark?" Sydney asked, still puzzled by the number on her caller ID.

"A pay phone near the office. That wasn't your computer was it, Sydney?"

"I didn't bring my laptop with me, Mark."

"I just thought I'd share that computer breach with you," he said.

"Thanks, Mark."

"Anytime." When they hung up, Sydney looked at me with a frightened expression on her face.

"Scott, the director would never call Mark to tell him about a security breach."

"I thought about that. This is not good, Sydney."

"I knew they would pick up the breach, but not that fast," Sydney responded.

"I wasn't talking about the breach when I said not good. I was referring to the director calling Markham. They've connected us to him. They've also traced the connection to their server by now, which means they know where we are."

"I guess that means we're moving again."

"As soon as possible," I answered. She shrugged her shoulders, opened one of the dresser drawers and started removing some of her clothes.

"It was probably a bad idea to try to get back into the system. I'm sorry," I said.

"It's not your fault. I thought it was our next best move as well."

"Sydney, I'm running out of hotel suggestions."

"How about we check back into my place. If we're going to have to make a stand, we may as well be somewhere that has plenty of firepower," she said.

"I assume that means you have some additional weapons there."

"The linen closet in the hall isn't locked to keep people from getting into my towels, Scott."

On the drive back to Sydney's, chills ran up my spine thinking about what she had said in the hotel. She was preparing to a hunker down in her house to make a last stand if the killer returned. I was sure he would.

CHAPTER 25

The house was still in disarray, but the smile on her face indicated that she was happy to be home. I sat my luggage down in the living room and went into the kitchen. I would have taken the bullet out of the wall before we left, but we were trying to get out quickly. Now I had the time. I was aghast at what I saw. Not only was the bullet gone, the bullet hole was gone. I rubbed my hand across the wall. It was smooth and totally repaired.

"Sydney, come take a look at this!" I shouted. She entered the kitchen and stood next to me. I pointed to the wall. "No bullet hole," I said, again rubbing my hand across the smooth surface.

She stepped closer and looked in amazement. Then she ran her hand across the surface, spun around and looked at the window the bullet had shattered when it entered the house. "James Markham's been here," she said.

"How do you know that?"

"The bullet in the wall wasn't just removed. The wall was repaired and painted, and the broken window was replaced. Mark used the spare key and had all this fixed."

"I hope you're right. Why wouldn't he tell you that he took it?"

"We didn't tell him that we were on the NSA server earlier either, did we?"

"I'd like to see the ballistics report on the slug."

"Scott, Mark wouldn't hide any of that from us. If you want to take a look at it, I'm sure he'll show you whatever he has."

Sydney took me to the spare bedroom. I laid my luggage on the bed. "Let me show you the weapons closet," she said. She picked up a key that was sitting on the molding on top of her bedroom door. She unlocked her linen closet, revealing a cache of weapons, from high-power handguns to shotguns and ammunition.

"I'm going to try to read a little and relax, what about you?" Sydney asked.

"Think I'll spread out on the couch, Syd."

Sydney's cell phone rang about three hours later. I heard her say, "Hello, Mark," so I scrambled to the bedroom. Sydney told Markham that she was going to put her cell on speakerphone, so we both could hear.

Markham said, "The director is really fired up about the NSA computer breach. It seems the agents in the IT department didn't get a good trace on the incoming breach."

"That's too bad," she said.

"Yeah, isn't it," Markham replied slyly. "Sydney, why don't you come in and let me get you and Scott a little protection until we can work this out."

"Not a chance, Mark. I appreciate everything you've done for us, but other than you, I don't trust anyone at the Bureau anymore."

"Sydney, come on. Sometimes things aren't what they seem."

"Scott's parents were killed, and I was shot at by operatives of the United States government. Scott and I are planning on finding the shooter."

"If he doesn't find you first," Markham said.

No one spoke for a moment. "Talk to you later, Mark."

Before she could disconnect he, spoke again. "Sydney, are you still there?"

"I'm here, Mark."

"I almost forgot to tell you. The lab guys confirmed that little device under your car was one of ours. I know you and Scott are good, but this guy does this kind of thing for a living. I wish you'd reconsider my offer to come back in." He was sincerely fearful for her welfare.

"Mark, I've got to go." Sydney punched the off button, flipped the phone closed, and looked me right in the eyes.

"We got away with the breach."

"Yeah, but this guy has missed with a bullet and bomb. Chances are he's pissed," I said.

"You're right, Scott. And this is not a guy you want to piss off." Sydney's voice quivered, and her right cheek twitched. That beautiful face was consumed with a look of stress. I came close to offering to fix us a cup of coffee until I remembered how ugly our last experience had been in her kitchen. I decided to try to reassure her. "You're a damn good partner, Sydney Sloan." Finally a smile reappeared on her face.

"How about we check all the windows and doors to make sure they're locked and covered," Sydney said.

"Good idea." I made sure the blinds were closed and I checked the locks on all the windows in the kitchen. Sydney checked the bedrooms and I followed up in the living room. She joined me there. I sat on the couch and she sat in a chair across from me. I looked into her eyes again.

"This place doesn't offer our best defense, but if you're comfortable here, we can make it work."

"I'd rather take my chances right here, Scott."

"Have you considered what could happen to your neighbors or the possibility of more damage to your home?"

"This is where I want to be," Sydney said pointing straight down. I looked at the pile of damaged antiques, and I had a sick feeling in the pit of my gut.

"Should we lay down some ground rules?"

"Scott, I've protected federal witnesses in safe houses, so please don't make this too basic."

"I didn't mean anything by that, just that we know what to expect from each other."

"I'm just a little on edge right now, Scott, but I'll be okay."

"We should each keep a weapon on us at all times; when one of us goes to the bathroom or showers, the other should be on watch. Try to stay away from the windows whenever possible and only go outside when the other person can cover. Use the deadbolts when we're inside and take turns sleeping while the other person stays on watch."

"That wasn't basic?" she asked.

"Sorry, Sydney. I suppose I said all that to reiterate how careful we need to be. Is there anything I left out?"

"Apology accepted, and I think you have it all covered," she said.

"Why don't you leave the weapons closet unlocked while we're in the house?"

"I'm used to keeping it locked, Scott. You know where the key is."

"Tell me again what all is in there."

"I have extra ammo, a thirty ought six rifle, a twelve-gauge shotgun and a Smith and Wesson three fifty-seven magnum hand gun."

"Mind if I take another look?" I asked.

"Help yourself."

I strolled over, picked up the key and unlocked the linen closet. Underneath the shelves of neatly folded sheets, pillowcases, and towels was a sizable cache of firepower.

"I should have some flashlights and spare batteries in there too," Sydney said.

"What do you think about running to the supermarket to pick up a few things, since this could be a long wait." I asked.

"Probably wouldn't hurt to pick up some fresh batteries too," she said.

"Do we need a shopping list?" I asked, locking the linen closet door and returning the key to her hiding place.

"I don't do lists," she said. Another similarity. I was looking forward to discovering more of them and hoping we wouldn't run out of time before I had the chance.

CHAPTER 26

Sydney drew her Glock and stood in the doorway of her townhouse. I drew my weapon and made my way to the passenger's side of her car. I reached for the door handle, but I heard Sydney say, "No, no, no." She was wiggling an index finger from side to side. I waited for her to come out. She hustled to my side, took a makeup mirror out of her purse, bent over, held the mirror close to the ground, aiming it under the car, then headed around to her side to complete the search.

I was admiring her beautiful body when I saw a little red dot reflect off the hood. The dot trailed in her direction and rose up her torso. I slung my door open to crouch behind it shouting, "GUN, GUN, GUN!" Sydney dove to the ground, rolling against the bumper, then under the car. I opened the back door, giving myself more cover from behind and dropped down against the back tire on the passenger's side.

I raised my head just enough to look through the window, hoping to see where the beam had come from. Nothing. There was a stand of sapling pine trees about a hundred yards across the parking lot, and every one of them swayed in a gentle breeze. That was the only movement I detected.

"You okay?" I asked.

"I hope that wasn't a drill."

"Laser beam reflected off the car as you were coming around," I said. Sydney was sitting on the ground leaning her back against the front passenger's side tire. She was wearing a blue top that was very close to the shade of her eyes and a pair of white slacks. Tiny pieces of gravel and dirt were scattered all over her shirt and on the knees of her slacks. Blood showed through the right knee of her slacks. This was a helluva way to have to go to the supermarket.

"See anything?" she asked.

"Nothing, no movement anywhere."

"You sure that laser beam couldn't have been the traffic light changing to red?"

"It was a laser beam. I saw the reflection off the hood. The beam followed every step you took, Sydney—give me a little more credit than that. A traffic light for Christ sakes."

"Had to ask," she said.

"Let me make sure it's clear, and we'll go back inside and take care of your knee."

"It's okay. Don't worry about that," she said, holding pressure on her bloody knee.

I raised my head again to scan the trees. A bright flash lit up the woods. A muted popping sound immediately followed. I must have looked like a deer in the headlights, frozen in time. I heard the bullet tearing through the air in my direction, followed by a piercing sound. My legs buckled underneath me. I ran my hand over my forehead and then across the back of my head, but I couldn't find any blood. A fireball explosion rocked the car as the gas tank exploded into flames.

Sydney yelled, "Let's make a run for the other side of that car!" There were two empty spaces and then a green Ford Explorer that she was pointing at.

"No stay down. That's what he's hoping for. He set the car on fire just so we'd do that." The heat was getting unbearable, I could understand why she wanted to get farther away.

"Scott, we can't stay here. This thing's probably going to explode."

"He hit the gas tank, Sydney. Fire is all he's going to get. We have a better chance here than we do running."

I stayed crouched behind the back tire, occasionally raising my head to peek through the flames. I couldn't see anything through the smoke and haze of the fire. If the shooter was still there, he was waiting for us to run. The fire billowed ten feet into the air, and the car had gotten so hot that I had to scoot away from it. The sheet metal felt like it was four hundred degrees. Sydney crawled away from the front tire as sweat streamed down her red face. With her head cocked to one side, she froze, saying, "Hear that?"

I could faintly hear a siren in the distance, so I raised my head, searching for the emergency vehicle. "Sounds like you've got a damn good fire department," I said.

"The siren's from the fire truck, the blue lights are from Alexandria's finest," Sydney said, pointing towards the road where an Alexandria police car was speeding into the parking lot. It skidded to a stop between us and what I thought was the shooter's position. I jumped up and ran towards the police car, keeping an eye trained on the trees. The officer pulled his gun, holding it in both hands and resting it on the hood of his car. "Drop your gun now," he shouted at me. I tossed my gun on the ground in front of me. He had no way of knowing I was a cop. Damn. I wanted to get closer to the trees to see if I could spot anyone leaving on foot, but I wasn't about to take another step and get shot by a nervous city police officer.

Sydney reacted the way we had both been trained to respond. She jumped up, holding her badge high over her head and in front of her, and yelling to the officer, "We're cops. Don't shoot. FBI, don't shoot."

This cop had probably saved our lives, but all I could think about was how he'd blocked our view of the shooter, who was surely gone by now. A second cop screeched to a stop at the shoulder of the road and jumped out of his car. Simultaneously, both cops shouted for Sydney to lay down her gun. The officer who had arrived first moved towards Sydney with his gun trained on her.

She cautiously bent over and laid the gun on the ground in front of her.

"Step back!" the cop shouted before she had completely stood up. She continued holding her badge in her right hand, raising her now empty left hand above her head.

"Who set the car on fire?" one of them asked as he slowly approached me and snatched up my gun.

The other officer moved towards Sydney, "Turn around," he hollered at her. She lowered her credentials and tossed them towards him and then complied by turning her back to him. He picked up her gun, studied her ID, and asked, "What the hell happened here?"

A fire truck arrived and three firefighters who'd been hanging onto the back of the truck jumped down and immediately went to work. One of them reeled off about thirty feet of hose. A second fireman tugged and twisted a valve at least a dozen full turns, while another knelt down in the middle of the hose to hold it in place. The firefighter who'd removed the hose opened the nozzle and held on with both hands as a white foam shot out at Sydney's car. He waved the nozzle back and forth until the hood and trunk of the car was completely layered with the thick foam and the fire was totally extinguished.

"Where's your ID?" the first cop asked me.

"My back pocket," I said.

"Take it out slowly," he hollered. I lifted in out of my pocket, holding it between my thumb and index finger and letting it dangle from my left hand. He stripped it out of my grasp. "Sheriff's department, huh?" He looked at me comparing my current looks with the photo on my sheriff's department ID.

"Yes, sir. Bay County, Florida."

"Here's your ID, Lieutenant," he said handing my wallet back to me. I had the feeling these local cops were bonding with me since I was one of them, albeit a lieutenant and an investigator from Florida. Sydney was a female and a fed, and none of that was in her favor with these guys.

A wrecker turned into the parking lot, and a short overweight driver stepped down from his vehicle. He was wearing a black cap with the number three on the front, and a tee shirt with the words, *I'm a Bud Man* across his chest. He was chewing on a toothpick and garbled the words, "Where ya want me ta take at thing?"

"How about the PD vehicle holding compound?" the cop who was talking to Sydney yelled over.

"You got it, boss," the wrecker driver said as he got in his vehicle, turned it around, and backed up directly behind Sydney's car. He moved some levers, and the bed of his truck dropped to the ground under her bumper. He picked up a chain from the deck and crawled under her car and hooked it onto the frame.

"That son of bitch is red hot," he hollered sliding out from under the car. There was no response from anyone, so he yanked a lever and the chain tightened making an irritating grinding noise until the car was hoisted onto the deck. When the driver moved another lever, the wrecker bed lifted back into place with Sydney's car piggy backed on top. He hooked a chain underneath the back of what was left of Sydney's car to secure it, before getting in his cab and driving away.

The firemen took out a water hose and rinsed the parking lot. After it was thoroughly soaked, they scattered something that looked like cat litter over the area.

Sydney stood next to the second cop and filled out a report. The other cop went back to his car and began talking on his radio. I walked to the trees where the shot had come from, and then along the edge of the parking lot. When the report was taken, the cops both pulled to the shoulder of the road just off the apartment complex property. They got out of their cars, stood and chatted with the firemen. One of the cops reached in his car and handed the firemen a copy of his report. They spoke a few minutes longer, before everyone shook hands and the got back in their vehicles and drove off.

Sydney and I walked back to her townhouse, watched closely by several of the neighbors who had gathered in their respective front windows. Apparently they had watched the excitement that had transpired on the front lawn. As we made eye contact, blinds closed, shades were drawn, and people scattered.

Sydney went to her room and pulled off her shirt and slacks. I stood in the bedroom doorway, concerned that she might have been hurt worse than I thought. She went into the bathroom and I heard the water running.

"Sydney, can I help you?"

"I'm washing up, then I'm going to clean the cut on my knee."

"Do you have a first aid kit?" I asked.

"In the linen closet," she answered. "Is there a doctor in the house?"

"First aid first responder is about all you're going to get today, lady."

She came out of the bathroom wearing a forest green long sleeve shirt that must have been a men's extra large. "First responder it is," she said, picking up a pair of jeans. Instead of putting them on, she held them in her hand and walked into the living room with nothing on the bottom half of her torso but her panties. Thank goodness she wasn't modest. She sat on the sofa, tucked her left leg under her and stuck her right one out in front of her. I knelt down, poured hydrogen peroxide on some gauze pads, cleaned the cuts on her knee, and taped a couple of broad Band-Aid squares across the wounds.

"All set," I said.

"My God, Scott, I don't even have a car now." She bounced up from the sofa and ran over and opened the front door. It had taken awhile for everything that had just happened to sink in, but now she stood half naked in the open threshold shaking her head in disbelief. "I loved my car," she said.

"Close the door, and we'll talk about it, please." She closed the door, leaned against it and slid down to the floor in heap.

"Sydney, I'll get you a new car. That's the least I can do for you."

"For me? Who was it that saw the little red dot? I owe you again."

"You don't owe me anything. I feel responsible for all the crap that's happened to you."

"None of that was your fault, but I hate losing her so prematurely. I only had two hundred thousand miles on her. I even gave her a name," she said as she caught her breath, stood, and pulled on her jeans.

"You're kidding?"

"I did. I gave her a name."

"No. I mean about two hundred thousand miles." She turned away from her empty parking space, looked at me, releasing a little smile.

"Okay, what was the name?" I asked.

"Trusty Rusty," she said with a sad smile.

"What about the trip to the Safeway?"

"Somehow right now that sounds like an oxymoron," I said. We both laughed. It wasn't very likely that the shooter was still hanging around after all the emergency vehicles that had been gathered there, so we went straight to my rental and on to the supermarket, hoping he wouldn't try to ambush us in the Safeway parking lot, or be waiting for us in the house when we returned.

CHAPTER 27

Sydney and I returned from the store with enough food to allow two people to hibernate for a couple of months. I backed in towards her front door to limit our exposure before unloading the Taurus. She lugged in five overflowing bags, and I had six. The groceries covered her kitchen counter. I offered to help put them away, but she knew where everything went.

"Scott, I haven't had this much food in my apartment since the day I bought it."

I picked up a clear bag of fresh shrimp in one hand and a box of penne pasta in the other. "I'm going to fix you some wonderful Italian tails and snails—but not tonight. I want it to be fabulous, and I'm afraid I'd be too distracted tonight."

"I love any kind of pasta, Scott, so the wait will be worth it. I'm like most guys I know when it comes to cooking. Pretty good with the hibachi, but not so great in this kitchen."

"Well, Sydney, I wouldn't recommend any outside cooking tonight. That might be a little dangerous tonight."

"Did you mean because of the shooter or my cooking?"

"Oh, I'd trust your cooking, maybe not as much as your ability to disarm small explosive devices, but I'd trust it."

"Thank you. I'll take that as two compliments. I should nominate you to be the president of my fan club," Sydney said with a laugh. She took a bottled water from the refrigerator and took a sip. "Right now I'd rather rest than eat. Mind taking the first watch, Scott?"

"I'm not that hungry either, and I'd be delighted to take the first watch." She folded all the grocery bags into a neat pile and stuffed them into her plastic recycling bag under the counter.

She gave me a kiss on the forehead. I fought the urge to grab her and return her kiss, but below her nose, not above it. It wasn't easy, but I maintained my composure.

"Nighty night." She waved over her shoulder as she headed toward her room.

"See you in a few hours," I said.

A huge bag of white seedless grapes caught my eye as I opened the fridge. I snagged the bag and took them to the coffee table, setting them next to my gun. I lay on the sofa, picked up the remote control, hitting the power and reduce volume buttons simultaneously, trying not to disturb Sydney. The twenty-four hour cable news networks were my stations of choice, so I surfed between CNN, MSNBC, and Fox News for about an hour until headlights shined directly through the blinds of the front window.

Grabbing my gun, I rolled off the sofa onto the floor, crawling over to the front window. I flicked the safety button to the off position. The headlights went out just as a car door slammed, so I raised my head up to the windowsill lifting one blind slat slightly to give me a little view. There was a car in Sydney's parking space. A guy got out and immediately climbed into another vehicle. The brake lights on that vehicle washed the front window in a red glow. What the hell was that all about?

"Sydney!" I shouted. There was no answer. "Sydney!" I shouted even louder. I peered out through the blinds again. There was still a strange car in Sydney's space, but no sign of the other car or the guy. I ran to Sydney's bedroom and knocked, pushing the door open slightly. "Sydney! I yelled even louder than I had from the living room. No answer, so I stormed in. She was curled up in her bed, but she wasn't moving.

Oh no. Had the car switch out front been a diversion? Had someone come through the window? Oh my God, Sydney, please don't be dead.

CHAPTER 29

I reached for her shoulder and shook her hard. She rolled over and wiped her face with the backs of her hands. "Getting a little fresh aren't we?" she said, trying to wake up.

"A car just pulled up in your space and the driver got out and then got in with someone else and drove off."

"I do have neighbors that have real lives, Scott. Just because I have no life doesn't mean my neighbors don't."

"Would you come verify that this car sitting out front is a neighbor's? Then I promise to start my watch over again?"

"Okay, okay. I'm coming, but be careful with that damn gun. I hate being woken up by someone with a Glock 19 in his hand."

"You are one incredibly deep sleeper, Sydney Sloan."

"I was wiped."

"The car, Sloan." This time she pulled both hands through her blonde hair, and it seemed to fall perfectly in place. She was amazing. She had rolled out of her bed from a deep sleep and looked terrific. Her muscles must have been stiff, because she walked clumsily from her bedroom to the living room. She stood next to the front window peeking through the blinds.

"Never seen that one before," she said.

"Great."

"That doesn't mean it can't belong to a friend of one of my neighbors, Scott."

I stepped behind her and looked over her shoulder through the opening in the blinds. "Did you see the windshield?" I asked.

"Windshield?" She pulled the blinds open and looked again.

"What the hell is that?" she asked with her eyes fixed on a large white piece of paper tucked under the wiper of the tan Nissan.

"I have no idea. Maybe your neighbors like to leave each other notes," I said.

"Come on, Scott, let's take a look." She turned and we stood chest to chest.

"At what?" I asked.

"Don't be a wise guy."

"Oh yeah. The paper." I turned and reached for the doorknob.

"Wait!" she said forcefully, before running into her bedroom and returning with her Glock.

I opened the door about six inches and looked out to my right. I pushed the door all the way open and stepped out. Sydney put her back to mine and went through the same routine behind me. I panned my gun across the parking lot, looking for any kind of movement. "Clear," I said.

"Clear on my side, too," she replied.

Sydney approached the car and leaned close to the paper. "It's an envelope," she said.

Headlights shined in our direction from across the parking lot, and we both scrambled to the front of the car, kneeling down next to the hood. The car passed us, driving to another apartment.

Sydney stood, returned to her position next to the windshield, and continued examining the envelope.

"What do you see?" I asked.

"Hang on, Scott."

"You think it might be anthrax or something lethal?"

"No I don't." She snatched the envelope from behind the wiper.

"What the hell are you doing? Aren't you being a little clumsy?"

"James Markham has written a lot of notes over the years, teaching me to be an FBI agent. I'd recognize his handwriting anywhere, Scott." She tore open the envelope. Her smile sparkled in the moonlight.

"Anything you can share?" I asked.

"Mark must have heard about Trusty Rusty. He sent me a car." I looked at the four-door Nissan parked next to my rental and wondered what Mark had to do with this.

"Is this Mark's personal car?"

"He drives a Crown Vic."

"Don't we all?" I answered.

"No. Not all of us. It looks like I'm driving a 1996 Nissan these days," Sydney said, studying a piece of paper with some type of seal stamped on it.

"Is that a car title?"

"Made out in my name. The seller is the US Marshall's Service. James Markham is some kind of good, isn't he?"

"Provided that Markham was actually the one who sent you that car," I said.

"You could have gone all night without saying that."

"Sydney, you've taught me more in two days about being cautious than I learned in a year and a half of law enforcement." That statement made me remember that we'd dropped our guard. I scanned the parking lot and was jolted by a view I couldn't believe we both had missed.

"Sydney, go back inside, very calmly and slowly." She looked startled, but she didn't question me. She went straight in. I followed her walking backwards. When we were inside, I closed the door. "Across the street." I said.

Sydney peeped through her blinds.

"Any idea who they are?" I asked.

"No idea. I can't believe we were out there, and I didn't see them."

I leaned over her shoulder and looked between the blind slats farther up on the window. Two guys wearing coats and ties were sitting in what appeared to be an unmarked police car. "Coats and ties in an unmarked. They look like cops to me."

"Scott, that doesn't make sense. Even rookie cops would have better cover than these guys."

"You're right, it doesn't. That's why we're about to find out who they are."

"What's your plan?"

"How's your acting?" I asked.

"Not very good. Why?"

"I need a distraction to hold their attention. Could you recreate that bomb inspection you did in Connie Collins' driveway?"

"Sure, but why do you want them looking in our direction?"

"Your direction. Give me three minutes, then go back out there and look around under the car in your parking space."

"Where are you going?"

"Out back, then around the building, and over to meet our new neighbors across the street." Without saying another word, I turned, walked through the apartment and out the back door. I stole across the yard to the tree line behind her apartment. I had followed the shooter there a couple of days ago, and I remembered the woods paralleled the entire length of the complex. About three yards into the cover of the trees, I ran using the light from the apartments to see where I was going. There were two other buildings next to Sydney's, all lined up in a row. When I was even with the end of the last building, I came out of the woods and ran towards the street, running close to the side of the complex. I made sure there were no cars coming as I crossed. Being exposed by a set of highlights would have ended this mission.

Fortunately, the pair was focused on Sydney, who had come out of her apartment and crawled underneath the Nissan. She continued looking busy, checking the newly delivered car. There were twelve stores and four parking rows in the strip center that faced Sydney's apartment. I dashed behind a parked car about ten cars down from where the two men were sitting watching Sydney. I stayed low and ran two more rows behind them to make sure I was behind their peripheral vision. Sydney slid out from under the Nissan, hesitated, walked to the doorway of the apartment, and stood there, staring right at them. She knew that would clearly draw their attention. I maneuvered over directly behind them and ran towards their car. They were still sitting in the front seat and both windows were down. Sydney waved, turned, went inside and shut the door. By the time the door had closed, I'd reached their car. I stuck my Glock against the driver's left temple.

"Hands on the dash, boys." The guy on the passenger's side hesitated. "I really wouldn't do anything stupid if I were you."

"Look, put the piece down. We work at the same place she does," the driver said.

"You guys work at Wal-Mart? Hardware or lawn and garden?"

"We work at the Bureau. Same place as Agent Sloan."

Keeping my gun trained through the window, I took a few steps back so I had a better look at both of them. "Put your right hand very slowly behind your head and use your left hand to pick up your weapon and lay it on the dash. Not you!" I told the passenger, jerking my gun in his direction. "You need to keep both your hands on the dash." The driver carefully laid his handgun on the dash in front of him. "Push it all the way to the window," I said. He complied, and I noticed sweat was beading up on his forehead. It was dripping in his eyes, and he started squinting, knowing he couldn't move his arms anywhere he wasn't told. "Okay, Eager Beaver, now it's your turn." The second man moved faster than the driver, so I reminded him, "Slowly, I said." He placed his handgun on the dash in the same fashion. "Now credentials, badges, IDs, whatever we have. Sweat poured down the driver's face from his forehead. Moisture was showing through his shirt as he looked down the barrel of my Glock. I stole a quick look at the apartment. Where the hell was she? Sydney was my partner, and she should have been here to back me up with these two guys. This was the first time her police work had pissed me off, but there was no way I could let these guys see that.

He fumbled for his wallet. "Shit," he said, dropping it on the seat next to him. I stepped closer and shoved my Glock in his window. "Left hand only," I said.

He picked it up and laid it in front of him. "Open it." He opened his wallet and laid it flat on the dash. I glanced back and forth between the two men and the badge. It was an ID exactly like Sydney's. "Step out of the car," I instructed the driver. Once he was out, he started telling me they had been ordered to conduct a surveillance of Sloan's apartment.

"You guys are pretty sneaky," I said sarcastically.

"We don't know why, but we were told us to be obvious."

"Well you can tell your boss that you two are really good at following directions."

The driver said, "You're not even licensed to carry that in this state, so why don't you..." He was trying to act bold, but his sweat-soaked shirt gave him away.

"Get in your car and get out of here. Tell whoever sent you over here this was a dumb idea," I said. He got back inside, started the engine, and said, "You know we'll probably be back, and you'll probably go to jail."

I watched them drive off, collecting their weapons and badges from the dash. Markham apparently wanted to protect Sydney until he could find out more, so he sent two guys out here to scare away the shooter. The same shooter we were waiting for. Checking to make sure they weren't circling around and coming back, I headed across to Sydney's. This task was tough enough, without having to try to separate the good guys from the bad. I was going to let Markham know how I felt about that.

CHAPTER 29

I jogged through the front door, spun around, and locked it behind me. It was time to give Sydney Sloan a little refresher on how to be a good partner. I couldn't believe she had left me out there that long without backing me up. I yelled from the bedroom doorway, "Hey, partner, thanks for the backup." I could hear the whirring sound of the exhaust fan in the bathroom. "Our friends across the street were coworkers of yours from the Bureau." There was no reply; probably too noisy with the exhaust running.

I was going to need a strong cup of coffee to keep me awake through my watch, so I headed to the kitchen. Christ, the backdoor was standing wide open. "Son of a bitch!" I screamed. "Sydney! Sydney! Goddamn it, Sydney, answer me!"

Turning to run to the bedroom, I banged into a barstool, knocking it against the other stool, sending them both crashing to the floor. I ran as fast as I could to the bedroom. I yanked my Glock from my waist and grabbed the bathroom doorknob. I tried to turn it, but the door was locked. One step back and I kicked the door with my right foot. The door flew open and slammed into the wall behind it. My body followed the momentum of my foot and I fell into the bathroom. I raked my gun across the shower curtain revealing an empty shower. "Sydney!" I shouted loud and long, holding the word until I had run all the way back into the living room. I pivoted on my left foot and took off again, racing toward the kitchen. I ran full speed toward the backdoor, grabbing the molding around the threshold to stop myself. The backdoor was still open. I surveyed the back of the complex from one end of the building to the other. She wasn't there.

My head fell in disgust. Dear God, I'd forgotten about the key under that damn hibachi grill. I knelt down, turned it over, and examined it for the key hider. It was gone. I tore open the grill and nearly dismantled it with my bare hands. Nothing. James Markham and his wife were the only other people who knew where that key was. The killer could have easily followed Markham to Sydney's and noticed him retrieving the key from underneath the hibachi.

I ran back to the front door, flung it open and looked for the car with the two agents who had been parked across the street. No such luck. Those two had called in the run-in they had with me, and they were probably cleared to go home for the night. I wondered if those two guys could have been part of a set up to snatch Sydney. Markham knew where the key was and those guys could have worked for him. He could have been doing this to protect her, but how would they have known I would be the one who approached them, leaving Sydney alone in her apartment? Markham couldn't have known that.

I stepped back inside the apartment, sat on the floor, and leaned my back against the sofa. Withdrawing my cell phone from my pocket, I scrolled through to Markham's number. If James Markham wasn't involved in this, the phone call I was about to make was going to be gut wrenching. He had depended on me to protect Sydney, and I'd failed. This was one of the lowest days of my life. Why hadn't I seen this coming?

Dammit! I should have known when she didn't show up at the car across the street that something was wrong.

Before I pulled myself up off the floor, I noticed one of Sydney's business cards lying next to my shoe. She could have dropped it accidentally, but unless the entire contents of her purse were down here, a single card seemed a little odd. Maybe it was a clue—a clue she left for me. But what the hell was she trying to tell me with her business card? Damn you, Sydney. How could you let this happen?

Picking up the card, I was struck with some sort of sweet smell. There was a wet spot on the floor near the card. I crawled closer to the spot almost touching my nose to several small drops on the floor. Whatever it was, I knew I'd smelled that scent before, I just couldn't remember where. I could rule out urine or blood because it was completely clear like water. Hopping up off the floor, I grabbed a paper napkin from the kitchen counter and placed it over the drops. Once the napkin had absorbed the liquid, I dropped it in a plastic baggie, sealed it, and tossed it on the table.

Suddenly I was feeling exhausted. My head was so woozy I fell backwards onto the sofa. This must have been what it was like to take a knockout punch. I was tired, but I wasn't so fatigued that I would end up on my ass. What else would cause that? What was the connection between the cards and the drops? Where had I smelled that sweet scent before, and what was she trying to tell me? .

Christ, I remembered the smell; high school biology. I snatched the bag open, ripped out the napkin and smelled it again. Chloroform.

Whoever took Sydney must have knocked her out with the chloroform, but before she was out, she dropped the card. She was marking the spot for me to find it. She wanted me to know she'd been abducted.

This was as far as this investigation was going to go. There was no way to put off calling Markham any longer. Damn, I dreaded making that call. I wiped my eyes with the back of my hand and dialed his number. A sinking feeling raced through my body leaving me with an empty pain in the pit of my stomach. It was the same feeling you got when you had to inform parents that their child had been killed.

This was all my fault. If she'd never said anything to me, or if I hadn't pursued her so aggressively, demanding she tell me what she had discovered, she'd still be here. Her apartment, her antiques, and her car would all be intact. I felt terrible about placing Sydney's life in danger. Now with a shooting, a car fire, and Sydney's disappearance, there was a chance the media might get involved. God, I hated to make this call.

Taking James Markham's card out of my wallet, I dialed his number.

"Hello."

"Mark, this is Scott Downing."

"Did she get the car?"

"Yeah. She got it."

"Well, I know how hardheaded she is. You tell her she has to keep it. She lost hers in the line of duty. She's not giving it back."

"We have another problem right now."

"What now?"

"She's gone."

"The car?"

"Mark, Sydney's gone."

"What exactly do you mean by gone?"

"Gone as in abducted from her apartment."

"How the hell could that happen, Scott?"

"Mark, I went across the street to find out why two clowns had her apartment under surveillance, while I was gone, someone slipped in the back door, put a chloroform rag over her face and took her out through the back.

"How do you know it was chloroform?"

"I found a few drops on the floor. I'm not a scientist, but I had enough years of biology in high school and college to recognize the sweet smell."

"Why wasn't the back door locked?"

"It was. The key was missing from the hibachi. I thought you and your wife, and Sydney and me were the only ones who knew about the key."

"We were. Someone probably had you two or me under surveillance and aimed a shotgun mic at us. We talked about that when we met."

"Mark, this is my fault. I'm so sorry."

"It's nobody's fault. You stay put. I'll be right over."

After we hung up, I looked around the empty apartment. Her broken antiques were still stacked against the living room wall. I couldn't just sit there. I had to do something, so I went to the linen closet and took out a large, square flashlight. It was too dark to find any clues in the woods behind her apartment, even with a flashlight, but I was determined to look anyway. This was futile. My body ached, my knees trembled they were so weak. I fell to the ground, landing on my butt in a pile of wet leaves and dead tree limbs. Somewhere between physical and metal fatigue and sniffing the chloroform, I was spent. I turned off the flashlight and shook my head in disbelief. A few minutes passed, and I forced myself to grab a skinny pine tree, pulling myself up off the ground. I stumbled back inside and try to recreate her actions from the last time I saw her.

Sydney's gun was lying next to her holster and my briefcase on the table in the foyer. I stared at the tabletop where she placed her belongings. Something was missing. There was only one cell phone there. Her work phone was missing. Unless she'd left it in her car, it was either in this apartment, or she had it with her.

Car lights flashed into the front window. A car door slammed. James Markham stormed in without knocking. I understood completely how he felt. "Anything, Scott?"

"I'm not sure. I may be reaching here—"

"There's no such thing as reaching. Run it by me. We don't have any time to waste."

CHAPTER 30

James Markham hadn't moved up to the rank of assistant director in charge because of political favors. He was an old-fashioned lawman. He believed in collecting all the evidence and working the case. That was also the way I'd been taught.

I showed him where I had found her business card on the floor, and I handed him the baggie with the chloroform-soaked napkin. Then I told him about the missing cell phone.

"I bought a couple of phones for us to use, in case someone was listening in on her Bureau phone."

"So the phone that's missing is her work phone?"

"Yeah, the one listed on her card."

He wanted me to walk him through what I'd found when I came back in the apartment and discovered her missing. I went over everything, from the grill out back, to the chloroform, to the missing cell phone.

"Scott, have a seat. I've got a confession to make."

"Confession?"

"The two guys across the street were from me."

"What do you mean from you?" My feeling of guilt was rapidly changing to anger.

"I sent her the car, and then I sent those two agents and told them to be obvious because I didn't want anything else to happen tonight."

"Well you did a pretty shitty job of that. Why didn't you tell us what was going on?"

"Scott, I don't know you, but I know Sydney Sloan. There's no way she would have allowed that to happen. With everything that's happened to her in the past forty-eight hours, I thought she needed a break. That's the only reason I sent those guys. I figured the shooter would see those agents sitting across the street and back off, at least for tonight. I have unfettered access to the NSA server, and—"

I heard a buzzing sound and held my hand up for Mark to stop talking. Sydney's new silver cell phone was vibrating on the table in the foyer. It had nearly bounced off the table by the time I reached for it and flipped it open.

"Hello." Whoever had placed the call had hung up. "Mark, no one knew this number but Sydney and me." I handed him the phone. He looked at the incoming number. It was Sydney's work cell. It vibrated again while Markham was holding it, but he didn't answer it. Instead he snatched up his own cell phone and hit one number before lifting it his ear.

"This is James Markham, I need a tower check." He paused and then called out Sydney's work cell number. He listened to the response and a baffled look covered Markham's face.

"It's moving where?" he asked.

"Can you get me a GPS location?"

Another brief pause, and then it looked like all of his blood rushed to his face. "Goddamn it, this is an agent who may be in danger that we're following. I need you to stay with me on this phone. We're rolling right now." He motioned to me, and I picked up my Glock, shoulder holster and keys. We both ran to his car and I climbed in on the passenger's side. "Talk to me, Richard. Don't leave me hanging here," Markham pleaded into the phone. "Okay, Richard, I'm driving now, so I'm going to give the phone to Scott. You give him the information, and he'll relay it to me, are we all clear?"

He handed me the phone, and I said, "Richard, this is Scott.

"Richard, are you there?" When he answered, he stuttered a hello and I sensed he was busy tracking instead of talking.

"He said he just set up a GPS on us, Mark. Richard, you can set up a global positioning satellite on this phone that fast?"

"Ask him something about where the hell we need to be going," Mark hollered.

"He said he's got us going north on the George Washington Parkway."

"Scott, I know where I'm going. Ask him about Sydney."

"Richard said to take the Fourteenth Street Bridge toward the District." Mark nodded his head in agreement.

"Fourteenth Street Bridge. We're turning now, Richard. Hey, if Sydney's moving, are we gaining on her at all?" Richard hesitated again. When he spoke he sounded excited and voice was high pitched.

"He says we're under ten miles from her, and the target is fixed."

"Ask him if he's sure the target is fixed?"

"He heard you, Mark. He said the target is definitely fixed."

"Damn," Mark groaned.

"What's the problem, Mark?"

"I don't like it." Richard spoke again and I relayed his input.

"He says we're pretty close, but her phone just disconnected, and that makes it a little harder. Doesn't that mean he has no more GPS tracking ability?" I asked.

"Goddamn it!" Mark shouted. "Put that phone on speaker, and lay it on the seat." I hit the speaker button and laid it next to Mark, keeping my hand on it to prevent it from falling off the seat.

"Richard, you punch that phone number into our agent surveillance system and tell me what you get."

Richard's voice sounded a little faint and hollow through the speaker.

"Sir, am I allowed to do that without all of the protocols for using that tracking system?"

"Mark, what's the agent surveillance system? He was already tracking her using GPS."

"That was based on a phone signal relayed through the cell towers. When she disconnected, Richard lost that signal. He has another method of tracking an agent. Sydney's phone has a chip inside that sends a signal to our computers. It allows us to track our agents. Richard, I need you to punch that number in now!"

"I already did, sir. Her location hasn't changed. You should get off on Ohio Drive at East Potomac Park." Richard's voice was trembling.

I remembered my way around the District pretty good, but I had no idea where these directions were taking us. "Where the hell is that, Mark?"

"I think it's the little road that runs down to the point of the park. If they're down there this could be an ambush," Mark snapped. "Richard, put it on the grid."

"Sir, I have it on the grid."

"Is this location at the tip of the park?"

"The very tip," he answered.

"Shit," Markham said.

My body was tight and tense. I had no idea why he was so pissed. "Are you going to tell me what's going on?" I asked.

"I'm not saying an ambush isn't a possibility, but I don't think this guy wants a face off out in the open. He operates covertly. I think he discovered the phone and tossed it."

I gritted my teeth and spoke without opening my mouth. "I hope it's an ambush."

"Me too," Markham countered softly. When we reached the tip of East Potomac Park, Markham picked up his cell phone. "How close, Richard?"

"Jesus Christ, Mark, you must be right on top of it."

"That's what I thought."

We got out and walked along the shoulder of the road. It was a very dark night with a cloudy sky. That made it much easier to spot the little green light blinking in the mud close to the river.

"There it is," I said pointing to the light. Our law enforcement training kicked in and we both searched for tire tracks in the soft shoulder of the roadway. Making a mold of a tire print might help us later on in the search. But we didn't find any.

"You mind getting it, Scott?"

I put my foot on the muddy bank, and it slipped away from me. I was beginning to do the splits, and I threw my arms up in the air and waved them wildly until I caught my balance. I wanted to race down and grab the phone, but this was the proverbial slippery slope. It was not going to be a quick retrieval. Each successive step after my first one was slow and deliberate, careful to not lose my footing. I was about fifteen steps away when my foot slipped in the mud. I skidded down the slope about ten feet before I shoved my hands into the mud to brace myself. Traction was non-existent. Between stepping, sliding and falling, I finally reached the phone. I picked it up and tried to trace my way back up the slope stepping in my own muddy footprints. I handed it to Markham.

On the point of that little island with the wind gusting into his face, I heard this big tough man make two quick sniffling sounds like he was fighting back tears. I sat back down in the car. Markham stood out there for a couple of minutes, looking at the phone and then gazing out into the Potomac River. I remembered my grandmother giving me all the time I needed the day I buried my parents. She'd never rushed me. James Markham was soul searching, and I wasn't about to push him now either.

A Boeing seven forty-seven was on short approach to Washington Reagan National, flying low over the river. Markham never looked up. He never flinched. He just stared out at the blackness of the river. He held the phone up and squeezed it. I thought he was going to crush the tiny plastic device into a hundred pieces with his bare hand. Finally, he turned toward the car, but before he took a step, he spun back around and threw the phone as far as he could into the river. I heard the splash and wondered if the phone was the only thing that was gone.

CHAPTER 31

We headed back toward Sydney's apartment. Neither of us said a word. When we pulled up in front, Markham put the car in park and looked at me. I saw hurt, pain, anger, and determination. We barely knew each other, but there was no doubt we had kindred souls. "You staying here?" he asked.

"Until we find her," I said. His head bobbed in agreement.

"We're going to find her alive, Mark."

"I hope you're right."

"This guy wants me. He can have me, but he'd better not hurt Sydney."

Markham slowly nodded his head in agreement again. He had little to say. He was staring at Sydney's apartment like he had stared at the Potomac. I stepped out and closed the door, holding my Glock in my right hand. Easing the door open, I reached inside the foyer and turned on the lights. Pushing the door all the way open, I pointed my Glock around the room, making sure it was clear. I checked every room in her place. Mark's headlights were still shining on the apartment, so I opened the door and gave him a thumbs up. Poking my head farther through the doorway, I watched him drive away, his taillights getting smaller and smaller until they became intertwined in a myriad of lights flickering on the horizon.

I plodded into Sydney's room and turned on the lights. It felt eerie sitting there surrounded by her things. Her scent was everywhere. The weirdest emotions consumed me. For some reason I was certain that she was about to appear out of her bathroom, wearing that long tee shirt and panties and asking me what was wrong. She didn't. I crawled into her bed; my head plunged onto her pillow. I buried my face in it, inhaling the scent again. Something inside of me was trying to convince myself that if I could establish enough of her smell, her touch, her feel, and her look that she would somehow materialize. It wasn't working, so I rolled over on my back, staring at the white ceiling fan with the round light fixture. I watched it slowly revolve. I even started counting the times it made a complete revolution until I became dizzy, so I closed my eyes. I wanted to stay awake, but my body gave up.

The phone rang at five minutes after six Tuesday morning. Sydney had been missing for six hours. It startled me when I heard it, and I scrambled out of bed. Where was the damn phone? Which one was ringing? I ran toward the sound and found it on Sydney's kitchen counter.

"Hello." There was no answer. "Hello, Sydney, is that you? Hello." I almost hung up, but it hit me, that there was silence but no dial tone. "Whoever you are, you need to stop being a chicken shit and talk to me." This time there was a dial tone. I walked back into Sydney's bedroom and picked up my Glock and my cell phone. I thought about calling Markham, but I opted to wait and see if I was going to get a call back. If that was the mercenary, he'd probably move around to another phone before calling back.

A cup of coffee might help settle my nerves and wake me up. I had been with Sydney when she put the groceries away, so finding everything was easy. Finding the coffee maker was more of a challenge. She had an appliance garage under the cabinets, so I looked there first. It was filled with case files, FBI manuals and paperwork. Finally, I located the coffee maker on the floor of the pantry. I measured enough coffee and water to make four strong cups. Two was my limit. Sydney wasn't going to join me, but I couldn't convince myself of that.

Waiting for a phone to ring was excruciating. I poured myself a cup, sat down at the counter and took a sip. It was too strong for my taste, but I didn't care. I wasn't getting up again.

Ghastly thoughts plagued my mind. Was he killing her because I had called him a chicken shit, or had he killed her earlier because the phone was tapped? She couldn't be dead. I had come to Washington in search of my parent's killers. I couldn't allow anyone else to be killed, especially Sydney. My heart began to conjure up positive thoughts. Markham would call and tell me they located her and she was all right. The Secretary of Defense and the director of the FBI had turned themselves in. My mother used to say I had a romantic and optimistic heart, but my father would always remind her that I had a powerfully logical brain.

The side of me my mother described was fading with every passing minute. The logical side my father spoke about was kicking in and bringing back thoughts of what had more likely happened to Sydney.

My cell phone rang at seven fifteen. "Hello."

"Scott, this is Mark."

"Mark, did you hear anything?" He said he had, but he didn't sound happy. "You sound like your night was as good as mine. I didn't sleep a wink," I said.

"I've been at the Bureau all night, so I'm running home now to take a shower. How about I stop by and tell you what I learned over night?"

"That would be terrific. How long before you get here?"

"About thirty seconds?"

Holding my coffee cup with one hand, I opened the blinds with the other. The rays of the morning sun broke through the branches of the trees on the east side of the parking lot. Mark's car turned into the driveway. His call wasn't as positive as I'd hoped for, but at least he hadn't delivered the news that Sydney had been killed...at least not yet.

CHAPTER 32

I unlocked the door and Markham hobbled in. His face looked grim and the bags under his eyes were puffy. Without a word he went straight to the kitchen, opened a cabinet and realized there were no coffee cups. "Bastard broke all her dishes, didn't he?"

"Morning, Mark. Let me clean this one for you," I said, pointing to my coffee cup.

He held up his hand signaling me to halt.

"Forget it. I'm about to float away already. I don't need another cup."

"Mark, I had a hang-up call this morning, but there wasn't a call back."

"There wouldn't be. He wanted to know where you were, Scott."

"Did he call you on Sydney's home phone?"

"Yes."

"He was checking to see if you would answer her phone. That was the safest way to locate you without risking being seen in the area again. Scott, let's go sit in the living room. What I have to tell you is not good."

My heart raced, and I dropped into a chair as Markham sat on the sofa. Something terrible must have happened to her, but he didn't want to tell me over the phone.

"Please don't tell me..."

"Don't jump to conclusions, Scott. We have a pretty good idea about what happened last night, and you and I need to talk about that."

"What happened to Sydney?" I curtly interrupted.

"I'm pretty sure the person who has Sydney is the same person that killed your parents."

"You know that for sure?"

"Five people in this country possess a security clearance allowing them to delve into the bowels of the NSA computer system; I'm one of them. Some items that have been deleted are still retrievable, albeit not without the help of a young techno-geek who works for us."

"Mark, has he hurt her?"

"He's had her for close to eight hours, but I don't think he's hurt her. She's his bait to catch you, Scott. I had my tech person go back beyond the files Sydney had discovered to also retrieve the emails between Fisher and Runnels. I uncovered the name of the consultant they hired to kill your parents."

"What's his name, Mark?"

"You know better than to ask me that, Scott. I can tell you he's a really bad guy. When I saw his name in the emails, I researched him in detail on our system. He's got a helluva pedigree in killing people. Twelve years in the military in Special Forces. He's also an ordinance and demolition expert. This guy can blow up a battleship at sea and the shipbuilder's wife who christened the vessel almost simultaneously from a thousand miles away. His sharp shooting scores were the second highest ever recorded in the US military. He is very proficient at hand-to-hand combat, has extensive jungle training and expertise, and is darn near a computer genius."

"With those kinds of skills, I'm sure he's a prize consultant of our government. I believe that's what you people call him, isn't it?" I said, giving Markham the most sarcastic look I could work up.

"Our government and quite a few others often have the need for a person possessing those kind of skills I'm afraid." When I'd first met James Markham a few days ago, he had a poker face, never allowing his emotions to be revealed. This morning he was biting his bottom lip between sentences, and he grimaced as he described the man who had taken Sydney.

"He's been an independent contractor for about ten years."

"I understand using a guy like that to take out a nasty dictator or to retrieve a US citizen who's being held in a foreign country, but what he did to my parents and now to Sydney makes him nothing more that a lowlife despicable criminal."

Markham took a deep breath and blew out a strong exhale. "Unfortunately, that's where the rub comes in. He's not a criminal in the eyes of our government. He takes his orders from high-ranking government officials, both from our country and two or three others. He's a renegade who we have little control over, which presents the problem of what to do if he gets arrested in the US. I can assure you that Fisher would do all that he could to see that this guy never makes it to his first appearance. He knows too much. Way too much, and if he started talking to save his ass, well we don't even need to go there. The files I retrieved indicated he's handled over a dozen assignments for Fisher."

That meant he's killed over a dozen people for our government. This was all preposterous to me. There was a dark side to federal law enforcement and while most Americans knew it existed, none of us wanted to come face to face with the reality of it.

"Damn, Mark, are you insinuating that if this guy were to get arrested, he'd barter his release using the information he has about *Operation Freedom Flows*, *The Burning Post* or *The Osprey's Nest*?"

"Scott, two of the most powerful men who ever worked in Washington would never allow this guy to be interrogated by anyone. In order for him to clean up this assignment, he has to kill you and Sydney. Then and only then does it all go away."

"Are you telling me that if Sydney and I were both dead and this killer gets in a bind with law enforcement that he wouldn't start talking about the conspiracies to save his ass?"

"It'd be his word against Fisher and Runnels. He'd have no credibility and no one to back him up"

"Even more reason for Fisher and Runnels to see that Sydney and I are killed."

"That's exactly right, Scott."

"So you really don't think he's killed her?"

He stood, walked to the window, placed his hand on the wall bracing himself as he leaned against it. There was a long pause before he answered.

"I think he assumes you're close to Sydney, so he's going to use her to lure you to him. Then he'll try to kill you both. There's a slim chance that he might let Sydney go because she's an agent, someone he thinks the director has control over. But either way, he has to kill you."

He jabbed me in the chest repeatedly with his index finger. "Whether Sydney lives or dies depends mostly on you."

I stood to look him in the eye. I wanted him to be damn sure that I meant what I was about to tell him. "Mark, if this guy will guarantee to release Sydney unharmed, I'll meet him anywhere. She should never have gotten caught up in this in the first place. This whole goddamn thing is my fault."

He rubbed his forehead with his left hand, pinching his fingers together over the bridge of his nose. He couldn't look up and face me when he spoke again.

"Runnels and Fisher duped the President of the United States and convinced him to invade Iraq. The only way to ensure they had no culpability was to kill your parents, Collins, and now the two of you. The killer also has to protect himself from you two discovering who he is."

"Mark, I've got all my personal business in order. If I could just find him and spit in his eye, I wouldn't need any more than that. As for Sydney, she could go back to the Bureau and keep her oath of silence."

"Scott, we don't know for sure what he's thinking, but he's already fired at Sydney once. Agent or cop, he's probably not planning on letting either one of you live."

"What if I kill him, Mark? What happens then? Does Fisher find another guy just like this one to come after us?"

"Probably not."

"And why is that?"

"Fisher has the file and he knows that Sydney didn't copy it."

"How does he know that?"

"A good agent doesn't create additional opportunities for future problems by doubling evidence that's sensitive or pertains to national security, and Sydney's a good agent. If you take out the killer, he's buried without a name or affiliation to any agency, you get some justice and satisfaction, and Fisher has the file, which is the only evidence except your testimony. If neither you nor Sydney bring the conspiracy information up again, it goes away. He knows you want closure in your parent's murder case, and he's counting on the patriotism of you, Sydney, and me. As for the shooter, Fisher Probably wouldn't mind if you killed him. Since he's got the file, he can win regardless of who comes back with the other person's head on a platter."

Markham moved toward the door and opened it. He was staring at the blackened spot in the parking lot where Sydney's car had burned. "Scott, when you said you'd give yourself up for Sydney, I believe you. But the last thing I want right now is for anyone else to be hurt, especially Sydney."

"So how do we find Sydney, Mark?"

"He's setting up his next move, but he won't attempt anything until he's comfortable with his escape options if anything goes wrong."

"What do you mean escape?"

"Trust me, Scott, he's got an escape plan, all the way out of the country. He knows the type of people he's been working for, and he understands he can't trust them."

"Mark, I can't imagine how could he get out of the country if the FBI was on guard trying to prevent him from leaving?"

"Some other government who wants his services will get him out of the country, and if he goes this time he may never come back."

Mark reached for his wallet, took out a business card, and wrote some additional phone numbers on the back. I now had his direct line at the Bureau, his home number, and his personal cell. He promised to call me if he heard anything, and I did the same. I closed the front door, walked to the couch, sat and stared at the phone. I was hoping to will it to ring. It didn't.

CHAPTER 33

Twenty-four hours had passed since he'd taken her. It was now just after midnight early Wednesday morning, but the phone remained agonizingly silent. Every time I heard a car in the parking lot, I flew to the window. None of them stopped near Sydney's townhouse.

I needed a hot shower, so I took my cell phone and Sydney's cell to the bathroom. Passing through her bedroom I reached into a closet and grabbed an empty wire clothes hanger. I laid my cell phone and Sydney's phone on the vanity closest to the shower stall, and left the door to the shower stall partially open. Before I stepped in I dropped a towel on the floor to catch the water that might spray out the open door. This was Sydney's townhouse, and I was counting on her returning and finding it just as she left it. I squeezed the sides of the hanger together to force it into a vertical shape instead of horizontal. Then I turned it upside down and hung it over the showerhead, sliding the hook that normally hung over the clothes bar through my trigger guard, letting the Glock dangle next to the tile wall. I turned the shower on, and checked the spray to make sure it was aimed out and not down.

When I finished my shower, I dried off, picked up my gun and the phones and laid them on Sydney's nightstand. It had seemed like an eternity since the phone first rang this morning around six, so I made sure they were on and fully charged. They were. I knew I wasn't going to get any sleep, but maybe I could at least rest my body for a while.

If this guy was really as good as Markham said he was, he'd keep changing the pattern. He had fired at us during the morning and afternoon. He kidnapped Sydney during the evening. Maybe it was time for a late night contact. After a couple of hours of tossing and turning in Sydney's bed I caught myself dozing off. I was frazzled and exhausted, and even though I was afraid to allow myself to fall into a deep sleep, I couldn't stay awake.

Sydney's cell phone rang out, startling me upright in bed. I leaned over and took a close look at the digital alarm clock on the nightstand. It was twelve thirty-seven in the morning, on Wednesday. The glowing green numerals eerily illuminated the dark room. Reaching for the phone I knocked my Glock and my cell phone on the floor.

I cleared my throat and answered, "Hello."

"Is this the gentleman from Florida?"

I was normally calm and collected in tense situations. Ramer, my partner, often lost his cool with suspects, and I would always rein him in. Tonight it was my temper that was raging out of control.

"My name's Downing. I think you're familiar with that name."

"It rings a bell, I just can't put a face with it."

"You're an asshole. Where's Sydney?"

"Easy. I don't have the patience or the time for crude comments, Mr. Downing."

"You don't have any time at all if you've hurt her because I'll track your ass down and rip your heart out if she's so much as got a bruise."

"I didn't know you two were so close. Let me put her on for you, so you two love birds can talk."

That was a mistake to let him know how I felt about Sydney, but I couldn't control myself. I heard sounds like the phone was being fumbled around, and then I heard her voice, "Scott."

"Sydney, is that you?"

"It's me. I'm fine." Her voice sounded rapid and tense. Then there were more extraneous sounds and he was back.

"Mr. Downing, I hope you're satisfied that your little sweetie is doing just fine. We've been on this phone line too long. Sydney's friends like to trace calls, you know. Stand by for further instructions, and let's keep this on a professional level, shall we? You communicate with any of Ms. Sloan's colleagues at either the FBI or CIA, and she's dead. No questions asked."

"I'm the one you want. You let her go, and I'll meet you anywhere in the District unarmed."

"In time, my friend."

"You're not my friend, and if you so much as—" He hung up. I picked up my gun and my cell phone from the floor and started getting dressed. There was no way of really knowing what her condition was, but at least she was alive.

Two minutes later my cell phone rang.

"Hello."

"Scott, this is Mark. The Bureau just called me. Was that Sydney's voice?"

"Yeah, it was her, Mark. She said she was okay, but she didn't sound good."

"Our agents haven't had time to do a voice recognition analysis, but if you're sure, that's good enough for me, Scott."

"Mark, thank God she's alive."

"My sentiments as well. You pick up anything else, Scott?"

"Yeah, I heard a noise in the background. I'm pretty sure it was a commercial airliner. I assumed that meant he was near Dulles since National still has the noise abatement rule that prohibits flights after ten p.m."

I thought I had given Mark a significant piece of news. His response made me aware of how thorough the Bureau actually was.

"My people heard that too, Scott. Actually, some aircrafts are permitted after ten o'clock at National because they meet the noise abatement guidelines. Hell, for that matter this guy could be at BWI in Baltimore or anywhere in the world by now."

"Mark, you were right."

"About what?"

"This guy sounds cold blooded and calculating. If he thinks you're backing me up, he'll kill her."

"I've been here before, Scott, maybe not with Sydney but with other agents who worked for me. You're gonna have to trust me. I already have a team in place."

"What kind of team, Mark?

"That's the Bureau's business, Scott. Sorry."

"I'm confident you know what you're doing, but I don't know about a team. Why not let me meet with him alone and see if he'll exchange Sydney for me."

"We've already discussed that. This guy isn't planning on letting either of you live, Scott. Keep your cell phone on, I'll be in touch."

I hung up, finished dressing, and made my way into the kitchen, placing Sydney's phone, my cell, and my gun on the counter. I pulled up a barstool and waited. I was a pro-active cop, so being re-active was really difficult for me. But tonight I'd do whatever it took to save Sydney's life. Moving through the apartment, I looked out every window trying to spot someone who might be on Markham's team. I was hoping I couldn't see any of them, because if I could spot them, so could the killer.

CHAPTER 34

My cell phones and gun sat on the coffee table, and I circled them like I was playing musical chairs, ready to pounce at the first ring. The waiting time dragged on throughout the day Wednesday and into the night. My thoughts were off the wall. Ridiculous thoughts that Sydney was working with this guy or that he was taking her to some tropical island and making me meet him there where the FBI and CIA had no jurisdiction and he could easily get away with killing me. Perhaps I'd read too many mystery novels. Whatever it was, I felt helpless, and I needed this waiting to end.

Five minutes after eight that evening my cell phone rang. Sydney had been missing for forty-four hours.

"Mr. Downing I need you to go to Metro Center at the intersection of F and 12th Streets. Oh, Mr. Downing, I need you to be there by nine o'clock. Take your cell phone with you and wait for my instructions."

"Why don't you just come here, leave Sydney and I'll go with you."

"My plan, Mr. Downing, not yours. If I see anyone following you besides me, she's dead—no further negotiating."

"How about if I—"

"Goodbye, Mr. Downing."

Markham probably already knew what was going on. Between tapped cell phones and shotgun surveillance mics, the Bureau had more than likely heard every noise I'd made today. I called Markham from my car to let him know where I was headed and remind him of the killer's warning about what he'd do if he spotted one of Sydney's colleagues.

"Hello, Scott."

"Mark, the killer just called."

"And?"

"He wants me to be at the Metro Center at F and 12th at 9:00."

"You'd better get going then, Scott."

"Mark, if your officers follow me, he said he'll kill Sydney." His answer to that shocked me.

"Okay. I won't send anyone then."

"Seriously, Mark?"

"Very serious," he said. "Something wrong?"

I was stunned that he would back down so quickly, but I was relieved that he wasn't going to send a couple of agents like the two who'd been parked across from Sydney's last night. "Everything's fine. I just assumed you weren't going to go along with anything like that."

"This time, you assumed wrong. You need to be extremely careful, Scott. Remember, he's an excellent shot. He may even use a long range sniper rifle."

"You really aren't going to back me up are you?"

"Nope."

"What about Sydney? Don't you give a damn about her?"

"Relax, Scott. I'm not sending anyone to follow you because he's testing you and me both."

"Testing. You mean he wants to know if I show up alone?"

"These are his rules. He wants to know if you're playing by them. If he doesn't recognize anyone from the Bureau who might be covering you, he'll set up another meeting. If he ambushes you, then I was wrong and you'll have to be as good as Sydney says you are to survive."

"You're quite a gambler aren't you, Mark?"

"It's an inherent part of the job I'm afraid. Good luck, Scott."

"Talk to you soon I hope."

I drove to the Metro Center and parked in the public lot. Two cops were walking ahead of me from the parking lot toward the Metro Center. They were having a heated debate over something to do with the Redskins. I didn't want to be seen walking with cops, so I slowed my stride to let them get well ahead of me. I had taken less than thirty steps went toward the terminal when my cell phone rang. I took a deep breath and answered.

"Hello."

"Very good, Mr. Downing. Now you can go back to Sloan's and wait for my next instructions. Oh, and tell the boys at the Bureau, good call on not coming tonight. Maybe I'll see 'em next time."

The killer anticipated the Bureau's every move. Before or after his military service, he could have been one of the Bureau's star students at FLETC, the Federal Law Enforcement Training Center in central Virginia. That was where most of the federal agencies trained new recruits or officers on special projects or missions. As badly as I wanted to check in with Mark right away, I was concerned that I might still be under surveillance. The call would have to wait.

My nervous habit kicked in and I turned into a McDonald's and entered the drive-thru window lane. I ordered a Quarter Pounder with cheese value meal, including fries and a Coke. I took them back to the apartment.

Locking the door behind me, I carried the food to the counter. I was in a city with some of the most magnificent restaurants in the country, and I was eating a burger out of a paper bag and drinking a soft drink from a wax cup. When I got Sydney back, I would treat her to dinner at the Palm.

Throwing the wrappers and trash in the bag, I compacted it into a little ball and tossed it into the can under the sink. I'd eaten faster than usual, anxious to get back to my post next to the blinds, where I continued to check out the traffic in the parking lot. It didn't take long for me to become bored with this task, so I found my favorite spot on the sofa and returned to the cable news networks. I thought about calling Mark, but if the guys at the Bureau were so smart, they probably already knew everything. I laid my head back and began to daydream. A vivid image of Sydney getting out of her car and strolling to the front door flashed before my eyes. I shook my head vigorously to chase away the cobwebs. I had to talk to someone about what was going on, so I picked up the phone and called Mark.

"Markham."

"You were right on. It was a test. I don't know how good that federal training is, but it's damn sure consistent."

"Yeah, I heard. My guys said they watched him turn you around."

"You mean you had people there after he threatened to kill Sydney?"

"Take it easy, Scott. This guy was checking out the cleaning people, the hot dog vendor, even the homeless people sleeping on benches. There was no way he was going to pick up on the two Metro cops who were arguing over the Washington Redskins."

"Those were your guys?"

"They were."

"You really are a helluva gambler, Mark."

"Keep in touch, Scott." He hung up. All day long I'd been so intent on spotting members of Markham's team. Now he told me that I'd only been a few feet away from two of them at the Metro Center, and I never had a clue. Thank God, the killer hadn't figured out who they were either. At least I hoped he hadn't, for Sydney's sake.

CHAPTER 35

Another long and sleepless night was facing me. I picked up a David Baldacci novel, but terrible thoughts of Sydney's demise made it impossible for me to stay focused. Clock watching was nerve-racking, but it was the only thing that held my attention. I stared at those green numerals on Sydney's digital clock when they rolled over to midnight, making it officially Thursday morning.

The next time I looked, the numerals rotated from 12:59 to 1:00 a.m., a little over forty-eight and a half hours since he'd taken her. At that instant my cell phone rang. I said a prayer that this would be Sydney, calling for me to come get her. Before I flipped the phone open, I took two deep breaths, filling my chest with air, and exhaled hard. On the third ring, I answered. His voice was now so familiar, and every word reverberated through my skull.

"Good evening, Mr. Downing. I need you to get back to the Metro Center."

"Come on. Can't you bring her here? You send her in unharmed, and I'll come out, an even swap."

"That may work where you're from, Mr. Downing, but not here."

"I'm a man of my word, what about you?" I asked.

"I'm a man of my word until I'm backed into a corner. I'd much rather go to your funeral than have you come to mine saying he was an honorable man and he wasn't a liar."

"Metro Center—I'm on the way," I said. But this time before I took off, I stepped into the bathroom, turned the shower on full blast like Sydney had done at the hotel, and dialed Markham. If anyone from the Bureau had a listening device aimed at the house, I was at least going to make it a little more difficult. He answered on the first ring.

"Markham."

"I'm on the way to the Metro Center."

"Here comes the chase, Scott."

"What kind of chase?"

"The chase is a series of directions where he runs you all over the District, although it might be too early for him to try that. He uses that tactic to wear you down mentally and physically, and to make sure you don't have any law enforcement following you."

"Who teaches these guys this crap?"

"I did for about fifteen years."

"I thought you taught spy stuff."

"That's the CIA. The Bureau teaches cop stuff."

"I'm on my way to the Metro Center. Don't do anything to get her hurt, Mark."

"You take good care, Scott. I expect to see both of you in a few hours."

Mark sure had a positive attitude. I hoped he was right. I took the clip out of my Glock and checked to make sure it was full. I took an extra clip from my briefcase and dropped it in my pocket.

There wasn't nearly as much traffic heading in or out of DC at this time of morning. Parking in the same lot, I got out and sauntered toward the terminal, anticipating another call before I got inside. It didn't happen. I purchased a three dollar one-day pass, turned back around and sat on a bench, waiting and watching. Checking my watch, it was a few minutes after two a.m. The number of riders at this hour was limited, which made it easier to check every one of them out as they boarded and exited the trains. I knew there was no way I'd be able to identify this guy by looking at everyone getting on or off the trains, but it helped to pass the time. One guy burst off of an incoming train the second the doors opened, ran over close to me, and leaned against a support column. He was a little less than six feet tall with a small waist and broad shoulders. He had dark curly hair, bushy black eyebrows and squinty eyes that seemed to pierce my skin when he gazed in my direction. He'd look away for a minute or two then he'd stare at me again. This routine was a little unnerving and became even more so when he picked up the pace, looking at me more often and holding his stare a little longer each time.

No one else was paying any attention to me, so I decided to try my lost tourist bit. I stood and turned towards him, mustering up my best confused expression. Then I asked if this was the train to the zoo. His answer was even more shocking. "No inglese." Christ, this guy was Italian. I'd lived in such a small town with so little ethnicity for so long, I'd forgotten what an eclectic and diverse melting pot DC was.

I nodded and said, "Scusi. Buona notte."

"Grazie," he said, releasing a huge, disarming smile.

When the next train came in, a gentleman exited, held up a photograph and looked at it before calling out to my Italian friend. They boarded the red line together and headed north with several dozen other passengers. I was still waiting for my next instructions. After another train came and went, I was beginning to feel beleaguered and lost. I continued to watch the passengers boarding and disembarking. They all appeared to be weary souls seeking their way home. I had almost given up when my phone rang.

I dug my hand into my pocket and snatched my phone out. "Hello."

"Mr. Downing, take the next train to Dupont Circle and wait for my call. You didn't notify any of Ms. Sloan's friends, did you, Mr. Downing?"

"Of course not."

"And you are still a man of your word, correct?"

"Correct."

"Dupont Circle." Then the phone went dead again. I saw the next red line train coming, and I stood there fidgeting as I anxiously waited for the door to open.

Dupont Circle was two stops away. The well-known residential section of the District featured palatial mansions, row houses, and freestanding residences, built in the styles popular between 1895 and 1910. I first discovered this little circle when I was attending Georgetown. It was known for its unusual architecture, artsiness, and unique bistros. My reminiscing briefly took my mind off the uncertainty of what was coming.

All through college and law school, and throughout my first few years in law enforcement, I was a big believer in planning and organization. Now I had none. Not only did I have no plan in mind, I had to idea what I would do next if the killer approached me. Several people milled around in the circle, a circular road intersected by New Hampshire, Massachusetts, Connecticut Avenues and P Street. The killer could have been any one of them. Trains stopped briefly as passengers came and went. The only travelers who lingered in the station were two guys who appeared to be having a lover's quarrel. I was certain they weren't connected with my mission. I sat again and waited.

A few moments later a hand landed on my right shoulder. I slowly slid my right hand inside my jacket and gripped my Glock, using my thumb to flick the snap off the leather strap that held it in place in my holster. I turned my head and looked up at the stranger who'd approached me from behind.

CHAPTER 36

He must have fallen asleep holding a bottle of cheap wine because his clothes reeked of alcohol. The gray pants he wore looked like pajamas and were covered with food stains; at least I was hoping they were food stains. He smiled revealing two upper teeth and only one lower tooth. His face was pockmarked, and he had what appeared to be a week to ten days growth of a beard. His nose was running, and he repeatedly used his jacket sleeve to wipe it. Watching that, my thoughts went to the hand that had been on my shoulder. I made up my mind to throw away the jacket I was wearing as soon this was over. I would have taken it off then and there, but I needed it to cover my shoulder holster.

"Could you spare a little change for a cup of coffee, cousin?" I removed my hand from my Glock, reached into my pocket and took out a couple of bucks.

"You make sure you go get coffee with that, and not something else, cousin."

He smiled widely, exhibited all three teeth, and staggered out of the station. I sat on the bench, praying that my phone would ring. Maybe he wouldn't call again.

It had been three long agonizing years, but I'd never given up hope that one day I'd have the chance to track down the person or persons who murdered my parents. There was a time in my life when I'd have wanted to bring the killer to my own form of justice, but not anymore. Now all I wanted to do was make sure Sydney's life was spared.

I wondered how long it would take for America to regain her position of prominence in the world if the true reason we invaded Iraq got out. What would the people around the world think about America if they learned that two of our top officials had hired a mercenary to murder three innocent people? What about the soldiers who'd been killed in the war in the Middle East? How would America, and the rest of the world for that matter, feel about a country whose leaders allowed that many soldiers to die over the personal greed that inspired *Freedom Flows*?

If other countries suspended trading with us, millions of jobs would be lost. What if the top oil-producing countries stopped selling crude to us? The price of gasoline could skyrocket to ten or fifteen dollars a gallon.

Markham was certain there was no way I could convince the killer to take me and let Sydney go. But the killer had been around the Bureau and the CIA enough to appreciate how dedicated the agents were. He had to know that Sydney would keep the oath she'd taken when she was sworn in as an FBI agent promising to obey the lawful orders and directives of those appointed before and above her. If she was ordered to keep her mouth shut, she would. America would be spared its reputation, its world prominence, and its economic stability, and I would join my parents in a different form of silence.

On the other hand, I wanted to be with Sydney. She'd become more than a partner in the past two weeks. She was a very special woman, and I wasn't ready to give up on where our relationship might be going. If I offered to trade myself for Sydney, I would never know what might have been. Markham was right. The trade was not an option.

Acknowledging how I felt about Sydney made waiting for the next phone call even more stressful. Maybe this guy saw the bum and thought he was a cop. If he had, Sydney might already be dead. I needed to focus on keeping those negative thoughts out of my head. I started counting the bricks on one of the walls. Somewhere around one hundred and fifty two bricks, my cell phone rang.

"Downing."

"Sorry for the delay, Mr. Downing. Circumstances beyond our control prevented me from calling you sooner." I looked around surveying the area to see if I could spot someone on a cell phone or a pay phone. If he was nearby I couldn't see him.

My frustration level had reached an all-time high, and it was showing as I snapped back at him. "If you want me to keep playing your game I need to talk to Sydney."

"Oh, Mr. Downing, how can I convince you that this is not a game. This is very serious business, and please understand you are not the person in charge."

"We both know that's bullshit. You need me. If I took a cab over to *The Washington Post*, you'd never work for this country again. In fact you'd probably never be able to come back to this country again, and the same guys who hired you to kill my parents would find another asshole just like you to make sure of it."

"Giving the story to the media would be your decision. I'd merely kill Agent Sloan and quietly slip away to another beautiful country where, I assure you, I'm quite welcomed.

"Let me talk to Sydney."

I heard some mumbling and then I heard her voice.

"Scott, I'm okay. Don't come it's too—" There were scuffling sounds in the background. He must have snatched the phone away. I heard a scream. It was Sydney. I wanted to kill him.

"I hope you're satisfied, Mr. Downing. Agent Sloan is fine. However, she came very close to needing a reprimand for being a bit too verbose. It would not be in her best interest to ask her to speak to you again. My reprimands have, shall we say, an electrifying effect on people."

"Don't hurt her, you piece of shit! Tell me what you want me to do."

"Ah, ah, ah, Mr. Downing, you're again forgetting who's in charge."

"Okay. You're in charge. What's next?"

"Take a metro bus south on New Hampshire Avenue to the Foggy Bottom District. Get off near the Watergate Hotel and wait for my instructions. We'll talk again when you get there." The phone again went dead. The process of running me around like this was exactly as Markham said it would be, and I felt sure he had carefully chosen each move. I caught the first Metro bus headed south on New Hampshire.

Sitting alone in the back of the bus, I meditated on thoughts of the emerald green waves of the Gulf of Mexico, gently rolling in and lapping onto sandy beaches. It was my way of combating the psychological fatigue he was attempting to inflict on me. I focused on something I loved, Panama City Beach. I could smell the unique aroma of the salt air. I heard the cheerful sounds of seagulls circling overhead, calling out to the tourists below, begging for a morsel of bread or chips or whatever offerings they might spare

The first time I opened my eyes, we were at the intersection of Washington Circle and New Hampshire Ave. I got off at the next stop, Virginia and New Hampshire, and crossed over to the Watergate Hotel. I remembered there was a bakery and deli on the ground floor.

It was a little after five o'clock Thursday morning, fifty-three hours of captivity for Sydney Sloan. A man and a woman were busily moving around in the bakery. I tapped on the door and a large man with black curly hair seeping out from a maroon Redskins ball cap approached the door brushing flour off his hands onto his white apron. He unlocked the door and asked if he could help me. I apologized for interrupting him so early, but I offered to pay ten dollars for one of their incredible cappuccinos. He pointed to a table with two chairs still stacked on top of it. There were about a dozen tables in the little deli, each with two to four chairs stacked on top, probably to allow employees to clean the floor at closing. A couple of moments later a short lady with gray hair delivered my cappuccino. I reached in my wallet, took out two five-dollar bills, giving both of them to her. She laid one of the fives back on the table. Before I could say anything, she scurried across the room to a counter where she rolled green cloth napkins around silverware.

The burly fellow who had let me in was the baker. He took a tray of croissants out of a Blodget oven and the smell of fresh baked pastries seemed to transform the room into a French boulangerie. As fabulous as they smelled, I was not in the mood for food.

I set my phone on vibrate before laying it on the table. Sipping my cappuccino, I stared through the window fantasizing about being with Sydney in a different time and place, and wondering what kind of place she was in, and how much time she had left.

CHAPTER 37

It had been nearly an hour since the last call. His pauses between calls had grown obnoxiously erratic. I asked God to please get me to the end of this chase, and to make it come soon. It occurred to me that maybe the killer was in a position to watch my every move. He might have been uncomfortable with me being inside the bakery. I left the five-dollar bill on the table, picked up my phone, and pushed the door open, standing in the doorway gazing up and down New Hampshire Avenue. Traffic was sparse and foot traffic was almost nonexistent.

I felt a sudden nerve spasm in my right thigh. My cell phone was vibrating in my pocket. Maybe my prayers to end this laborious cat and mouse game were being answered. I grabbed the phone and flipped it open "I hope we haven't detained you, Mr. Downing."

"Actually, I'm enjoying my tour of the District. I haven't seen it for a while."

"Good. I'm glad. Now you are ready far a little walk, Mr. Downing?" The way he enunciated every word and addressed me as Mr. Downing was irritating, but I wasn't about to let him know that.

"A walk would be very nice, thank you. Since you're able to call me by name, don't you think it's only fair that I call you by your name?"

"I don't play fair, Mr. Downing, and I don't care what you call me. You'll have a better idea of who I am when we met and complete this transaction, Mr. Downing."

"Is that supposed to scare me DMT?"

"DMT?"

"You'll have a better idea of what DMT stands for when I complete my transaction."

"Fair enough. As for scaring you, Mr. Downing, I already know you well enough to be fully aware of the fact that I couldn't possibly do that. If you're ready to continue, I need you to walk toward the end of New Hampshire Avenue."

"Which way would that be?"

"If you got off the bus as I suggested, you should have a relatively short walk, Mr. Downing."

"Are you going to tell me where I'm walking to?"

"Give me a landmark, Mr. Downing."

"I'm in front of the Cup'A bakery and deli at the Watergate."

"Very good. Turn your back to the café, then face right and start walking. Walk leisurely, don't call attention to yourself and I'll call you soon with final instructions. Mr. Downing, let me reiterate my position. If I have the slightest indication of someone or anyone following you or shadowing your movements in any way, Agent Sloan is dead."

"I'm alone. I haven't spoken to a soul. This is between us."

"Good attitude, Mr. Downing. Are you walking yet?"

"I'm walking in the direction you just instructed me to walk."

"I'll be in touch, Mr. Downing." He hung up again, so I flipped the phone closed and put it back in my pocket. I was about to pass a vacant lot encircled with a black temporary construction fence that looked like it was roofing tar paper. I noticed an old bronze statue standing alone in the center of the property. I'd driven this road in the past, and never noticed that statue. Before I could take another step, a blunt metal cylinder the size of a gun barrel was forced into the small of my back. A chill shot up my spine. An arm wearing a black sleeve reached around from behind me and shoved me hard through an opening in the black enclosure that concealed the vacant property. The grass was knee high inside the fence and the lot or park or whatever it was looked like it had been deserted by the community.

"Face the fence and don't you turn around, else I'll shoot your ass." Christ, this wasn't the killer; I was being mugged. This poor bastard had picked the wrong person at the wrong time. I felt his warm breath on the back of my neck as he stood close to me trying to lift my wallet out of my back pocket. I stealthily lowered my right hand and slid it inside my jacket on my left side and flipped the leather tab holding my Glock. It dropped into my hand at the same moment that he lifted my wallet out of my pocket. Pushing off the fence with all my force I spun around and shoved the barrel of my gun into the face of an African-American teenager. In his right hand he was holding a short piece of pipe he'd used to simulate the barrel of a gun. He was holding my wallet in his left.

"What was it that Clint Eastwood said in that *Dirty Harry* movie?" I growled at the kid through gritted teeth. He hesitated a few seconds, debating what to do next.

"Put the wallet down, punk, or I'll shoot it out of your hand."

He threw the wallet at my feet and took off running across New Hampshire Avenue and up the opposite side of the road. In less than ten seconds, he disappeared in the direction of an apartment complex. I holstered my gun, picked up my wallet and squeezed back through the fence to the sidewalk. Continuing to walk south on New Hampshire as directed, I approached a tall white stone building. It was probably an embassy or some sort of foreign government offices because an unfamiliar flag was flying from the center of the building. I walked closer.

The sign on the front was written in English and Arabic. This was the Saudi Arabian Embassy. I didn't think that could be my destination, but I didn't see any other buildings in the immediate area, so I continued. Looking toward the embassy as I strode past, I observed two men who appeared to be guards just inside the doors. Fifty yards beyond the building, my cell phone rang.

"Downing."

"Mr. Downing, how unsociable of you to walk right by us and not stop for a visit."

"Where's Sydney?"

"I can see from your expression, Mr. Downing, that those armed guards make you as nervous as they do me. That's why I always use the back entrance."

"Back entrance to what?"

"The embassy you just passed is the home of some very dear friends of our country, well friends of mine at least."

Son of a bitch. He was in the Saudi Arabian Embassy. Very dear friends of our country my ass.

"Are you American?" I asked.

"Mr. Downing, I was born in America, but I have citizenship papers from a number of nations friendly to the US."

"What kind of American would support the greedy bastards behind something like *Operation Freedom Flows?*"

"We're wasting precious time with this trivial stuff, Mr. Downing. You need to come back toward the embassy and follow the tree line around to the rear of the building. Ghazi will meet you at the gate and see you inside." I couldn't believe what I was hearing. The Saudis had given this guy refuge, and with a kidnapped female no less. This certainly confirmed what most Americans suspected about the Saudi government.

"DMT, I don't go inside until Sydney comes outside."

"Mr. Downing, I look forward to being enlightened as to the meaning of your acronym. I'm sure it is most clever."

"I'll explain the acronym when I see you. What about Sydney?"

"As soon as you come inside, you'll be reunited with your dear Sydney, Mr. Downing. You have my word on that."

"I need to talk to her."

"Again, you'll have to take my word for it that Ms. Sloan is in good condition, but you won't see her until you're safely on the inside of the embassy."

"Do you work for the Saudi government?"

"I work for many governments, Mr. Downing. The Saudis are very generous and have provided me with special services and assistance from time to time. We get along quite well."

"I think they're back-stabbing whores."

"Calling them such names could prevent them from extending their warm hospitality to you, Mr. Downing."

"They're whores. They screw us at every OPEC meeting, they screw us on the oil we buy from them, and they support terrorists and killers just like you."

"I wouldn't advise you to share those thoughts with Ghazi. He's doing us both a huge favor by letting you enter the embassy. Your point of view would definitely engender ill will."

"I take it your Saudi friends aren't aware that you're working for two Americans who want to take over all the oil production in the Middle East."

"Wanted to, Mr. Downing, as in past tense. Currently, my clients only desire is to put their activities in the Middle East behind them and remove any possibility of their connection to those activities."

"Who's to say if you kill Sydney and me that they won't go after that oil again? How would your Saudi friends feel about then?"

"We gain nothing by this speculation, Mr. Downing."

"Get Sydney to a window. I want to see her." This was like a rattlesnake inviting me into a pit full of the deadly reptiles, and there was a good chance Sydney might already be dead.

"Ms. Sloan is alive and well. There'll be no showing in a window. You're on my turf now, and these are my rules. Ghazi will be expecting you any minute. If he doesn't see you waiting for admittance, he will revoke your invitation, and then I'm afraid you'll have to assume the responsibility for Ms. Sloan's welfare."

I had no choice but to go along. "You and the Saudis deserve each other. You're all whores."

"Name calling will get you nowhere, and for a man of your background, I'm frankly surprised to hear you repeatedly speaking like that. I'll see you momentarily." He disconnected.

Based on how much Sydney and I knew, there was no question he planned to kill us both. For us to survive we had to kill him. For America to survive we had to make sure that the knowledge of all the conspiracies died with him.

Chapter 38

The double doors at the building's rear entrance opened electronically. Immediately inside the door, two uniformed guards stood facing each other standing next to a tall, gray metal detector. The guard on the left was holding the stock end of an automatic rifle in his right hand, while his other hand supported the barrel. The other guard seemed to be armed only with a holstered handgun. He must have been the guard in charge of the security at the rear entrance of the building, because he barked orders in Arabic, and the other guard responded by dropping one of his hands from his rifle and pushing me forward to the metal detector.

A man was rapidly approaching from the far end of a hallway that looked as long as a football field. His shoes clicked and echoed off the marble floor with every step of his brisk stride. He had an air of confidence, head held high, shoulders drawn back. He was as tall as me, around six feet four or five. His thick, black, wavy hair looked like it had just been permed. His bulky physique was stocky but not heavy. He had an olive complexion with eyes that were as black as the suit he was wearing.

I paused in front of the detector. The other guard stepped to the far end of the metal detector and said, "Come forward."

Every sweat gland in my entire body released copious amounts of perspiration. I could either turn and run in the opposite direction, pull my gun and get into a shoot out with all three men or step through the detector and acknowledge my weapon. I took a deep breath and stepped toward the machine, knowing that an alarm was about to echo through this hollow hallway.

I was inches away from reaching the center of the detector when the man in the dark suit dashed to the side of the detector and without hesitation flipped the power switch, turning it off. I cleared the detector and gave a startled look to my new friend. What the hell? Why would he do that?

"Mr. Downing, I'm Ghazi. Come in please," he said with a smile as he extended his arm.

"Thank you," I said with my body still quivering, as I followed him down the hall.

Massive chandeliers were spaced equally along the hallway hanging down from the thirty-foot ceiling. The floor was made of large two-foot-square marble tiles that were snow white with streaks of gold that looked real. We passed seven sets of large mahogany doors, all closed, on either side of the hallway. A beautiful young woman with dark hair and mocha skin was sitting at a desk at the end of the hall. The wall behind her was covered mostly by white ceramic tiles, broken occasionally by a triangular pattern of blue and yellow tiles. Ghazi pointed to the woman and said, "Mr. Downing, would you please be so kind as to let Ms. Attar here store your weapon and your wallet while you are visiting our embassy." She pulled out the top left drawer of the desk, waiting for me to comply. I contemplated my options and the woman raised her brows in anticipation of my next move.

"I assure you, Mr. Downing, that Ms. Attar will return them to you at the conclusion of your visit," Ghazi said firmly. These people knew what they were doing. They would have both my weapon and my credentials. If anything went wrong, I had no way of proving I was a law enforcement officer, but I reluctantly handed over my gun and wallet.

"Please, this way, Mr. Downing," Ghazi said pushing in the direction of the wall at the end of the hallway. A five-foot section of the wall rotated open into another long hallway, this one made of concrete block, with a concrete floor and Spartan looking light fixtures. About fifty steps put us in front of another guard in military dress. He was blocking the entrance to a huge set of brilliantly polished wooden doors. Ghazi knocked once and opened one of the huge doors. He stood in the threshold, ushering me inside. I was awe struck by the six-inch thick impeccably polished mahogany wood. The next sound I heard was the giant door slamming shut behind me. Ghazi was gone.

I stood in front of the doors and surveyed the room. It must have been one hundred feet across and seventy-five feet deep. It was as enormous as a hotel ballroom. The lower three feet of the walls were covered with cherry wood wainscoting. A gold chair railing divided the wooden lower portion of the walls from the red floral wallpaper that extended to the ceiling. Directly across from me was a mammoth fireplace with a white granite mantle and hearth, large enough for someone to stand upright in. Three sofas and four high-backed chairs were clustered around the fireplace. I didn't recognize the artist of a painting over the mantle, but I recognized the subject. It was Saudi Arabian King Fahd bin Abd al-Aziz Al Saud. Way too much CNN I guess. There was one tall, narrow window near the fireplace. Dark red drapes were gathered by gold braided rope on each side of the window. A sweet smell filled the air. Not incense, more like vanilla candles or potpourri. Neither of which I saw anywhere in the room. I wasn't sure whether to step farther into the room or to just stay put. I took two steps forward trying to imagine what the plan was from here. I was here to save Sydney's life, but I couldn't help but wonder how much he really knew about *Operation Freedom Flows*. If he killed both of us, what would stop him from blackmailing Runnels or Fisher, or holding our country hostage over the information he had? The Saudis would more than likely pay him a fortune to use his information to stop the US from continuing to interfere in the Middle East. From our conversation on the phone, I wasn't sure how much he actually knew, beyond simply being paid to kill my parents, Collins, and now Sydney and me.

I had a creepy feeling that I was being watched. It felt like I had a dozen cameras aimed at me from all around the room.

I knew that if I found Sydney alive in here, our chances of us getting out were poor at best. Employees of a foreign embassy were granted immunity to most of our country's laws.

The Saudi government was one of the few friends America still had, or thought we still had, in the Middle East. When you combined the Saudis' immense influence over OPEC oil prices and production and their strategic military importance, which allowed the US to have base operations in the Middle East, there was no doubt Sydney and I were in a place with absolute invulnerability. This killer was covering all his bets to see that he had backed us into a corner we couldn't escape from. He was the only person in my life I had ever wanted to kill, and I wanted to do it today.

CHAPTER 39

He was probably watching my every move. I looked around for the places where surveillance cameras might have been installed. I gazed up at the chandelier above my head. It must have been fifteen feet in diameter with hundreds of crystal pieces sparkling like giant prisms. If there was a camera mounted above it, I couldn't see it.

Standing alone in the gigantic room, I wondered where the hell he was. Three loud beeps startled me. Then a female voice spoke in Arabic over the PA system. My eyes chased across the ceiling until I noticed the round white flush-mounted speakers. I didn't understand a word of Arabic, but I totally comprehended the next sound I heard. The dead bolt to the door behind me was electronically slammed shut. I wasn't sure, but I thought I heard the same sound coming from other rooms as well. I turned to go toward the door to check the lock, but I was stopped in my tracks by Ghazi's voice booming through the speakers.

"Mr. Downing, I apologize for the inconvenience, but we are experiencing a slight security interruption. I need to ask that you step to the fireplace across the room." The question of cameras had been answered.

He obviously knew I wasn't leaning against the mantle. There was no point in checking the door. It was certainly locked, and my options were pretty limited, so I walked to the fireplace as he asked.

"Very good, Mr. Downing. I thank you for your cooperation. Now, I am going to ask you to do something you might find a bit unusual, but I assure you it is for your safety and welfare."

"Ghazi, somehow I doubt your top priority is about my safety and welfare."

"Mr. Downing, truthfully you are correct. That is not my top priority, but it is certainly among my priorities. If you would be so kind as to step inside the hearth of the fireplace."

"Ghazi, I used to tell people I wanted to be cremated, but I was hoping I'd already be dead when that happened."

"Mr. Downing, we do not use that fireplace for providing warmth to the room you are standing in, so you may eliminate that worry." Then what the hell would you use a fireplace for? I hesitated in front of the hearth, examining it closely, but there was nothing that would indicate this was anything more than a fireplace.

"Please step in, Mr. Downing." Reluctantly I followed his instructions and backed into the fireplace, keeping my eyes on the door.

"Please face the back wall, Mr. Downing."

"Ghazi, this whole thing is getting to be a little too much for me. I'm standing inside a damn fireplace in a foreign embassy and taking instructions from someone I can't see."

"My apologies, Mr. Downing. Requesting that you face the back wall of the hearth will be my last instruction for you." If he was telling the truth, I had to be closer to getting to the end of this journey. Again, I did as he asked.

Immediately, I had the sensation of dropping into a black abyss. My stomach felt like it was in my throat. The fireplace was some sort of elevator. Whining noises shrieked above me and I noticed flashes of light from floors passing by. It took only a few seconds, but it seemed to go one for minutes, before the elevator thudded to a stop. Light poured in from behind me. I turned around, looked into the room and was astonished at what I saw.

I was in what seemed to be a basement with unpainted concrete block walls and a concrete slab floor. Hanging on and stacked against the walls were some of the latest and most pieces of powerful military equipment in the world. Signs printed in English acronyms stood in front of each column of equipment. Huge crates reached to the ceiling along the wall to my left. There were ATGMs or anti-tank guided missiles, MAAWS or multi-role anti-armor anti-personnel weapons systems, and LAWs or light anti-tank weapons. Dozens of boxes of ammunition were stacked in front of those crates. If this guy had anything to do with the Saudis having access to this stuff, he was more connected that I had ever dreamed.

Hanging on the wall to my right were M1A1 submachine guns, M16 semi-automatic rifles, and something I had only heard of but never seen before. The OICW stood for the objective individual combat weapon. It was an unusual looking, lightweight weapon. When I went through training at FLETC in Virginia, I had a weapons instructor who told us some stories about the OICW. It wasn't just another high-powered rifle. It weighed twelve pounds and fired 20-millimeter high-explosive bullets with a kill range of one thousand meters. I was pretty sure this weapon had only been in the testing stages for a couple of years and had not yet been issued to our own military personnel.

He obviously wanted me to see all this weaponry to illustrate who and what I was up against. This showing was definitely designed to unnerve me. He had succeeded.

The room went black and I heard the killer's voice directly across from me. Then one lone, brilliant beam of light focused on my face. It was like an aircraft light, so powerful that I could feel my face flushing. My eyes watered; I was forced to look down to avoid being blinded.

"Sorry for having to greet you this way, Mr. Downing. Apparently your friends with the FBI thought they could follow you into the embassy."

"What are you talking about?"

"The building is in lockdown, and the FBI has it surrounded. Unfortunately for you and Agent Sloan, they won't be allowed inside. When the ambassador calls the President and informs him of what has happened, the agents outside will be instructed to vacate the premises."

"They're not my friends, and I never called them. Where's Sydney?"

"In due time, Mr. Downing. I am curious as to that little nickname you gave me over the phone. I'd love to know what DMT stands for."

"DMT stands for Dead Man Talking."

He laughed out loud and then responded, "Very clever and exceedingly positive I might add. I admire your attitude. It's your ability that disappointments me."

"Where's Sydney, asshole?"

"I thought you would want to visit with me a while, Mr. Downing. You know, maybe learn a little bit about that fateful night on Panama City Beach. Your parents were very courageous."

"Fuck you." My adrenaline was surging through my body. If I could get close enough to him, I was sure I could break his neck.

"Now, now, Mr. Downing, that profanity is not your style. You're a well-educated, well-traveled, professional law enforcement officer. Using such foul language is not becoming of you."

"Where's Sydney?" The veins in my neck felt like they were going to erupt. I could feel them pulsating.

"You'll see her soon enough. First things first; turn around and face the fireplace."

Before I could get completely turned around, I felt a painful stab in the back of my neck. My head suddenly felt like it weighed fifty pounds, and I saw the floor of the fireplace racing toward my face.

CHAPTER 40

I was sitting, bound with metal cable or chain to a gray metal chair in a dimly lit, cold, damp room. A disgusting musty scent triggered my sense of smell as I regained consciousness. The scent was sickening. My pupils were opening wider as I struggled to let in more light. A single dim lightbulb attached to a black electrical cord hanging from ceiling rafters provided minimal illumination. This was a different room from the one where the weapons were stored, although the wall behind me only extended about two thirds of the way across the room. If that wall was a divider, he could have dragged me around it and sat me in this chair.

The damp, musty room reminded me of some of the dungeons I had seen in castles when I'd traveled with my parents to Europe; only they smelled better than this. There was either no bathroom down here, or there was one that wasn't working. God only knew what the Saudis had used this place for. Unpainted concrete block walls surrounded me like a fortress.

I attempted to move in the chair, but the cable tugged on my back when I leaned forward and at my chest when I sat back. There was a sting in the back of my neck. Dammit! The pain was from a needle. He'd drugged me, which meant that while I was out, he could have moved me hundreds of miles. I had no idea where I was. Why was he wasting his time tying me up? He could have easily poisoned me instead of drugging me. There had to be some reason he was letting me live. He wanted something, but what? The more important questions: where was Sydney and was she alive?

"Scott." I heard my name being called from behind me. The voice was weak and shaky, but it sure sounded like Sydney. Maybe she was in another room and he was forcing her to talk over a PA system. I searched through the darkness looking for Sydney. There was no one in the room. I wondered if I was hallucinating. That was probably the answer. I wanted to hear Sydney's voice so badly; I was fantasizing about it.

"Scott." I heard it again. There was no doubt it was Sydney's voice.

"Sydney, is that you?"

"Scott."

"Goddamn it, Sydney, where are you?"

"Behind."

"Behind where?"

"Behind you."

I dug my fingers into the metal seat, collecting all of the energy in my body and trying to twist the chair around. Nothing. Not an inch. Why couldn't I turn this chair? I tried again and again. It didn't budge.

"Scott. Bolts." What did she mean by bolts? I looked around my chair. Jesus, the chair was bolted to the floor. That's what she was trying to tell me.

"Sydney, are we in the same room?"

"Yes." Her voice was barely a whisper, but I couldn't tell whether or not she was drugged, sleep deprived or injured.

"You okay?" I asked.

A weak voice responded, "Okay, Scott."

"Sydney, do you know where we are?"

"That's enough questions, Mr. Downing. Ms. Sloan isn't up for any unnecessary chitchat." His voice was coming from the same direction as Sydney's.

"Turn me around and let me see her you asshole."

"I think you've already discovered that that's impossible."

"How about you? Why don't you step over here and let me see what a gutless, lowlife, chicken shit looks like."

"Mr. Downing, your profanity is totally inappropriate for mixed company. I think we should try to improve your language, don't you?"

Sudden fire shot through my body. Electricity jolted me from my thighs to my waist and up through my arms to the tips of my fingers. The pain from the electrical shock felt like a hot knife had slashed through my lower body. When the current stopped, I was soaked with sweat. I struggled to breathe.

"Stop it." I heard Sydney's voice, much stronger than when she had called my name. Then, I heard her scream. The son of a bitch must be doing the same hideous electrical shock thing to Sydney.

"I'm the one you want. Leave her alone." Another burning dose of electricity scorched my body. I trembled with pain until it ended. I could smell burning flesh—mine.

"I am the only one talking from this point. Mr. Downing, if you speak out of turn again, you'll be responsible for what happens to Ms. Sloan. Ms. Sloan, the same goes for you. Do we all understand?"

"Go to hell," I said. Sydney screamed again.

"Okay, okay that's enough," I shouted.

"That's better, Mr. Downing. Now that we have an understanding, I need you two to tell me who you shared information with about the classified file called *The Osprey's Nest.*"

"Go to hell," Sydney mumbled.

"Oh GOD!" I screamed at the top of my lungs as the voltage riddled my body again. This time he wasn't going to turn it off. He was going to fry me in this chair. My body was convulsing violently. Then it stopped. My head dropped to my chest.

"Don't kill him," Sydney shouted, using her strongest voice yet. I wanted to tell him about James Markham, but I knew if I did, he would be dead before morning. The chances were pretty good that so would we.

CHAPTER 41

The effects of the drug had dissipated and the pain had subsided enough for me to focus on my surroundings. Blood dripped from the bend in my elbows where a metal cable bound my upper torso and arms to the chair so tightly that it cut into my skin. Another cable stretched across the tops of my legs to under the chair, and yet another cable bound my legs to the chair. My watch indicated it was four-thirty. I wasn't sure how long I'd been out, but I assumed it was Thursday afternoon. I'd only been subjected to this for about nine hours. I didn't want to even think about what Sydney must have gone through for the past two and a half days.

I listened for his footsteps and tried to smell his scent. Now that I knew what I had to work with, I came up with the only plan I could think of. I was going to turn myself into an electrical conductor. If he stood close enough to me when he was frying me with the electricity and I could touch him with my head or shoulders, maybe I could get a jolt into him. If I was lucky he might not be able to let go, which could knock him out. Then maybe Sydney and I could collaborate on a way to escape. Enduring another long blast of that electricity again wasn't something I was looking forward to, but right now it was all I could come up with.

"Mr. Downing, I don't suggest that you continue trying to turn around. Ms. Sloan isn't a very pretty sight at the moment."

"Fuck you!"

"Mr. Downing, please, there's a lady present. Now, you have ten seconds to give me the name of the people with whom you and Ms. Sloan discussed *The Osprey's Nest*."

"Forget it." I responded.

"Seven seconds, Mr. Downing." He was nowhere near me. I couldn't see him, let alone try to touch him to shock him.

"Four seconds, Mr. Downing."

"Sydney and I talked about my parent's murders and the Middle East invasions, but we never discussed that stuff with anyone else," I said. The instant I had gotten those words out of my mouth, I heard Sydney scream. It was so loud and shrill that it hurt my ears. This had to stop.

"Okay, okay, that's enough, I'll tell you."

"Excellent decision, Mr. Downing. Until now, you two have only been getting half the charge of 120 volts. The full charge I just gave her is so much more exhilarating. You can tell by the intensity of the scream, don't you agree?"

"I'll give you his name, but please don't do that to me again," Sydney unexpectedly interrupted from behind me. That last charge must have been unbearable.

"Ms. Sloan, I'm surprised at you. I thought your federal hostage training would allow you to handle this better."

"James Markham," she shouted. Jesus Christ, Sydney had given up her best friend in the Bureau.

"Thank you, Ms. Sloan. Now, how about the names of the other people you spoke to about this."

"That's all. He was the only one I trusted."

"Speaking of trust, I trust you're telling the truth, Ms. Sloan."

"Why would I lie now?"

"Good point, Ms. Sloan."

"How old is this Markham fellow now?"

"Sixty-two."

"You realize he'll probably talk much sooner than you two, and if he gives me another name, I'll be very unhappy when I return."

"He's the only one," she shot back.

I sat silently in the chair, dumbfounded by what Sydney had just done. Every muscle in my body was aching from the electrical shocks, the cuts where the cable was binding me, and from pure fatigue. I heard noises like our captor was moving around, perhaps preparing to leave. In a few minutes the noises stopped. I visualized this mercenary breaking into Markham's home and slitting his throat. Even if Markham had a good security system, this guy was good enough to get in.

I still couldn't get over how easily she'd given up Markham. The way this guy has operated in the past, he'd probably kill Markham and also his wife.

I was about to call Sydney's name when I felt the cables loosening across my chest. He grabbed my right arm, yanking it behind my back. Then his hand smacked my left wrist, and he pulled that arm behind my back. The metal cable sagged into my lap, and a plastic handcuff was drawn tight around my wrists. The taut cable around my feet went slack, and he grabbed a handful of the back of my shirt, lifting me up from the chair.

"We're going for a little ride, Mr. Downing. You might be valuable to me, should I incur any problems." He prodded me toward the wall across the room, using the barrel of a pistol. The wall was about twenty-five feet away and appeared to be solid concrete block with two tarnished brass lanterns mounted about seven feet from the floor and five feet apart. Neither lantern was lit. Halfway to the wall I caught a glimpse of something to my left. The room had an L shaped angle. The ell was dark and shadowy, but I could make out the silhouette of a female sitting in a chair like the one I had just left. I desperately wanted to run to her, but doing something to make him shock Sydney again would be stupid. For that matter he could shoot her with whatever type of weapon he was shoving into my back. I had to turn my eyes away from Sydney to keep my emotions in check.

Each step was more painful than the last. My muscles had drawn tight from both the bindings and the shocks. We stopped in front of the back wall and his arm reached for the lamp above me and slightly to my right.

A voice came from the lamp, Ghazi's voice. "Yes," Ghazi said. The light was an intercom. I should have known that the wealth Saudi Arabia derives from oil sales would make this embassy one of the most high-tech facilities in DC.

"Ghazi, I need a favor. If I'm not back in one hour, I need you to turn the breaker on to electrify the floor down here."

"How long would you like it left on?"

"Leave it on until I return and tell you to turn it off." That would slowly and agonizingly fry Sydney to a crisp. This guy was a sick human being. He had all the leverage. I needed to come up with something to take it away.

He reached over my left shoulder and grabbed the other lantern. It tilted down like it was hinged on the wall. The right side of the concrete wall moved inward, screeching like chalk scraped across a blackboard. Its opening was only about ten inches, but enough for one person to squeeze through. He continued to hold me by the back of shirt, pushing me through the opening.

Once we were both clear, he snatched me to a stop, and my neck whip lashed. He must have touched or pushed something that made the wall close behind us, but he had me facing the opposite direction, so I had no idea how he made the door close. Instantly inhaling the fresh air from outside the building, I felt guilty that I was free of the stench in that dungeon and Sydney was still being held captive in there. He clung to the back of my shirt and pushed me with the gun barrel across a manicured lawn to a set of concrete steps leading down to a parking lot. A taxi passed on a side street, and I thought about hollering for help. He must have read my expression as my eyes followed the cab. "If we're not back in an hour, Ms. Sloan's beautiful body will begin bubbling. It won't take long for her soft skin to turn black and crispy. A few minutes after that her insides will explode through her burnt skin. I wouldn't do anything to prevent our timely return, Mr. Downing."

CHAPTER 42

He opened the door to a silver SUV and thrust the gun barrel deeper into my back. I refused to move so he slammed his knee into my tailbone. I bit my lip, fighting the urge to scream. Then another upward swing of his knee into my tailbone had me clawing my way into the seat. I was sure it was broken, and the pain of just sitting on the seat was nearly unbearable. The gun was a nine millimeter, and he pushed the barrel against my kneecap. If I tried to kick him right now, there was no doubt in my mind that he would blow my kneecap off. I sat as still as possible while he reached under the seat and lifted up a pair of metal handcuffs that were connected by a chain to the floor or maybe bolted to the bottom of my seat. I tried to get a look at him, but there was nothing for me to see but the top of his head. He cut the plastic cuffs and freed my hands. I glanced at my watch. It was straight up on six p.m., probably an hour before sunset.

"Remember, one hour and Ghazi turns the lovely Ms. Sloan into a French fry."

"I remember," I said, holding my hands together in front of me, allowing him to snap the cuffs on my wrists. He pulled out another pair of cuffs attached to a chain, raised my pants legs and shoved them onto my ankles, locking them in place so hard it felt like he'd cut off my circulation. Closing my door, he walked around the back of the vehicle to the driver's side. He looked towards some windows across the back of the Saudi Embassy and casually displayed a thumbs up sign.

The overhead light came on as he opened the door and slid behind the wheel, giving me my first good look at the man who had killed my parents. He was clean-shaven with sharp cheekbones and thin facial features. The haircut was close, military style. His green eyes were deep-set and beady with crow's feet sprouting out from the corners. The wrinkles were identical to those of every sniper I'd ever known who'd spent countless hours squinting down rifle sights. His military green tee shirt fit skintight on what seemed to be all muscle mass. His body was medium size, maybe a hundred and seventy pounds, but extremely fit. His thigh muscles bulged in his green camouflage trousers.

We drove out of the parking lot onto the Beltway. The directional signs indicated we were heading toward Reston. He picked up his cell phone and punched in a number. A moment later he said, "It's a wash." Then he hung up. That was bizarre. My mind raced wildly trying to make sense of an obvious covert code he'd just used.. What would it's a wash have to do with me?

We pulled into a strip mall and drove to the parking lot of a freestanding restaurant. It was a Chili's restaurant. He parked, turned, stared at me with those piercing beady eyes and said, "Mr. Downing, you do anything or say anything, and she's dead. One phone call to Ghazi and Ms. Sloan gets her name on a plaque at the FBI headquarters for dying in the line of service. If a cop car as much as slows down in front of the embassy, Ghazi will light that floor up before the Saudi ambassador can finish reading a search warrant. Do we understand each other?"

"What makes someone like you so screwed up?" I asked. He must have enjoyed being called screwed up, because it was the first time I'd seen him smile. It was an arrogant prick sort of smile.

"Do we have an understanding, Mr. Downing?"

"Yeah."

He stepped out of the car, looked back over his shoulder and squeezed his key holder, activating the horn and locking the doors, and went inside the restaurant. I followed his moves through the windows. A hostess started to escort him toward the back, but he stopped and pointed toward a table near the front. She seated him at the table he had requested, and he sat in a chair facing the window. I saw him craning his neck to look toward me.

Less than five minutes later, a long black Ford Excursion pulled into the parking lot followed by a black Ford Expedition. A gray-haired gentleman exited the Excursion, walked around and said something to the man who was driving. Next he went back and spoke to the men in the Expedition. That's when I got a good look at him. Son of a bitch! It was the director of FBI. One of the two men who had planned the conspiracies known as *Operation Freedom Flows* and *The Osprey's Nest*. This must have been a meeting place for the killer and him.

His security team got out of the Expedition, followed by the driver of the Excursion. Fisher crossed the parking lot and went inside. Two of the security men lit cigarettes and they all talked with each other while they waited for their boss. It seemed odd that none of them were observing what was going on in the restaurant, but I was. Through the window I saw the killer leave his table and go toward the back of the restaurant. The hostess seated Director Fisher at a booth along the front windows, and a waitress poured him a cup of coffee and handed him a menu.

When she was gone, Director Fisher stood and headed towards the back of the restaurant just as the killer had done. Two minutes later, Director Fisher returned to his booth. Now Fisher more than likely had James Markham's name as our accomplice. I guessed that a plan to kill Markham was in the works. The director left some money on the table and exited the restaurant.

His officers all climbed back in their vehicles, they made a left turn out of the parking lot and disappeared from sight. My guy returned to his table and chatted with the waitress. Moments later she returned with his order, placed it on the table and followed it with the check. I looked at my watch. It was six thirty-five. We only had twenty-five minutes left. This meal better not take long. Thank God, for Sydney's sake it didn't. After a few bites, he placed some money on top of the check, stood and headed to the door.

He briskly strode in my direction, opened the door and climbed back in.

"Recognize anyone, Mr. Downing?"

I didn't know what to say. He gave me an arrogant prick smile, and I badly wanted the chance to remove it. We pulled out and headed back toward the District.

"You like music, Mr. Downing?" I gave him a hatred glare, but I said nothing.

"I like music. Since you don't seem to be much of a conversationalist tonight, let's listen to the three tenors." He pushed in a CD and the powerful voices of Placido Domingo, Jose Carreras, and Luciano Pavarotti reverberated through the vehicle.

"The Tenors are very soothing don't you think?"

"It's a little loud," I said.

"Sorry." He reached toward the sound system and reduced the volume. "I find them so relaxing, I listen to them with my headphones while I'm looking through the scope of my sniper rifle."

He followed that disgusting statement with roaring laughter. All of his laughter, smiles, and comments were designed to keep me angry and off balance, and he was succeeding. Even though I knew better than to let him get under my skin, just sitting next to him infuriated me; his comments made it even worse.

"You're a sick piece of shit," I said as we turned into the embassy parking lot where we had begun this trip. He came around and unlocked my ankle bracelets, dropping the chain from the handcuffs, but leaving them on my wrists. I slid my feet over to step out and he yanked me to the ground. He picked me up by my shirt collar again and I felt the gun barrel return to the small of my back. I took a few steps and he yanked back violently on my collar. I stumbled to the ground. "Better hurry, Mr. Downing, time is running out." I scrambled to my feet and continued towards the building. He turned me around to face away from the entrance while he opened the doorway, making sure I had no idea how to get inside. As it screeched open I checked my watch. The time was five minutes before seven; too close for me to the hour he'd instructed Ghazi to electrocute Sydney. She should still be alive, but there was no way to trust the word of a guy like this.

He prodded me back into the basement, calling to Sydney, "Ms. Sloan, we're back." Nothing. Not a sound. My heart raced wildly. This time I was grateful to receive the same old disgusting smell. That meant that it hadn't been replaced by the odor of burning flesh. I struggled to see through the darkness in the direction of the ell where she had been, but she wasn't there. Surely those Saudi Arabian thugs hadn't electrocuted her. I couldn't wait any longer.

"Sydney!" I shouted.

"Scott," she responded. Her voice actually sounded stronger than before we had left her.

"You seem nervous about Ms. Sloan's welfare, Mr. Downing."

"You've got me. I'm the one you want. Be a man of your word and let her go."

His laughter roared through the basement. "Mr. Downing, how could such a well-educated man make such a ridiculous statement. I don't just have you, I have both of you, and soon I'll have Mr. Markham too." He continued shoving me towards the metal chair in the center of the room. He put his hand on my shoulder and pushed downward hard until I landed in the chair.

"Ms. Sloan, Director Fisher was very disappointed to hear that you shared the details of *The Osprey's Nest* and *The Burning Post* with Mr. Downing."

"Do you understand what *Operation Freedom Flows* was all about?" I asked.

"I'm not a politician, Mr. Downing."

"You don't even know what led to the order for you to kill my parents, do you?"

"I was briefed, but the specific details of what happened before my assignment weren't really of a concern to me. *The Osprey* and *The Post* were the only missions I was concerned with," he said.

"That's what I thought. *Operation Freedom Flows* was a conspiracy conceived by the Secretary of Defense and the director of the FBI to invade several Middle Eastern countries and take over their oil production."

"Like you and Ms. Sloan, I get paid to do my work, not to evaluate the politics behind it. As long as I'm compensated nicely for my efforts, I couldn't care less what the motives are behind the orders."

"You were a soldier once, weren't you?"

"What's that got to do with anything?"

"Young men and women are being killed every day in Iraq and Afghanistan. Blown up by car bombs and RPGs. You killed my father before he could stop the invasions into Iraq. As far as I'm concerned, you're responsible for the death of every American soldier in the Middle East, you piece of shit."

"I'm a silencer, Mr. Downing. That's what I do, okay? I stop people from talking, and I don't get involved with the politics. Do you understand?" On the outside he looked nonchalant, cool and collected. But mentioning the soldiers dying must have gotten through to him. His voice quivered now with each response. He was circling my chair, securing the cables. He leaned close and I watched as his eyes narrowed; he squinted as he stared back at me.

I tried to keep a conversation going that might give him more reason to have second thoughts. "Director Fisher lied to the President of the United States; what makes you think he didn't lie to you?"

"It's time to put an end to this political bantering, Mr. Downing, and time for you and Ms. Sloan to tell me everyone you talked to about *Freedom Flows* or *The Osprey's Nest*."

"You sound a little testy there, DMT. Let's see, the President and I had a chat the other day. Come to think of it, he might know about both of those plans. Hey, maybe you could get another job out of this," I said. "You wouldn't kill the President of the United States, would you?"

"It's never the person, Mr. Downing. I weigh the percentage of being successful without getting caught against the money offered for the job. If I like my odds and the money's right, I take the assignment. It doesn't matter who the target is."

"You are one helluva loyal American." I thought I might have gotten him distracted enough with the conversation that he would forget to lock one of the cables around me. "The President wanted any kind of victory after 9-11 and after Osama Bin Laden slipped through his fingers in Afghanistan. That's why Fisher and Runnels had such an easy time convincing the President to invade Iraq. He thought it'd be over in a flash like Desert Storm. Now the blood of thousands upon thousands of dead and wounded soldiers from units just like the one you served in is on your hands."

"I'm not a politician, those aren't my problems."

"All of this mess is your problem. But if you think Director Fisher wouldn't have you killed because of what you know, you'd better think again," I said.

"I'm quite comfortable with Director Fisher. He's my American boss. I answer directly to him when I work for the US government, and he needs my services quite often. And now I need to put your seat belts back on so you don't fall out of your seat, Mr Downing."

I couldn't wait any longer to take some kind of action. When I caught him bending over and focusing on the cables, I gripped my hands, cuffs and all, and swung them toward his face with all the energy I had. The blow missed his head and glanced off his shoulder as he ducked the punch.

He kicked me in the groin, and I reached for my crotch and doubled over onto the floor in excruciating pain. I raised my head in time to see the black waffle pattern of the bottom of his boot surging toward my face.

"Stop it!" I heard Sydney holler as the back of my head slammed into the floor. The warm moisture running into my mouth was my own blood. I took my cuffed hands and brushed the backs of them across my face.

"You're a disgusting gutless bastard," I said, trying to get back up but wobbling badly.

"Ms. Sloan, I understand you're a very good friend of James Markham."

"I worked for him once," she said.

"Let's hope Mr. Markham still considers you a friend."

"What do you mean by that?" Sydney asked. The darkness of the room made it difficult to see her, but I noticed her voice had cracked as she spoke. She must have been dying inside.

He lifted me off the floor and body slammed me into the chair. I bit my lip as I hit the chair and blood spurted out of my mouth. I rolled back onto the floor, so he reached down, grabbed me by the hair of my head and held me up. I scrambled to my feet and clawed my way back into the chair. I sat motionless, my head throbbing, while he finished securing the cables around me.

"Ms. Sloan, I'm going to give you a chance to convince James Markham to come here alone and join us. If you can't convince him to do as I say, I'm going to kill Mr. Downing right before your very eyes."

"You're going to kill us all anyway, you asshole," I said, slurring the words so badly that I wasn't sure if either of them understood me.

"Watching someone you care about die a gruesomely painful, slow death is not the way anyone wants to spend your last moments on this earth," he said, pointing to an empty chair off to my right. Ghazi must have added the chair while we were gone.

He really wanted to wrap all this up neatly. Once he had Sydney, Markham and me together, he could use torture to learn the names of everyone who we might have talked to about *Operation Freedom Flows*, *The Osprey's Nest* or *The Burning Post*. That would mean the tech person at the Bureau who recovered the files for Markham, Ms. Collins, and perhaps even the woman at the Mailbox store. His need to know thier names was the only thing that had kept Sydney and I alive.

"Now, Ms. Sloan, I need you to call James Markham and invite him to join us."

"I gave you his name. Isn't that enough?"

"Enough is when Mr. Markham has taken his place of honor in that empty chair, Ms. Sloan." I heard Sydney crying.

"There's no need to be upset, Ms. Sloan. Remember you've already given me his name."

"I gave you his name because I knew that outside of here you weren't good enough to take him. In here you have an unfair advantage."

"That's the way I like to work, Ms. Sloan."

"I won't do it. I can't!" Sydney yelled.

He stepped closer to the wall and reached for a box about the size of his hand that was attached to a black cord extending up into the ceiling. Fire and sparks flew from the bottom of my chair.

"My God!" I shouted squeezing my hands together as tight as I could.

"Stop!" she cried.

"Are you ready to call your friend, Ms. Sloan?"

"Can't you just—" He hit the button on the box again.

I tried not to scream, but I couldn't contain it.

"Okay, I'll call, I'll call, just put that thing down," Sydney begged.

He released the button. I smelled my flesh burning. Tears mixed with sweat streamed down my face.

"You give me the number, and I'll punch it in for you. Then I'll put it on speaker phone and hold it up where you can chat with Mr. Markham. Is that understood, Ms. Sloan?"

"Understood."

"Now, the number, Ms. Sloan."

Sydney was crying louder now, and her voice quivered between each number she called out.

"Ms. Sloan, let Mr. Markham know that I'll be cutting off a finger, or a nose or an ear with each thirty minutes that passes following your conversation, and if he brings the cavalry, or even notifies them, I'll fry you both."

CHAPTER 43

I heard James Markham answer in his usual gruff voice, "Markham."

"Mark, Scott and I are in the basement of the Saudi Embassy. The shooter wants you to join us."

"Sydney, are you okay?"

"He says he'll cut off a body part every thirty minutes you don't show up."

"I'll be there," Markham said.

"Mark, you can't notify the Bureau or the local police."

"I wouldn't think of it. I'm on the way. How do I get in?"

"I'm sure they're going to roll out the red carpet for you."

I heard the phone flip closed. The call was disconnected. The killer stepped next to me. It looked like he was checking his watch. If he was marking time, this bastard wasn't kidding about cutting off a body part every thirty minutes.

I was sure Markham would arrange for some type of backup, but Director Fisher would probably be informed the minute that happened. Fisher would probably make up some diplomatic lie and see to it that Markham's backup never arrived.

"James Markham is a good law enforcement officer. He won't let you, or the director, or the Secretary of Defense get away with any more killing," I said.

"I look forward to meeting him," he said as he disappeared behind me. I kept turning my head from one side to the other, trying to locate him out of the corners of my eyes. I couldn't see him, but I heard him whispering into his cell phone. I heard him call Ghazi's name, and he mentioned Markham's name several times before hanging up.

"Mr. Downing, Ms. Sloan, I want you to know I thoroughly enjoy your company, but I have a date with Mrs. Markham. Ghazi will entertain Agent Markham until I get back, and then we'll all be together."

"You bastard! Markham doesn't talk to his wife about work," Sydney yelled.

"Ms. Sloan, I think we've already established that I don't take chances. I have no choice but to drop by Mr. Markham's house while he's on they way here to rescue you and Mr. Downing. But I promise Agent Markham's wife's death will be quick and painless." His voice sounded like it came from around the back wall. When the dialogue with Sydney ended, I heard the screeching sound of the secret door again.

The activity behind me gave way to a loud commotion in front of me. Ghazi and two men entered the room in front of me, coming around the partial wall where I thought the elevator-fireplace might have been. They were rolling three large wooden boxes towards me. The men made no eye contact and didn't say a word. I wondered how many people they'd seen tied up in this basement. They seemed very matter-of-fact. Once they had dropped off the boxes, they disappeared on the other side of the wall.

There was something stenciled diagonally across the crates: I craned my neck, attempting to read the words. Embassy furniture—fragile. I had listened as they banged and bumped the big wooden boxes when they rolled them into the room. The sound was hollow. I was certain there was no embassy furniture in them, and there was no furniture in this basement that anyone was planning on shipping. The crates were for us. I was looking at our caskets.

CHAPTER 44

Sydney's attempt to muffle her crying now sounded as if she was struggling. She might have finally come unglued, and with good reason for all she'd been through. Loud clanging sounds followed her vocal noises.

"Sydney, are you alright?" She didn't answer right away, and I heard footsteps.

"I'm better now, how are you doing?" Sydney asked, almost whispering into my ear. I could feel her breath on my neck. What the hell? She squatted next to me, tugging on the cables wrapped around my chair.

"Sydney, how in the world did you—" I was so astounded I couldn't finish my question.

"All this jerk gave me for three days was a few sips of water. Maybe the diet he put me on caused me to lose enough weight to wiggle out of that cable. Whatever it was, it feels pretty damn good to be standing. One thing's for sure, I don't have the strength to rip these cables off this chair." She stood, massaged her thighs, and stretched.

"I heard you crying and I thought—"

This time she cut me off and whispered again. "As good as it feels to be out of that contraption, it hurt like hell getting out."

"Sydney, why are you whispering?"

"I'm not sure that his friend Ghazi isn't listening in down here."

"That's a comforting thought," I replied. "Let me tell you how to get out of that door back there."

"Save your breath, Scott. I'm not going out that door without you."

"Sydney, that's going to be a little hard for me to do from this chair." She got down on one knee, followed the cables with her hands, crawling around my chair and ending up behind me.

"My cable was twisted around me and the chair," Sydney said. "He's got some kind of huge lock on the back of your chair where all the cables come together. Maybe I can find something to pry it off." Before she stood up, she frantically tugged once more at the cables, but they didn't budge. "If I had my Glock I'd get you out of there in second."

"Sydney, why don't you pull the wires up that are attached to the legs of this chair? That way if Ghazi decides to light the floor up, I won't get fried."

She stepped around in front of me and ripped the electrical wires away from the chair legs.

"That was a good idea. Now I wish you'd come up with some kind of brainstorm to remove that damn lock from the cables."

"I've got one if you're up to it."

"Hurry, Scott, I'm worried. He's coming back."

"When he brought you down here, did you see a cache of weapons on the other side of that wall in front of me?"

"Scott. I woke up in that chair. That's all I remember."

"I need you to take a look on the other side of that wall, and I hope to God I'm right."

Sydney reached the corner of the wall and peered around it. Then she disappeared from sight.

CHAPTER 45

If the weapons were still there, Sydney wouldn't need any further instruction.

The sound of wood cracking and splintering was non-stop. Sydney groaned out loud followed by more cracking and splintering. I wanted to holler to ask what her plans were, but I refrained, in case Ghazi was listening in.

"Holy Jesus!" Sydney exclaimed loud enough for me to hear. "Where in the world did all this come from?"

"Just bring back something to shoot this damn lock off before that idiot comes back."

She returned carrying an M16A3 rifle, slapping the ammunition magazine into place.

"Have you ever fired one of those?" I asked. I couldn't see her facial expression that well, but there was enough light for me to know I'd asked a stupid question by the way she planted her free hand on her hip.

"How are you going to do this without killing me?"

"You just sit still. This is what I do for a living, remember?"

"I hope you don't have to do this that often," I quipped.

"Only with my closest partners." Sydney was facing me holding the stock of the gun with her right hand and the barrel in her left. She stood straddling me, with one leg on each side of my body.

"If I did this from behind the only angle I could get would probably nick you."

"For Christ sakes, not with that damn thing."

She held the rifle over my shoulder and pushed her breasts into my face, sitting in my lap for better balance.

She clamped her arms against my ears and said, "This isn't a lap dance. It's the only way I can keep from destroying your eardrums." She fired into the lock. The sound was tremendously loud, but nothing like it would have been had she hadn't thought to protect me. The cables dropped to the floor, she withdrew the gun from over my head and stepped back. I fell onto the floor. The circulation had been cut off to my arms and legs. I flexed my hands to get the blood to flowing again and pushed myself up off the floor. I was wobbly, but I was moving. That was all that mattered.

I pointed to the wall that was really a door. "There, Sydney, let's hurry." We staggered toward the wall and I told her, "We should try to get to a phone and call Markham's house, if we're not already too late."

"Scott, when Mark learned the details of what we were involved in, he sent his wife to her sister's house in Chicago."

"Why didn't you tell me that?"

"I didn't think it was relevant to anything you were doing. Scott, how the hell do we get out of here?" I yanked the light fixture on the left, and the wall screeched open. Sydney went through first. I heard footsteps running and men speaking in Arabic. The sounds grew louder as I forced my body through behind her. Our legs were wobbly and we had trouble getting traction running across the slippery dew-covered back lawn of the embassy. I ran like I was trying to zigzag and after about thirty yards I fell flat on my face. Sydney used the rifle as brace to support both of us as she helped me up. Before we took off running again, I glanced back and saw Ghazi and the uniformed security guards coming through the door. I had my arm around Sydney's shoulders and she held on to my waist. We must have looked like we were in a three-legged sack race. The guards were twenty paces behind us when we reached New Hampshire Avenue. We were off their property. Ghazi shouted something in Arabic, and the guards stopped in their tracks before slowly retreating. I looked at Sydney. She was still clutching the M16A3. There was no way to conceal a semi automatic rifle, but I was okay with that, because it increased our chances of drawing the attention of law enforcement.

I gestured in the direction of the Watergate. Sydney looked at the hotel then back towards the embassy. "Oh my God," she shouted. I turned to see what had startled her. There was no movement that I could see. A black Ford Crown Victoria was sitting next to the curb in front of the embassy. Sydney planted her feet so abruptly, we both tumbled onto the asphalt.

"That's Mark," she said.

"Sydney, we have to keep moving."

She stood her ground, refusing to budge.

"That's his car, Scott. I'm going back after him. We can't leave him there."

"Sydney, give me the gun, you go to the Watergate and call for help. I'll go back in."

"No, Scott. You're not going without me."

"Sydney, we have to do it this way. This guy wants all three of us in the embassy. We can't let him have that. Think about it. What does good law enforcement logic tell you to do in this situation?"

"Call for backup, but, Scott—" I put a hand up and stopped her.

"You've been in there for three days without food. You go to the Watergate and call for backup. Besides, this isn't a 9-1-1 call, and you know the right numbers, I don't."

"Crap, I don't even have any money for a pay phone," Sydney exclaimed.

I patted my pockets. "Neither do I, Sydney. The Saudis have all of my cash and my credit cards in my wallet along with my ID."

"Me too," Sydney replied. Her thoughts were on another subject, but she paused a moment before she spoke. "Scott, asking me to go to the hotel and make the call isn't about you're a male and I'm a female is it?"

"You know me better than that. Sydney, you're very weak right now. Please, let's do it this way."

"Promise me you'll get him out of there."

"I will, Sydney. I promise. Now, you go get some help on the way." She tried to run, but it was more like a painful, brisk hobble. I was seventy-five yards west of the embassy moving back towards the side of the building. There was no traffic in front of or behind the embassy. I looked on both sides to see if I could spot any backup. A helicopter roared overhead about two miles south of me, but it had call letters of a local radio or television station painted on it, and it moved farther south away from us. If Markham had called for backup, it hadn't arrived.

Doing this by the book meant that I should wait outside until the backup that Sydney had called for arrived. Sometimes you have to deviate from the book. This was one of those times.

I crawled along the backside of the embassy, staying below the view of any of the rear windows. When I got to the open wall door, I slowly leaned my head in the gap to have a look inside. There was still no movement. I held the rifle in front of me, letting it lead my entry, looking down the barrel as I searched for Ghazi, his men or Markham.

The chairs were gone. What could have happened to the chairs in that brief amount of time? They'd been bolted to the floor. The crates were gone, too. They had removed everything. Markham must have shown up at the front door, leaving the Saudis scrambling, assuming the entire FBI staff would be coming after him. Holy shit. There was a solid wall where the fireplace/elevator had been. This was like the medieval castles that winched up their drawbridges during an attack, leaving a giant moat circling their fortress. I pivoted on my right foot three hundred and sixty degrees. There was nothing there but algae-covered concrete walls, and a single light bulb dangling from a rafter on a black cord—nothing else. I stepped to the corner of the partial wall and peeked around it. The massive amount of weapons that had been stacked on the other side of the wall was gone. How could they have removed all that stuff? This was like the Twilight Zone. With no elevator and no stairs, there was no way to access the upstairs from this basement.

I backed around the wall, all the way across the room and out the door. Once I was outside, I ran around to the front of the building. Markham's car was gone. My hope was that he was in it. Four DC Metro police cars pulled to the curb. Hopefully as a result of Sydney's call for assistance. When the officers saw me they leaped out, training their weapons on me. I dropped the rifle and shouted back that I was a law enforcement officer. They wouldn't let me speak. I'd been in that situation in Alexandria just a couple of nights ago.

"Lie down on the ground! Face down! Now!" the cop shouted. I complied and waited for them to approach me. I put my arms behind my back, and one of the officers cuffed me. I raised my head and saw one African American and one white police officer; each clutching their pistols with both hands and aiming at my head. The third officer was the one who had cuffed me. Two more patrol cars swerved to a stop next to the others. The newly arrived officers got out and ran in our direction. "Is that him?" one of the officers asked.

"It's him," the cop who had just cuffed me answered.

"Is that the weapon?" Another of the officers asked.

The officer who had me in custody picked up the rifle and smelled the edge of the barrel. "It's been fired recently. My guess would be this is the gun that was fired in the Saudi embassy basement, and this would be the burglar who fired it."

Burglar. What the hell was this about? I'd been set up, but I wasn't sure whether Sydney, Markham or the Saudis had done it. Markham's car was removed, there were no electrified chairs or weapons in the basement, and I had no ID. This did not look good.

"I'm a lieutenant with the Bay County Sheriff's Department and I—"

"Got any ID?" one of them asked.

"The Saudis took my weapon and ID."

"Oh so it wasn't a burglary. It was a robbery. The Saudis must have lured this man in their building to get his badge and his gun," another of the cops spoke like he was doing comedy at the Improv. He got a huge laugh out of everyone there but me.

I was being crammed into the back of a black and white squad car with no ID, no Sydney or Markham to vouch for me, and I had no idea if either one of them was safe.

"Officer, I'm a lieutenant and the chief homicide investigator with the Bay County Sheriff's Department in Panama City, Florida."

"Uh huh." There was no use wasting my breath on this guy. I'd have to talk to his superiors when I got to booking.

After several minutes, I decided to throw out another name to see if he'd recognize it. " I've been up here working with FBI Agent Sydney Sloan who is waiting for me at the Watergate Hotel."

This time he did respond. "She and G. Gordon Liddy over there going over what went wrong?" My head and shoulders drooped simultaneously in frustration at his comment. "Booking and interrogation should take about three hours. Then you can join them at the Watergate."

"Does it matter to you guys that I'm a cop?"

"Gordon Liddy was FBI. You got any idea how many cops we arrest every year? I'm sorry to say, including some of our own."

"Well can you at least check with your watch or shift commander and see if FBI Agent Sloan called in for backup support at the Saudi embassy?" I asked. He called a supervisor on his radio and asked if an FBI agent had called for assistance at the Saudi embassy.

"Negative. The only call we got was from the Saudi Embassy staff saying some guy had fired a rifle in their basement."

Ghazi and his men were good. They knew we had one of their rifles and would be back with law enforcement, so they turned the entire embassy inside out in a matter of minutes. They also knew I had no way of convincing any police officer who might have interceded in our skirmish on their property, because they had taken my credentials and weapon. When they called in and told the Metro police that someone had fired a rifle in their basement, I was toast.

I wasn't worried about my predicament, but I had no idea how bad it might be for Sydney and Markham. If they were in trouble, a long ride and booking process would make their chances of surviving that much worse.

CHAPTER 46

When we arrived at the Metropolitan Police Headquarters at 300 Indiana Avenue, I saw the sign identifying this as the Henry J. Daly building. Daly had been a homicide investigator like me, and he was gunned down and fatally wounded by a maniac who stormed into the DC police headquarters in 1994. Recalling that incident reinforced why cops up here didn't trust anyone, including someone with a rifle who claimed to be a police officer.

A muscular black officer took me into the building, leading me to the booking room. An older cop wearing captain's bars intercepted us just inside the door. They stepped away from me out of hearing distance, turned their backs to me and talked. After a brief conversation they turned to face me, and the captain asked the arresting officer to uncuff me. As he turned the key releasing my wrists from the cuffs, he gritted his teeth and backed away. Then he stormed out the door. I knew I didn't want this guy to catch me on the Beltway going one mile per hour over the limit. A dignified silver-haired man introduced himself as the deputy chief and ushered me into his office, closing the door behind me.

He walked past me and sat behind his huge desk, gesturing to a chair.

"Mr. Downing, please have a seat." His tone didn't have the ring of a one-cop-to-another conversation.

"Let me get right to the point. I understand why you had to come to DC."

"You do?" I asked. Surely no one would have told this guy the whole story.

"Mr. Downing, it's lieutenant, isn't it?"

"Yes it is."

"Very well then, Lieutenant Downing, I can appreciate your need for some answers, but you have no jurisdiction here. Fortunately for you, Director Fisher of the FBI called and told us about you." Oh my God, there was nothing fortunate about that. That bastard was on top of every move we'd made.

"He told me you were here investigating the murder of your parents, but he couldn't share any more details. Fisher is a good man; he asked me to look out for you until he could meet with you personally." Good man my ass. He was a lowlife traitor and I sure as hell didn't want to meet him without a weapon.

"Are you charging me with anything?"

"No, Lieutenant. You're one of us," he said, giving me a wink. "I believe Director Fisher placed a call to the Saudi Arabian ambassador, and they won't be pressing any charges."

My God, I had forgotten to check on Sydney.

"Where's Sydney?"

"I'm sorry. I'm afraid I'm at a loss."

"FBI Agent Sydney Sloan and I were being held captive in the Saudi Arabian Embassy by the person who killed my parents."

"I'll check with the director about Agent Sloan's condition."

"What about Markham?"

"You mean James Markham?"

"Yes, sir. He went into the Saudi embassy when Sydney and I escaped out the back, but we never saw him come out."

"I'll have the director look into that, but currently, I have no knowledge of Agent Markham's whereabouts either."

"I'd like to go back to the embassy and look for James Markham. There's a good possibility his life is in danger."

"As I said earlier, you have no jurisdiction here, Mr. Downing. Additionally, you're not authorized to carry a weapon in the District, and finally, the Saudis have diplomatic immunity on that property. If it weren't for Director Fisher, the Saudis would more than likely be pressing charges, and we'd be taking you before a judge for arraignment sometime during the next hour."

"I'll try to remember to thank Director Fisher when I see him. By the way, Deputy Chief, the Saudis have my weapon, my wallet, and the man who killed my parents isn't just visiting the embassy, the Saudis are knowingly harboring him."

"Lieutenant, are you saying someone in the Saudi Arabian Embassy admitted to killing your parents?"

I had come too close to giving this guy more information than he needed so I cut off the conversation. "Sir, I shouldn't have said anything. That information is for the FBI or the CIA to deal with."

"That's good because these diplomatic situations are very often beyond our authority. The type of accusation you're making belongs in the purview of the State Department."

"Sure," I replied curtly. This cop was a lifelong bureaucratic talking head with a badge and a uniform. He may have been a cop at one time, but that part of him had apparently dissipated over the years. Now he was a member of the establishment, and since he looked somewhat close to retirement, he didn't want to color outside of the lines.

"If you could give me a lift to Agent Sloan's townhouse in Alexandria, I could pick up my belongings." There was no way I could tell this guy that Sydney had a closet full of weapons and a vehicle that I could use, not to mention a place to stay.

"I can get you transportation to pick up your things, but Director Fisher asked me to find you a place to stay until he could speak with you personally."

"Deputy Chief, if you don't mind, I'd like to speak with Agent Sloan face to face before I share my information with Director Fisher."

"I suppose it doesn't matter whether Fisher meets you here or at Agent Sloan's home. I like you attitude, by the way. A good cop always wants to get his story straight," he said, patting me on the shoulder.

Hopefully that line of bull crap I'd just fed him would keep him from calling Fisher right away.

"You've been a big help, Deputy Chief, and I apologize for causing you and your department any problems."

"No problem at all. I'll get one of my officers to give you a ride to Agent Sloan's. Do you know the way?"

"Yes, sir, I do." I sat in a chair outside of his office, and within five minutes, a female officer introduced herself to me and informed me that she had been asked to provide transportation to wherever I needed to go.

I could tell the female cop wasn't sure about me. She was very cold in her responses to questions, like how long had she been a cop and did she have any desire to move up to investigations. Her answers were curt. It was clear that she had been told to deliver me to the apartment but not to participate in any type of dialogue. The minute I stepped out of her patrol car, she drove back toward the District without as much as a goodbye or good luck.

The apartment felt like a deserted island. There were no lights on, and no noise coming from TVs, radios, stereos, dishwashers, and most of all, from the owner of the apartment. I felt dejected and defeated. The only friends I had in this town were either dead or missing, and there was no one locally in law enforcement who I could confide in. I went to the linen closet and looked over Sydney's weapons. I chose a Smith and Wesson .357 magnum. I grabbed some ammunition, loaded the gun and put a handful of extra bullets in my pocket. I walked to the kitchen and pushed the voicemail button on her phone. There had been one call, but the caller hung up without leaving a message.

The Saudis not only had my gun and my ID, they also had all of my cash and credit cards. The first thing I had to do was call my hometown bank and arrange for a wire transfer to one of their branches in Virginia. I carried Sydney's phone over to the couch and picked up my day timer from the coffee table. Richard Neves was my banker, and he offered to call their credit card division and have a Visa and Master Card overnighted to Sydney's address as well. If nothing else, it helped to have someone recognize me.

Next, I called my partner Robert Ramer and promised to brief him on everything when I got home if he promised to Federal Express me a badge and my photo ID credentials. I kept a spare in my desk drawer. I gave him Sydney's address for the FedEx shipment. He asked me if I expected to make it home over the weekend. I wasn't sure what day it was, so I asked him.

"TGIF, partner, and payday. It's Friday, April sixteenth, two thousand and four in the year of our Lord," he replied.

"I just asked for the day, Robert, not an introduction to a court hearing." Sydney was abducted Tuesday morning a little after midnight. We escaped Thursday night, and now it was Friday. Keeping track of time through all of this was maddening.

He asked if I needed him to fly up to help, or if there was anything else he could do. I assured him that sending my badge and ID was a huge help. He gave me the classic line from one of the old TV cop shows, "Let's be careful out there." He wouldn't be joking around if I told him what had transpired over the past seventy-two hours. In fact he'd probably go ballistic over the phone. This wasn't the time for that.

I flipped through to Sydney's numbers, including the number of the phone I'd recently given her. I ruled out her old work number and tried the other two, not really expecting an answer. My expectations proved correct. There was also the possibility of a TV news story being aired about a shooting or an arrest at the Saudi embassy, so I picked up the remote for the TV and flipped it on. Finding Sydney and Markham was preying on my mind, but without my ID, credit cards, or cash, there was nothing I could do now but wait, and waiting was agony.

CHAPTER 47

Cars were coming and going through the parking lot just outside Sydney's window all morning. Every time I heard engine noise or gravel crunching under tires, I dashed over to take a look. Where could she be, and why hadn't she called? I was sitting on the sofa channel surfing when a car parked in Sydney's space directly in front of her front door. I raced over to the door, flung it open, startling a short plump Hispanic woman who was carrying cleaning supplies in a bucket in one hand and a vacuum in the other. Her bucket slipped from her grasp, crashing to the sidewalk, bottles and rags bounced out. She scrambled to pick up her things and I bent over to help.

We placed her things back in her bucket, she reached for the handle of her vacuum, and said, "Gracias, senor."

"De nada," I said. She turned and gave me a big smile before walking away. "Adios," I said as she knocked on a door two apartments over. The door opened, and she paused before going in and flashed me her warm smile again. I was glad to have helped her. After all, that's what my job is all about, helping people. That was the driving force that got me out of bed in the mornings, but today the person I wanted to help the most was no where to be found.

I returned to the sofa and tried to take a nap. I had been tossing and turning for about thirty minutes when I stretched my right arm over the end table, knocking something off. I leaned over to pick up whatever it was. The item on the floor was a framed eight-by-ten color photo of Sydney standing with a couple I presumed was her mom and dad at her college graduation. Her smile was infectious. I lay back down embracing the photograph like she was actually there in my arms.

This situation had turned out to be a total disaster. After all that Sydney and I had been through together, including being held hostage by a professional killer, we were almost back to where it all began with me trying to locate her.

Her home phone was standing in a charger on the kitchen counter, and I couldn't take my eyes off it. It felt like the phone was calling for me to come over and pick it up, so I did. Pulling out a barstool, I picked up the phone, trying all of Sydney's numbers again. No answer. I had no choice but to go back to the area of the Watergate and the Saudi Embassy to see what I could uncover. I showered, changed, grabbed the keys to the Nissan and headed toward the embassy. There was no way I could wait until tomorrow for my ID to arrive. I had no driver's license, no money, and no credit cards, but I had to go back and look for Sydney and Markham. At least I was armed again, and Sydney's extra cell phone was still on the foyer table, so I put it in my pocket.

It was midday on a Friday, as good a time as any to return to the scene of the crime. After all, it was the best starting point I had. I drove up and down New Hampshire Avenue between the Watergate Hotel and the Saudi Embassy. I thought Markham's car might have reappeared, but it hadn't. I drove to the Kennedy Center, but I remembered I didn't have money for the paid lot, so I parallel parked in an available space on the street. This time I was traveling up the same street on foot, checking behind buildings and places that I couldn't see very well from the car. Finally I reached the embassy. I walked around back to the parking lot. The silver-colored SUV the killer drove was gone. Markham's black Crown Victoria was nowhere to be seen either. The Saudis probably had the ability to drive the car into the embassy, disassemble it and ship it to Saudi Arabia without any questions asked.

I recalled what it was like in that metal chair with the electrical current running through it, and prayed that Markham wasn't in there having to endure that. At his age, it would probably kill him right away.

Walking in the alley parallel to the embassy back lot, I heard a vehicle coming at me from behind. A white block wall divided the Saudi parking lot from the alley I was in, so I stepped over and stood as close as I could to the wall to let the car pass. The car veered over almost touching the wall with its front bumper, coming right at me, and it wasn't slowing down. I looked up, but the wall was too tall to try to jump over. I turned and faced the vehicle, preparing to dive across the hood when it reached me. The sun was bouncing off the windshield, creating a fierce glare, preventing me from making out what kind of car it was or who was behind the wheel. I put all my weight on my right foot, preparing to push off and dive to my left. The car slammed to a stop about three feet away from me.

A voice muffled by the racing sound of the engine shouted, "Get in!" I thought about running, but I wasn't sure which direction would get me to safety quickest. Then I heard the voice again. "Scott, dammit, get in!"

Sydney stuck her head out the window of the driver's side of the car. "Now, Scott! I was too astounded to move right away. Finally I shuffled over and reached for the door, but the car was so close to the wall, I could only open it about three inches. She pulled up and over enough to let me get inside. I was filled with mixed emotions. I was thrilled to see her alive and well, but pissed off she hadn't called me.

"Where the hell have you been, and why didn't you call me?" I fired at her.

"Let me get out of here first," she responded, turning north on New Hampshire to the Capital Beltway.

"Sydney, are you not talking? What the hell is going on? I was worried sick. Did you ever make it to the Watergate?" She turned at the next intersection and we were headed west to Two Seventy.

"No. I started running that way, but when I'd gotten about half way there, I decided to come back to the embassy. I couldn't stand the fact that Markham was in there, and you were going back in alone."

"So you never called for backup?

"No."

"Sydney, when I went back inside everything was gone. The metal chairs, the crates, the room filled with weapons, everything that had been there before was gone, so I headed out on foot toward the front of the building. That's when several Metro Police cruisers converged on me. I laid down the rifle, and they took me to jail."

"I know. I saw the whole thing."

"Christ, Sydney, why'd you let them take me to jail?"

"I didn't have any more ID than you did, so those local guys had no reason to believe me either. As long as we were separated, and one of us was on the loose, the killer still had something to worry about. I found some change in Mark's car, stopped at a pay phone, called Bureau switchboard, and asked them to patch me through to Metro Police Headquarters. I got the deputy chief on the phone, and told him I was calling for Director Fisher and that one of his Metro officers had you picked you up on the lawn of the Saudi Arabian Embassy. I told him who you were and to make sure you had a ride, preferably to the airport, but anywhere away from the Saudi Embassy." I began to have a deeper appreciation for how good she really was.

"So, that's how I got out of there so fast?" Telling him that Director Fisher wanted to talk to me was a bit unnerving. You could have left that part out."

"I thought it added a little believability."

"Yeah, it did, for me anyway. Is this Markham's car?"

"Yeah."

"And Markham?"

"He's still in there, Scott."

"Shit! Why the hell didn't you answer your phone?"

"I was determined to stake out the embassy in case they decided to move Mark. The Saudis have the finest high-tech listening equipment in the world. I couldn't risk talking to you, and I couldn't run home to pick you up because I was afraid to break off my surveillance of the building."

"What made you give up on watching the embassy?"

"You did."

"I did?"

"Scott, if he hasn't moved him by now, I'm guessing that he's not going to. Fisher has probably already updated him on as much as he could. The next move would be a call to my cell phone or my house. My guess would be the house phone."

"What about the Bureau? Anybody else there that can help us?" I asked.

"No. Markham was it."

"We headed back to your place?"

"Yep. Scott, I'm worried about Mark."

"Do you think he's alive?"

"I think he has to keep him alive in order to lure us to him. He knows we'll come after Mark," Sydney answered confidently. James Markham may have been alive at the moment, but there was no doubt that the killer had plans to eliminate Markham along with Sydney and me.

We arrived back at the townhouse. Sydney went straight to her bedroom, so I followed her.

"Scott, I can't take much more of this. I thought I was a strong person, but I'm totally worn to a frazzle." I lay next to her on the bed and gently rubbed her back.

"It'll be okay. When he calls, we'll get Mark back, I promise."

She embraced me tightly. We looked deep in each other's eyes. I saw a kindred soul that was unlike any other woman I'd ever met. My lips met hers and we kissed, and then she whispered in my ear, "Make love to me, Scott." Making love wasn't something either of us took lightly, especially since we were working together. But deep down I had this fear that if not now, maybe never. I wasn't sure if the next hour or the next day would bring about the death of one or both of us. I felt sure Sydney must have been thinking the same thoughts.

We undressed, and I admired her flawless body. We slid under the sheets from opposite sides of the bed without a word. I held her tightly in my arms as our naked bodies touched. Looking deeply into her eyes, still without words, our lips came together in a kiss that seemed to last for an hour. Then we made love like there was no tomorrow—I hoped that wouldn't be true.

CHAPTER 49

It was one thirty Saturday morning. I'd fallen in and out of sleep from exhaustion, so had Sydney. The phone still hadn't rung. I stared at the ceiling, then at Sydney, then back at the ceiling again. I was filled with that feeling you get when you realize you've finally discovered that special person you thought would never come into your life. She had tossed and turned more than me, no doubt worrying about James Markham. I wondered if the Saudis might feel a little uncomfortable knowing that the killer was holding a high-ranking FBI agent in their embassy. On the other hand, if the Saudis had the ability to make hundreds of pounds of weapons and ammunition disappear in a matter of minutes, making a person vanish would present little to no challenge for them. Fatigue kicked in again and I dozed off.

Sydney's cell phone rang an hour and a half later at one minute to three. We both popped up like a jack-in-the-box with a new spring. I handed her the phone, but before answering she checked the incoming number on her caller ID window.

Tears welled in her eyes, she looked at me with fear on her face and said, "That's Mark's phone number." She pushed the talk button and spoke, "Hello."

The expression on her face turned from fear to total horror. Her body was rigid. Her hands trembled uncontrollably. The she dropped the phone like it was on fire.

I snatched it up and asked, "Mark where are you?" The voice that answered wasn't James Markham's, but it was the one I'd been waiting to hear from.

"Mr. Downing, I'm proposing a trade."

"Where's Markham, asshole?"

"Mr. Markham was much tougher than I expected, but he finally conceded that I'm in charge. You need to do the same, Mr. Downing."

"What do you want to trade?"

"You, Mr. Downing. Director Fisher believes that Mr. Markham and Ms. Sloan are loyal government employees. He's satisfied that the oath they took when they became FBI agents is omnipotent in their lives, and being exceptional government employees, they'll take our secrets to their graves. You, on the other hand, don't meet those standards. I am proposing an equal trade—you for Mr. Markham.

"If Fisher had you trying to kill Sydney, let you torture her and probably Markham too for that matter, he's not going to welcome them back to the Bureau with open arms. You may be a good at killing innocent people, but your bullshitting needs a lot of work. Besides, how do I know you haven't already killed Markham?"

"Agent Markham is alive and well for the time being."

"Well, if you don't set Markham free within an hour, I'm going to contact the State Department and have them blow that Goddamn Saudi Arabian Embassy down."

"Well said, Mr. Downing, and almost believable. Maybe I'm not the only one who needs to work on his bullshitting. You see, Mr. Downing, there are a lot of tentacles that hold the relationship between the US and the Royal Saudi family together, so there's no need to offer up that threat again."

"I want Markham out of there."

"Mr. Downing, I really wasn't bullshitting you about Director Fisher allowing Ms. Sloan or Mr. Markham to live. If he can come to terms with his employees, he'll gladly spare their lives for their silence."

"What makes you so sure they'll have long-term safety?"

"Mr. Downing, keeping secrets for life is what they do. However, that offer does not apply to you, Mr. Downing."

"How do we know that Markham is alive?"

"You'll have to take my word for that, Mr. Downing."

"Where do we make the trade?"

"Arlington House. You know it don't you?"

"Sure I know it. Robert E. Lee lived there in the mid-eighteen hundreds. It's on a bluff at Arlington National Cemetery."

"Very good, Mr. Downing. I can see your expensive Georgetown education was worth the money."

"Stop the background bullshit. I'm not impressed. When do you want to make this trade?"

"Mr. Markham and I can be there in an hour."

"So can we. Make sure Mr. Markham is still in good health."

"See you in an hour. Oh, and, Mr. Downing, if you take one hour and fifteen minutes, Mr. Markham will have been dead for fifteen minutes when you arrive."

I hung up knowing I'd promised to give up my life for James Markham's. A few hours ago, I made love to an incredibly beautiful woman whom I was now hoping to have a relationship with for the rest of my life—I had counted on that lasting more than an hour. When I explained to Sydney what he wanted, she refused to go along with the trade. I thought she might, but I was also sure she wanted to get James Markham back before this wacko killed him. Markham was the only person who'd helped us through all the tight spots we'd been in with this killer. He was Sydney's mentor and as close as a father to her. We couldn't let this monster kill him.

CHAPTER 49

Sydney was pissed off that I had agreed to the trade with the killer, but she was committed to coming with me and doing whatever she had to do. I watched her expression as she drove the Nissan back toward the District. The muscles and veins in her forearms bulged under her skin as she gripped the steering wheel tighter with every passing mile. We didn't talk. I knew I couldn't win a debate with her right now, and she knew she couldn't change my mind.

"The cemetery closes around sunset. We may have to cut a chain across the road or use the front bumper to push open a gate," I said.

"Fine. I've done that before." Her answer was abrupt and abrasive.

"Sydney, we had no choice. I wasn't about to let him kill Markham and neither would you."

"I wouldn't have agreed to the trade. I would have negotiated another deal," she replied.

"Sydney, I hope you know me better than that. I want him to believe we're making the trade, and one of us is going to kill this bastard tonight."

We were minutes away from the entrance to Arlington Cemetery. I broke the silence. "I've never been the type to go for a one-night stand."

"And what do you mean by that?"

"I hope to see a lot more of you, Sydney Sloan, so when I draw this guy's fire, I'm counting on you to take him out."

"I don't think I like this setup. No night vision, no night scope, unfamiliar surroundings. I like my time, my place, and my conditions. I don't like our chances, Scott."

"Well unfortunately you're not calling the shots, pardon the pun. None of us have come here to make a trade. You and I know that, and so does he. He has home field advantage by knowing his way around the cemetery, but we have two guns to his one. His first priority is to kill all of us and ours is to get Markham out alive. That's the only thing that gives him a little edge as far as I'm concerned."

"Scott, Arlington Cemetery is filled with obscure shadowy shooting positions. Who says it's two guns against one? This guy could have called Fisher, and there could be a half a dozen shooters waiting for us."

"Too much ego for that, Sydney. This guy wouldn't have the nerve to call Fisher and ask for backup. He's alone."

We arrived at the cemetery entrance at ten minutes before four in the morning. The gate was open. A broken chain was lying on the ground next to it. I reached into the back seat and double-checked the rifle for ammunition. It had a thirty-round standard magazine, which meant that she had twenty-nine rounds left after she spent one blowing the lock off my chair in the embassy. The M16A3 had a fully automatic mode, unlike its predecessors with three round burst modes. I was hoping she wasn't going to need the automatic mode tonight. It may have been naïve, but I was planning on a one shot victory.

She turned off her headlights and we drove slowly up the road. In the distance to our left we could see the tomb of the Unknown Soldier. The military honor guard was faithfully on duty. Last year a minor hurricane came across the Virginia coast and moved inland into DC. The military decided to suspend the guard detail until after the storm had passed. The young men assigned to the detail showed up for work despite the fact they had been allowed to stand down for the severe weather. They manned their post through the wind and rain, and the tomb was never left unguarded. I was certain they wouldn't stop their detail to get involved in our little skirmish that was about to break out on the hill at Arlington House.

The rolling hills of Arlington National Cemetery were covered with thousands of white headstones that marked the graves of fallen soldiers. It was in a cemetery in Pensacola where I'd promised my parents that I would try to do something to make a difference in people's lives to avenge unsolved deaths. Three years later I was preparing to have a final confrontation with their killer, in of all places, a cemetery.

I had never really been afraid of dying, even over the past several days when it seemed inevitable that Sydney and I would both be killed. Through it all I maintained the confidence that it would all work out. Tonight, I didn't have that feeling of self-assurance. Tonight I was expecting to die. Perhaps I was like the cat with nine lives, and I knew I'd used up eight of them. I had a nauseous feeling in the pit of my stomach; my head was lightheaded. All of my movements were difficult because it felt like my arms and legs weighed fifty pounds each.

We meandered up the hilly road with our lights off. Sydney was doing a great job of staying on the road, because there was no moonlight. She stopped the car about two hundred yards away from Arlington House. "I don't like it, Scott."

"Sydney, I can do this alone, but I could sure use your help."

"All of a sudden I'm afraid of so many things, Scott. The killer, something happening to Markham, the media getting hold of this story, and God knows what happens to America after that, and..." She hesitated, her bottom lip quivered, then she rested her head against the top of the steering wheel.

"And what, Sydney?"

She lifted her head and looked me in the eyes. "Scott, I don't want anything to happen to you." I reached for her hand that was resting on the seat between us, covering it with mine. I squeezed, and she squeezed back. The touch of her hand energized me. The nauseous feeling dissipated, the lightheadedness cleared up, and I was filled with determination.

"Sydney, this ends here, tonight. First we get Markham, then we take this guy out, and after that we figure out how we're going to deal with the conspiracy information. I promise."

"Okay." She gave me a faint smile. Now we were both focused on the mission. She pointed towards Arlington House.

"If he's in that house, he has the best cover and probably an escape route. He has the best shooting angle from up above us. You saw that equipment at the Saudi Embassy. He probably has night vision and high power scopes. Two guns to one, he still has a helluva advantage."

"He doesn't have us. That what's going to make the difference."

She gripped her gearshift and seemed to be debating between forward or reverse. I grabbed her arm, and rolled my wrist over so she could see my watch.

"Sydney, remember he gave us until four o'clock. If I don't walk through the front door of that old house in five minutes, James Markham dies. Let's make it good."

Reluctantly, she put the car back in gear and continued slowly toward Arlington House, parking parallel to the front porch. Sydney got out shielded by the body of the car, reached in and grabbed the weapon she had taken from the embassy. She squatted behind the rear tire, laid the rifle across the trunk and tapped on the side of the car to let me know she was in position. I eased out of the car trying to act calm, but I had no control over how wildly my knees were shaking.

The old stone house had six large white columns across the front and one on each end of the porch. The famous old home was perched on a hill above the cemetery. The front door was swung open, resting against the wall behind it. The closer I got to the house, the better my view was of James Markham. He was sitting in an old-fashioned ladder-back rocker, steadily rocking. That was the positive part. Rocking meant he was alive, although it was probably at gunpoint. I stared closer at Markham with every step I took. His hands were clinging to the ends of the rocker arms, but he wasn't tied up or cuffed. His head never moved and his eyes did not blink. None of that made any sense. Markham was the kind of cop who'd leap from that chair and take a bullet to warn a fellow officer about an ambush. Finally, I'd come all the way to the porch, using a wooden column for cover while the rocking continued just inside the door.

I was still puzzled by Markham's dormancy. Then the rocker slowed to a stop. Peering around the column through the door, I spotted monofilament fishing line coiled in a pile next to the rocker. He had tied the fishing line around the rocker legs and was pulling it to make it look like Markham was rocking himself. The line must have broken or slipped from his grasp. I could see Markham clearly now. There was no doubt he was already dead.

CHAPTER 50

Sydney was right. His timing, his turf, his conditions, all were in his favor, not ours. We were no longer there to save Markham, we were there to kill this guy and save ourselves. I pivoted back behind the column. When I refused to take his bait, this guy had to know that I'd discovered Markham was already dead. I dropped to the ground behind the column and yanked the .357 magnum I'd picked up at Sydney's from my belt. I had it stuffed behind me so I would at least look unarmed. The door slammed closed. There was no way to get back to the car, so now it was truly a waiting game. The column was about three feet across at the base, so it offered me a little cover. I drew my legs tightly against my chest, making sure I was completely covered by the column. I turned and waved my arm in a lowering motion for Sydney to stay down. I didn't want her to rise up and try to offer me cover with those twenty-nine rounds so that I could run back to the car. I was determined to get justice tonight for my parents, and for James Markham.

A shot rang out from inside the house. I moved my head far enough from behind the column to see smoke drifting out of the window left of the front door. He'd removed one of the glass panes from the window casing. I pulled my head back behind the column as another shot rang out followed by the sound of a bullet ricocheting off metal. I turned and looked toward Sydney's car. There was a hole in the rear quarter panel directly across from where Sydney had been kneeling on the opposite side of the car.

"Sydney, you okay?"

"I'm okay."

The window he was shooting from was about six feet to the left of the door, twelve to fifteen feet away from me. A third shot sounded, and I could have sworn that I was hit. A piercing pain traversed my body like a bolt of lightning.

I yelled to her, "Did that come from the window?"

"Yeah. It hit just over my head." If that was the case, I wasn't hit. In fact, the shot wasn't even in my direction. My mind was playing games with me. I felt pain when I heard shots fired. I was more afraid right now than any time in my life.

I'd been in shootouts before, but I'd never been pinned down like this. I needed to do something to draw the killer to a position that would give Sydney a shot at him.

I pointed to the next column over. Sydney was staying low so I didn't know whether or not she saw me. I hoped she did.

A second later she yelled, "Don't do anything stupid, Scott." This girl already knew me better than anyone I'd ever worked with. I ran to the next column to my right. I heard two quick pops. I was standing behind the column and looking at the car. There was no movement and no sound coming from Sydney's direction.

"Sydney." She didn't answer. "Sydney, are you okay?" There was no answer.

If I could get to the next column I'd have an angle through the open door and possibly through the window too. I ran toward the next column when I heard the pop. I was only inches away from the protection of the bulky column when the bullet hit me, spinning me around in nearly a full circle. I fell to the ground at the base of the column with my head facing towards Sydney. Beyond Sydney's car I could see endless rows of white head stones that seemed to stretch for miles. My legs had crumpled first and my shoulders were the last part of my body to pound into the ground with the force of all my weight. The ground was damp and cold and the sky was pitch black but full of tiny flickering stars.

As I lay there and looked toward the heavens, I hoped that somewhere up there my parents knew I had done all I could to vindicate their deaths. That thought alone gave me peace and contentment. Then I heard a few muffled sounds like footsteps coming from the house, someone taking deep breaths, and then I heard a final pop.

One by one the stars began to go out and total darkness overtook the sky. I became very cold as the sounds faded, and it felt like I had fallen into a black hole.

CHAPTER 51

My eyes opened slowly. I saw an officer wearing a vest and a gun belt with a nine-millimeter handgun holstered on it. He was standing next to a white concrete wall. There was a radio clipped to his shoulder, and he spoke into it and then stood blocking the doorway. He looked immovable with his legs spread and his hands folded behind his back. A woman approached and he shifted to one side, letting her in the room. She stood over me and stared into my eyes before reaching up and squeezing a transparent plastic bag attached to a metal pole next to a bed I was lying in. Then she reached for my left wrist and held it in her hand. Another woman who seemed to have been moving briskly skidded to a stop at the doorway, and the officer stepped aside again. The two women spoke as a tall man wearing green scrubs with a stethoscope dangling from his neck entered the room.

He went around to my right side, leaned down close to my face and asked "How are you feeling?"

The words sounded distorted like he was speaking from inside a barrel. I wanted to answer, but I wasn't sure what to say.

He asked again, "Mr. Downing, can you tell us how you're feeling?"

Numb was the word that came out of my mouth, but I mumbled it so badly, I almost didn't recognize what I'd said.

"You're at Walter Reed Army Medical Center in Washington, DC. I'm Dr. Tullis. There are some people who want to speak with you. I need to know if you feel like talking yet."

"What happened?" I asked.

"You were shot. You lost a lot of blood, and you had some damage to the area where your clavicle connects to your shoulder girdle. We think we got you pretty well patched up," he said. "You want to ask me any questions?"

Dr. Tullis saw me licking my lips trying to get enough moisture to speak properly, so he reached across me and picked up plastic cup with a white plastic spoon in it. Then he scooped up a piece of ice and spooned it into my mouth.

"We're going to give you a little more than that in a few minutes, but right now that's the best I can do for you."

"Thanks, Doc," I said.

"Now, let's try that again. Any questions?"

"Sydney Sloan," was all that I could get out. Just saying her name took all the energy I had.

"I've been told that Ms. Sloan was your guardian angel. She had a minor flesh wound to the right side of her neck, but she was treated and released. Any questions about your health?" Relief raced through my body as every muscle relaxed at the same instant.

"The guy who shot me." I needed to abbreviate my question, but I thought he understood it.

"I'm afraid the people who are waiting to speak with you are going to have to address that with you. If you feel like talking for a few minutes, I'll make arrangements for them to come in. After that, I want you to get some rest, and I'll check on you before I leave this afternoon." He patted me on my ankle and left the room. I reached over and took another piece of ice from the cup and sucked on it to wet my throat a little more.

The doctor and the two nurses had been gone less than two minutes when another nurse and an orderly came into my room. "We're going to take you for a little ride," she said.

"Where?" I asked.

"To see your friends." They hustled around the bed and secured tubes and cords, and I wondered why my friends couldn't come to see me in this room. They wheeled me out into the hall, and whisked me away into an empty elevator. The orderly punched a button, and I could sense we were moving up. The doors opened, and they pushed my bed to the end of the hallway where it intersected another hall. The nurse and the orderly were fussing with an electronic monitor and the bag that had been hanging from the pole in my room. Suddenly the gurney shook violently and I heard a deep roaring sound. A stapler sitting on an empty nurses station counter across from me vibrated off onto the floor. Everyone in the room jumped and then froze in position momentarily. Another nurse approached from the hallway, knelt over and picked up the stapler. What the hell was going on? Could that have been an earthquake? The noise and the vibrations gradually lessened. A man in a business suit motioned to the nurses, and they rolled me down the next hallway and through two double doors. There was a large vacant room on the other side of the doors at the end of that floor.

"I don't think I have any friends down here." I said, hoping someone would tell me what was going on.

One of the nurses behind me said, "Oh, I think you do, Mr. Downing." There was a big room at the end of the hall, but they stopped short of pushing me inside. Two men in dark suits were moving around inside the room conducting some sort of inspection. They were taking switch plates off the walls and removing plates around electrical plugs. Then they stood on footstools, raised some ceiling panels and shined flashlights around in the space above the ceiling. Why were they conducting that kind of an inspection of a hospital room? All I could think of was that the killer was still at large. Two more men were standing outside the door of the room, and a third was coming toward us through double doors immediately to my left. Each man had an earpiece stuck in his ear, and they all appeared to speak into the ends of their sleeves. Someone important was coming to see me, and if it was Director Fisher, they may as well have let me bleed to death.

They gathered outside the room, huddled together and whispered to each other. One of the men then stepped away from the group and waved to the orderlies and nurses that it was clear to bring my bed into the room. They pushed me inside and hooked up all of my cords and hoses again. The orderlies and one of the nurses left the room. The nurse who remained asked me if I needed anything.

"You're not leaving are you?" I asked.

"You're going to be just fine," she said.

"Are you going to stay with me?" She smiled and brushed the back of my head.

"I'm getting a little nervous. Do you know who my friends are that are coming to see me?" If Sydney had made peace with Director Fisher, or if the Bureau felt I was a threat to the welfare of America because of what I knew, this would be the perfect way to get rid of me. They could put me on a military medical helicopter and dump me so far out to sea that even the sharks couldn't find me.

"This will all be over soon, and we'll take you back to your room," was her reply. They were going to kill me. How easy was this going to be for them. There was no fight left in me, Markham was dead and Fisher must have convinced Sydney to be a loyal FBI agent. I never dreamed it would end like this.

I checked out the IV tube and the little blue box that was constantly displaying my blood pressure and heart rate. I remembered it being one twenty-four over eighty when they disconnected it in the other room. Now it read One thirty-nine over eighty-one. It was bad enough to be nervous and fearful, but it was even worse to have a billboard sharing it with the world. One of the men outside the room put his hand up to his earpiece and then lifted his arm and spoke into the cuff of his shirtsleeve. A couple of seconds later, the double doors opened and my heart rate shot up again. Sydney Sloan came through the doors, holding her credentials up for the men to see. She entered the room where I was and came over and gave me a kiss on the cheek. When she bent over the bed, the large gauze patch on her neck wrinkled, and I could see a long row of black stitches.

"It's good to see you," she said.

"It's really good to see you," I said. "Sydney, I'm so—" She put her right index finger up to my lips, stopping me from continuing.

"It's over and we're both okay."

"You got him didn't you?"

"You drew his fire. I couldn't have hit if you hadn't drawn him out in the open."

"You did get him though."

"Yeah, I got him, Scott."

"Sydney—" She held up her hand and stopped me again. Then, several of the men outside came into my room, frantically looked around, even under my bed. They asked Sydney to please be seated, pointing to a chair.

"What's going on? Sydney, you can stand here if you want," I said, trying to utter my strongest objections, but sounding pretty pathetic.

"It's okay, Scott," Sydney said as she sat in compliance. Then the men retreated to the doorway and stood with there facing away from us.

"What the hell is going on, Sydney? Take me back to my room." Then the double doors in the hallway burst open, and two more men in dark suits almost ran through them.

I lay there and watched in awe as the President of the United States strolled toward my room.

CHAPTER 52

The President entered the room with an air of confidence yet disarming congeniality. He seemed to ignore all of the movement around him by the Secret Service, to focus totally on where he was going. Sydney had sat on the end of my bed, but promptly stood at attention and faced the President.

"Hello, Agent Sloan, Lieutenant Downing," the President said.

"Mr. President," Sydney said, shaking his hand. He reached across their handshake and laid his left hand on my arm just above my wrist so he wouldn't disturb my IV connections.

"May I call you Scott?" he asked.

"Scott's fine, Mr. President."

"You two have been loyal public servants, as were your mother and father, Scott."

"Thank you, sir," I said, fighting back tears.

"On behalf of the United States government, I want to extend my condolences for the loss of your parents, Scott, and I apologize to both of you for what you've been through the past two weeks."

I looked at the President and tried to muster a strong voice. "Mr. President, I never dreamed my own government would hire and protect paid assassins."

The President stepped closer to my bed before he spoke this time. "There's no way I can say to you that I understand how you feel. I could never conceive of losing both of my parents at the hands of a murderer, but I hope you realize two greedy men, and not your entire government, were involved in those conspiracies."

There was something on my mind, and I couldn't let this go by. "With all due respect, sir, the director of the FBI and the Secretary of Defense represent the government of the United States as far as I'm concerned."

"Scott, *Operation Freedom Flows* and *The Osprey's Nest* took place during my first term in office. I had no idea what those men were up to. That doesn't make it right, but I want you to believe me that I had no knowledge of those conspiracies. I've tried to do what was right to protect this country, and unfortunately some of my closest advisors led me in some wrong directions. Our men and women in our armed services, like your parents, have paid a huge price for those mistakes." He pursed his lips, fighting back sorrow over everything that had happened, here and in the Middle East.

"Mr. President, what keeps them from doing something like this all over again?

"Director Fisher's body was found this morning at Fort Marcy Park." Jesus Christ, the President must be ordering someone to kill us all off to make this go away.

The President was staring at me, waiting for me to respond, but I was too stunned to give him the lead in he was looking for. I broke out in a sweat, wondering if he was about to order one of the secret service agents to put poison in my IV.

"Fisher committed suicide. He killed himself about five feet from where Vince Foster took his life." I remembered Foster. He was Deputy White House Counsel to President Clinton.

"Scott, Director Fisher wasn't killed. I don't work that way."

I nodded, acknowledging his statement, but the news he had just delivered was so shocking and yet spoken so matter-of-factly, I didn't know what to believe.

"The Secretary of Defense has taken a teaching a position in the UK. He's agreed to quietly live out the remainder of his days without returning to the US."

"What guarantee do you have that Runnels wouldn't divulge this information for money from another country or a book publisher?" I asked as respectfully as I could.

"Scott, Secretary Runnels has already found the need to hire a body guard for personal protection based on his perceived legitimate involvement in the Middle East. If there was full disclosure about what the Secretary and Director Fisher had been up to in Iraq, he'd become the target of American and Iraqi families who lost loved ones in the war, not to mention the Islamic radical groups who would love to find justification for killing the man behind the invasion into their part of the world. Even living in seclusion in the United Kingdom wouldn't provide Runnels the safeguards he'd need if the information behind his fiendish plans were to get out. That brings us to you."

This had to be it. He may have just said "I don't work like that," but I couldn't see any way that he could afford to let me live with the information I possessed.

"I'm sure you understand what would happen to this country if anyone other than those of us in this room were to learn about *The Osprey's Nest*, *The Burning Post*, or *Operation Freedom Flows*." I nodded again in the affirmative. This time I simply couldn't speak.

"I'm deeply sorry about your parents, but I need your word that the bullet Agent Sloan put in the mercenary's skull at Arlington House gave you the justice you came here looking for. I need your word that for the sake of our country, you'll never discuss those three despicable plans with anyone ever again." He leaned over the bed, his eyes locked intensely onto mine. He was observing the movement of every facial muscle I had as I prepared to answer.

"Mr. President, you have my word."

He remained hovering over me for at least a minute without saying a word. I wondered if he believed me. Finally, he stood up straight, gave a nod to Sydney, and walked to the door, grasping the door handle. He turned and faced me once more and said, "You're an honorable man and patriot, Lieutenant Downing. You've given me your word, and that's a contract with your country I know you'll keep for life. On behalf of the United States of America, I thank you." Without waiting for a reply, he took two steps through the doorway and disappeared, surrounded by secret service agents.

CHAPTER 53

Sydney came to pick me up the next day. She brought some clothes she'd taken from my luggage for me to wear to leave the hospital. I'd forgotten that the shirt I had on when they brought me in was a little bloody and there was a bullet hole in it as well. The doctors promised to release me if I promised to start physical therapy on my shoulder right away. As far as I was concerned, it was one of the best deals I'd ever struck.

This time the trip through Washington Reagan National Airport with Sydney Sloan would be a little less nerve-wracking that the last. I cleared the metal detector, and as I was picking up my belongings off the conveyor belt, I recalled that was the exact spot where Sydney had shouted the news about my parent's murders the last time we were in this airport.

I was putting on my loafers after they came through the conveyor when I spotted Sydney in the crowd beyond the ticketed passengers entry. She was saying something to me, so I focused on her mouth, trying to read her lips. She said it again, then she gave me one of her fabulous smiles. I mouthed an answer, "I love you too, Sydney Sloan."

Printed in the United States
45027LVS00005B/74